To Bob & Carole
With deep
friendship and gratitude!

Richard

WORKS OF GENIUS

WORKS
OF GENIUS

Richard Marek

ATHENEUM
New York
1987

Library of Congress Cataloging-in-Publication Data

Marek, Richard.
Works of genius.

I. Title
PS3563.A6445W6 1987   813'.54   86-47951
ISBN 0-689-11889-9

Copyright © 1987 by Richard Marek

All rights reserved

Published simultaneously in Canada by Collier Macmillan Canada, Inc.

Composition by Maryland Linotype, Baltimore, Maryland

Manufactured by Maple-Vail Book Manufacturing Group, York, Pennsylvania

Designed by Marek Antoniak

First Edition

To Margot

Part

I

I AM MORE INTELLIGENT THAN MY FATHER.

This is not said boastfully; it is a matter of fact. But it explains, in part, why he, a passionate reader, an avid scholar, an acolyte to the minds of the masters, nevertheless never went to college and spent his life as a civil servant in the city's court system; while I, a graduate of the same De Witt Clinton High School my father attended, earned a scholarship to Cornell.

It explains, too, why I decided not to become the writer my father so passionately wanted me to be (since his own creative ambitions were constantly frustrated), but rather remained on the periphery of literature. I love it too much to insult it with genetic clumsiness. Instead, I was an economics major in college, and the business of books, as well as their content, remains my lifelong fascination.

My name is Anthony Silver. I'm a literary agent. Benedick Morley is my client; so are Adrienne Whitelaw, Max Harris, Cynthia Baum, Jody Monroe, L. L. Lustig—and dozens more, not so renowned.

I was Eric Meredith's agent, too. You've read his books, or you wouldn't be reading this one.

For, as is fitting, this is ninety percent Eric's story, ten percent mine. Eric's autobiography lies in his novels, but I venture you will find things here he would not have said—might not even have known—no matter how sincere or far-reaching his candor. And I, the man he called his best friend, witness to his greatness and cruelty, relish the task of biographer. He has consumed my life.

No, he did not ask me to write this book. Had he known I was doing it, he would have demanded I stop. Yet I would have continued anyway, with or without his permission, in hopes that he reads it. If he does, I trust he will recognize it as a tribute. *Only a tribute?* I hear my wife, Judy, asking.

All right, Judy. It is also an act of revenge.

When I first met Eric Meredith, I had been an independent agent for only ten weeks. In the nine years before that, I had worked for Oliver Bishop, an agent specializing in science fiction, horror, and movie star autobiographies. I liked him personally, but I loathed the books that made him rich and resented that part of my job which required me to fawn over the stars who so often prowled the office.

I eventually found a niche for myself as the "literary man" in the agency. My authors' books achieved good reviews and generally dismal sales, but Bishop welcomed their prestige. I loved most of my authors. They were fragile and earnest, talented but as yet unformed, my sometime solace from the gigantic egos that strutted so demandingly through the corridors and pretended that the pieties in their books were sincere.

My breakup with Bishop came suddenly and dramatically— over an issue so small it later made me realize that I must have been looking for an excuse to leave him. "I want you to negotiate one last clause in the Rachel Reynolds contract," he said to me one morning, appearing at my office door and tossing the contract on my desk.

Reynolds was a movie star turned born-again Christian. She was explicit in her depiction of the sins of her pagan youth and the venality of her co-stars.

"She called this morning. Wants a guarantee that her name on the jacket will be in larger type than the title, no matter what the title is."

"That's ridiculous," I said.

"She says she gets the same guarantee in movie contracts."

I had heard this argument before, and it made me wild. "Can't you teach these people that there's a difference between books and movies?" I asked him. "Isn't it part of your job as an agent to educate?"

He gave me a tired smile. "My job is to represent my client in negotiations with the publisher. You know that, Tony."

"I'm sorry," I said. "I think it's an unreasonable demand of hers, and I won't do it."

Something changed in his eyes. I had crossed him before, but never this brazenly ."I don't want to have to fire you," he said.

I took a deep breath. Judy and I had just become engaged, and I could not afford to give up my salary. "I don't think my crime's that terrible."

"I think it is." His eyes lost their expression, and he stood straight and still. He routinely negotiated with presidents of companies; he was not about to give in to me. My choice was to capitulate or leave, and I considered it carefully.

"Fire me," I said at last, conscious of the pounding in my chest.

He took one step back, a gymnast who had barely missed a perfect dismount. Otherwise he showed no sign of emotion. "If you take any of your authors with you," he said quietly, "I'll sue you. You brought them here while you were employed by me, and they remain clients of this agency."

Exhilarated, I met his stare. My tone was just as calm as his. "If they want to come with me, they'll come. They're not your slaves. They're *writers*."

He looked at me a long time. I did not flinch. "I want you out by this afternoon," he said. "You'll get two months' severance and whatever vacation pay is due you."

It was a generous settlement, but before I could respond, he had left. I called Judy and told her what had happened. If she was as apprehensive about the future as I was beginning to be, she didn't show it. "Good for you," is what she said.

I didn't know how many authors would come with me, how many would prefer to have Bishop's power behind them. But I knew some would remain loyal, and that as soon as I announced the formation of my own agency, manuscripts from them and from strangers would start coming in.

Indeed, eight weeks later, a manuscript called *Success* arrived from a writer named Eric Meredith, along with a letter asking if I would represent him. I like to meet my authors before I take them on, so after I read the manuscript, I wrote back, and we set a date.

Even though the day was cloudy, he arrived wearing sunglasses. The date was March 13, 1975, three months before my marriage. The place was my apartment/office at 16 West 84th Street, New York City.

Since I was too poor to afford a secretary, and because Judy was out on a job (interior decoration—she too used our apartment as an office, so we each doubled as receptionist and boss), I met him at the door myself. In his early thirties, as I was, he came bareheaded and coatless despite the winter wind, and the hand he extended was cold. He was an enormous man, well over six feet tall, and heavy—no, not heavy: *massive*. He must have weighed two hundred and fifty pounds, but it was solid weight, not flab; I had the sense he could run for miles without being winded. His black hair was already thinning, and the wind had whorled it on his head like tangled wire. His face and neck were the only parts of him that were puffy; his jowls had forced him to open the top button of his shirt, and his tie—blue background with red herons —hung beneath it, the knot off-center, though he had obviously made an effort at neatness before he started out. He wore a gray suit, clean but unpressed, and his shoes were unshined but not scruffy. He reminded me of a labor union negotiator after a tough bargaining session; I was struck by the sense of fatigue underlying his outward exuberance. He was smiling shyly, but because of the glasses, I could not make out the expression in his eyes.

"Coat's in the car," he said, noticing my glance. "Anne's with it. I've asked her to pick me up in an hour."

His voice was surprisingly high for so large a man, but it had a pleasant ring to it. I smiled involuntarily. "You could have asked her to join us."

"She'd have made me nervous. I wanted to hear your verdict alone."

For drama and timing I did not want to tell him too soon what I thought of his book. "Let's talk in the office," I said. "You must have a lot of questions."

He laughed. "Lots. I've never had an agent before, though Lord knows I need one." He paused and moved a step toward me. "You *will* represent me? You liked the book enough for that?"

Playing with him, drawing it out, I kept my voice flat. "Yes."

He seemed to take no satisfaction from it. "I hoped you might." He said it casually, not quite diffidently, and I liked him for it. Modest authors rarely have talent.

I led him down the hallway to my office. "Ask anything you want," I said, ushering him in. "There are no secrets in being an agent."

He laughed again. "Just in being a writer."

I took him seriously. "No. Writers *reveal* secrets. That is, the goods ones do. You do."

If he recognized the compliment, he did not acknowledge it. Rather, he looked around the bedroom-study. I winced. There were only the sofa bed, the desk and two chairs, a barren credenza, two lamps, and a closet, its door not tightly shut, revealing my clothes and some of Judy's. *Don't go*, I willed. *I need you.*

"I used to work in a large agency," I said, "Oliver Bishop's. My problem was that he was overloaded with movie stars and didn't have enough time left for real writers. No matter what, I'll keep this operation small."

He chuckled. It was a soft sound, agreeable, like a politician's. "But you plan to get *slightly* bigger?"

"Oh, sure! I'm only thirty-two. Just starting."

"Good," he said. "Me, too."

I couldn't tell if he was referring to his age or his work. "Why did you pick me?" I asked. "There are other agents."

"Two years ago I heard you speak at the Breadloaf writers' conference. I was impressed. You seemed straight. No bullshit. In fact, you were the only one there with anything to say. The classes were worthless."

I shrugged. "I try to tell the truth."

"Besides," he went on, "a friend once told Anne, 'When you go to France, go to the one-star restaurants, not the threes, particularly if they're run by young chefs. Those are the guys going up. Literally aiming for the stars. They'll break their balls to get them.' "

I enjoyed his ardor. "As with chefs, so with literary agents?"

"Precisely."

"But in your letter you said you had your first book published without an agent."

Another chuckle. "Right. And look what happened to it. No sales. No ads. No *shit*."

"The fate of most first novels."

He turned his face abruptly to the side, as though I had slapped him. "*Anderson's Luck* was not 'most first novels.' "

He was right. After I had read his new manuscript, I had called Doubleday, his publisher, for a copy of his first book. It was a simple love story, or at least so it seemed at first. But I felt when I had finished it that I had read it too quickly, that its underlying meaning, its central symbols, had eluded me. Underneath its easy melody lay complex orchestration, and two or three readings were probably necessary to understand it fully.

"True," I said. "*Anderson's Luck* is exceptional. But still, for all the beauty of style and care of construction, who'd want to pay ten ninety-five to read about a minister's son and a disc jockey's daughter?"

His face reddened; the slap had hit home. He stood up, his hands clenched, and he trembled. "If you don't like my work . . ."

His reaction surprised me. For all his seeming self-assurance, he was scared. "But I *do* like it. I *want* to represent you. Only if I do, I have to teach you the economic facts of life. *Anderson's Luck*, insightful and wonderfully written as it is, could not possibly attract a large audience. It's too subtle. Too quiet. You'll have to develop a body of more important work before readers will go back to it." He was still standing, unmollified. I cast about for something to make him stay. "Besides, think of James Joyce. *Portrait of an Artist* didn't sell when it was first published. It needed *Ulysses*. Well, think of *Anderson* as your *Portrait*. And *Success* as your *Ulysses*."

It worked. He sat down again. "I'm glad you think *Anderson's* as good as *Portrait*," he said, "but I don't see much comparison between *Success* and *Ulysses*. Shit, *Success* is accessible!"

I hadn't meant to compare him to Joyce, and not for the first time I marveled at what authors hear and don't hear in discussions of their books. But I merely said, "Of course it is. And I dare say that while *Ulysses* made its way slowly, *Success* will find a large audience as soon as it's published."

He took off his glasses. His eyes were light hazel, almost colorless, but I could feel them blaze at me. His hands still trembled. He needed me, and I rejoiced at his vulnerability.

"You really think so?" he asked. "A large audience?"

"I make it a practice not to tell authors anything I don't believe. It's bad technique to feed their dreams."

"A large audience." He was playing with the phrase. Suddenly, his eyes grew suspicious. "You've read it?"

I could not contain a laugh. "Certainly I've read it. It's difficult to decide whether or not to take on a client without reading his work."

He ignored the sarcasm. "And you like it?"

I could hold back no longer. I said what I had been bursting to tell him since he arrived. "More than like it. I think it's a master-piece. A fucking miracle."

He gave a whoop, then stood and began to pace the room, punching right fist into left palm as though beating a drum. When he turned once more to face me, I saw tears in his eyes.

"Holy God be praised!" he said. "A fucking miracle."

I was almost as excited as he; his pleasure was contagious. "Let's go for a walk," he said.

I smiled. "Why?"

"Because I can't sit still. And because I'll feel a little less like a supplicant to the throne."

"I'm hardly a king," I reminded him.

"You are to me." His grin was endearing. I led him to the front door, took a coat from the closet, and we stepped outside.

"You won't be cold?" I asked.

"I'm impervious to the elements." It seemed true. He radiated the warmth of joy.

"Then let's go." I led him toward Central Park. We were in an arcadian mood. I knew I had to slow us both down.

"I don't think we should submit the book yet," I warned. "There are technical problems in it. I wouldn't start with the trial, for example; you don't want to give away the verdict until the end."

He stopped and took my arm lightly, his gaze averted. "I don't like editing." His voice was calm, but I could sense his dismay.

"There's a difference between editing and suggesting. I'm sug-gesting. You don't have to change a word if you don't agree."

He let go of my arm, and we continued down the street. "I wel-come suggestions," he said. "Particularly from people I respect."

"You might do more with Alice's parents," I went on, feeling foolhardy and heroic. "It would make the reader feel more of her conflict when she decides to leave."

He *was* cold. At least he scrunched up his shoulders inside his suit jacket. "Noted," he said. "You're probably right."

"But don't change Ben or Alice," I said. "They're alive. I love them. And the sex is sensational. It may be the most erotic book I've ever read."

He glanced at me shyly. "They're me, you know. Both of them."

I smiled at his naiveté. "I know."

He stiffened. "You do? You've never met me before."

"All novelists write about themselves."

He thought about it. "I suppose they do."

"Sure. Even if they're writing thrillers or detective stories. It's *their* fantasies they're putting down on paper."

He walked on without comment. "I charge ten percent," I said briskly. "It's ten percent of everything you make on the book. I handle foreign sales—actually, I've arranged with agents abroad to represent my clients. They take ten percent, too, so on foreign sales you get only eighty percent. And I've got a representative in Hollywood. You get eighty percent of any movie sale, too."

He looked at me longingly, as though foreign sales and movie sales were beyond dreams. "You *like* it," he repeated.

"More than like. I've told you."

"I need to hear that. Over and over." He sighed, as though a great pressure had been lifted from his brain ."What do I sign?"

"You don't. There's no contract. I trust you, you trust me. If you don't like the job I do, then leave. But this book is mine. I'll send you a letter to that effect, and you can countersign it."

"Fine," he said. "Whatever. Do you think I'll be famous?"

His longing touched me. "Yes. Some day."

"You think *Success* will be a best-seller?"

"Hold on. I didn't say that."

"But you think so."

"I think it will sell better than *Anderson's Luck*."

"But how *much* better?"

"Anywhere between one thousand and fifty thousand copies."

His eyes glowed ."That's not very helpful."

"Sorry," I said, just a little frightened of him. "But it's the only honest answer. There's just no way of knowing. I've thought books would do splendidly, and they've failed. I've thought books would do poorly, and they've sold like crazy. So I really don't know, and I don't want to get your hopes up by pretending that I do.

"My hopes *are* up," he said. "I'm not asking for a guarantee— only an opinion."

"Then closer to fifty thousand. I love the book and think it could sell."

This time there was no fist in hand. He only smiled.

"So do I," he said. "I'm glad we agree."

We reached the park. Because of the weather, it was nearly deserted. A mother stood in the playground pushing two bundled-up children on swings; a messenger sped by on a bicycle; a lone teenage girl, dressed in leather skirt and leather jacket, stood on the grass, tossing up a ball and catching it. "It's sad to see something like that," said Eric, noticing my glance. "Mother at work, probably. The girl's either skipped school or ducked out when she could. That's one lonely kid. Look at the sag of her shoulders, the curl of her mouth. Jail bait, I'd say. She'll probably be hooking in three years."

Two young Puerto Ricans passed us. "Now *they*," he went on, "are heading up in the world. Look at their shirts, their shoes. Not much money there, but style. They're just as sure of themselves as the girl is unsure. It's a pleasure to watch them."

I smiled at his enthusiasm. "You see well."

"It's a writer's job." He said it without pretentiousness or pride. "How did you become an agent?"

Moved by his interest, I found myself talking of my childhood, about the particular combination of shyness and brains that drove me to reading when my comrades were playing ball or, later, fighting Irish and Italian kids in the street. I told him of the responsibility my father had placed on me—to write as he never could, to rise with words as he had never risen—and how disappointed I had been when it became clear I simply did not have the talent. "I knew I had to be associated with words nevertheless," I said. "The choice was editor or agent. I picked agent because I like the business side of things too." He was watching me intently, seeing things, I was sure, that I myself had never recognized. I felt uneasy and honored; intimate. "So I get my talent vicariously. I admire it and crave it, need it like oxygen. I think there are a lot of people like me," I added. "People who need books the way they need air, but can't create them."

We had turned and were heading back to my office. "You should count yourself lucky. Creating's *work*," he said, again without pretentiousness. "Once I've considered your suggestions and *Success* is ready to go, what are the next steps?"

I told him I would get him out of his option to Doubleday, as I supposed he wanted me to, then send *Success* to Arthur Collins at Diadem Press. Arthur, a senior editor, like us in his early thirties, blended commercial acumen with literary judgment. We had entered publishing around the same time. He was the first editor who had ever taken me to lunch, and I had admired his taste ever since.

"He's perfect for you," I told Eric. "He's got a terrific literary eye, and enough clout in the house to push the books he champions. Besides, he's a friend; I trust him. He would treat your book conscientiously."

"Does Diadem have money?"

"You bet. *Blood Lust*'s been on the best-seller list for three months, and they got half a million for the paperback rights. It's Arthur's book, needless to say."

He smiled. "*Literary* eye? With a title like that?"

I returned the smile. "Touché. But we all have to make a living. Arthur can teach you a thing or two, I'm certain."

Abruptly, the smile disappeared. "I don't want him touching a word of my book."

I grinned. "Not even make suggestions?"

To his credit, he shared my amusement. "Provided he knows I don't have to accept any of them. If I say I want the book to read a particular way, that's the way it reads."

"He'll respect that."

"But you'll make it clear to him that he has to. In so many words."

"If you wish."

The intensity had returned, the humor vanished. "Isn't that what agents are for?" he asked.

I felt a chill go up my backbone; there was more to his resentment of criticism than I had realized. "Oliver Bishop says that the agent's function is solely to represent his client in negotiations with the publisher."

He looked at me with warmth and humor, even affection. "But you think it's more than that."

I averted my eyes. "Yes."

"And that's why I picked you over Bishop. Over the whole lot of them. You're a humanist, Tony. You've got a soul!"

Ten minutes after we got home, the doorbell rang. "Judy," I said. "She wants to meet you." We went from my office to the door, and I opened it. Judy stood shivering, her arms too full of packages to dig in her purse for the key. She brushed past me, stumbling behind the weight of her bundles, and dropped them on a chair in the living room. Then she shrugged off the hood of her coat, and turned to face us, fluffing her hair with her hands and smiling first at me, then at Eric.

"This is Eric Meredith," I said ."Eric, my fiancée, Judy."

"Oh, how *nice*," she said, looking at him intently, as one would a painting.

"Hello," he said, staring at her with such manifest admiration that I longed to step between them. I thought of the fascination with sex in *Success* and vowed with an adolescent's heart to make sure he would see as little of her as possible.

"Usually, Tony doesn't let me meet his clients," she was saying. "That is, I greet them at the door, when I'm doing part-time work for him, and escort them to the bed—his office. Then he shuts himself in with them, and I see them only long enough to show them out." She unbuttoned her coat, revealing a tweed skirt and tan sweater; she looked ravishing. "But you," she went on, "are different. Last night, I made Tony promise he'd introduce us, but then I had to go out, and the subway home took forever to come, and I ran from the corner, and thank God I caught you before you left."

"Thank God you have," Eric said, beaming. "But why?"

"Because I read your book last night."

He glared at her, clearly astonished. "I sent it to Tony. It was meant only for him."

She seemed oblivious to his irritation. "And he was so excited he gave it to me. It's wonderful. Really wonderful. Brand-new. Real. Funny and moving and terrifically sexy." She blushed. "I'm sorry. I sound so vapid. As though I were describing an actor's performance, not a writer's novel. I'm usually good with words, but when I feel something deeply, I get tongue-tied." She took a breath. "Your novel moved me very much. I think it's the most important book I've read in years."

He shone, his anger forgotten. "Seems to me you're good with words now."

She shook her head. "No."

"There are faults," I said. "I've made a few suggestions for improvements, and Eric's promised to think them over before I send the book to Diadem."

"But you could get it published now," she said. "That is, if Mr. Meredith were hit by a truck, you could sell it as is. It'd still be sensational."

He took her hand and kissed it. It was neither a self-conscious gesture nor a theatrical one. "Come meet Anne," he said, barely including me in the invitation. "She's outside in the car."

I glanced at him, startled. "I thought she was going to come here," I said.

He shrugged. "But she didn't. Ergo, she's in the car. I saw it when you opened the door for Judy. Anne told me she was going to Riverside Park. She must have just come back."

Judy and I put on our coats, Eric his dark glasses, and the three of us moved toward the door.

"I presume you have a copy of the manuscript," I asked him.

He grinned. "Dozens."

"Then I'll keep the original you sent me. Do you want it back when you've finished the revision?"

"Why should I?" His smile was beatific.

"If you become famous, you can donate it to a university."

We were out the door. The car was double-parked across the street. Eric went over to it.

Judy and I watched the scene from the top of the brownstone steps. In the twilight, I could make out the shadow of a woman's head inside the car, but she had it turned to Eric as he stood in the street, his arms folded on top of the car, his head at window level, so I could not make out her features. He seemed to be talking animatedly, but we were too far away to overhear.

At last he straightened and beckoned us toward him. Anne got out of the car on the driver's side, leaving it double-parked, and the four of us, whose lives were eventually to be so intricately intertwined, met for the first time on the street, forming a tight circle less for intimacy than for warmth.

Anne Meredith was tall, five feet six or seven; she dwarfed Judy, who is only slightly over five feet, and I suppose most of you would say she was the more desirable, which simply proves the untrust-worthiness of surface appearances. In any case, she had a patrician beauty, blond and cool; despite hours in the car, she seemed perfectly neat—her wine-colored wool coat was unwrinkled, her hair meticulously combed. I could not discern her figure under the bulky coat; it turned out to be that of a model, small-breasted and small-hipped. Nor could I tell about her eyes. Like her husband, she wore sunglasses. But she was obviously nervous, smoothing nonexistent wrinkles in the front of her coat, her fingers scurrying across the fabric. She held out her hand, not as a princess but as a friend; first Judy, then I took it. "Eric tells me you liked his book," she said, including both of us in her statement, though she seemed to be looking between us and did not move her head. Her voice trembled as she talked, but it was musical nevertheless. "I can't tell you how happy that makes me. He's so mercilessly hard on himself and he won't believe me when I tell him how good he is."

"Better than good," Judy said, but I said only, "It's a vast step up from *Anderson's Luck*."

"Do you think he'll make some money from it?" she asked, then quickly added, "Not because we're greedy, but because it will finance him. He's got more books in him—many more—and I don't want him to have to work at anything but his writing."

"Are you working now?" Judy asked him.

"Actually, *I* am," said Anne with an embarrassed smile. "I'm a potter—ceramics—ashtrays and vases. Nothing fancy."

"Anne works at home, just like me," Eric said. "It gets crowded."

"Do you sell from home?" Judy asked.

"No. The outlets are department stores, novelty shops, et cetera. I sell to them wholesale. The things aren't really very good."

"Her stuff's gorgeous," Meredith said, no inflection in his tone. "But it's still a small business."

"But fun," Anne added. "I wouldn't want it to get much bigger. But it hardly floats the three of us, and Eric's had to take odd jobs —substitute teaching, carpentry . . ."

"Jesus, waiting on *tables*," Meredith said.

". . . so we could make ends meet."

"The three of you?" Judy asked.

"There's David," I said. "He's six." Meredith's covering letter had mentioned a son. It wasn't the usual sort of information one included with a submission, and I had wondered at it.

We established quickly that David was in public school, first grade, good in math, not a writer like his father. The talk was cordial and desultory. We stood in our circle, moving against the cold, exercising. No one seemed to know how to end the conversation. Meredith in particular spoke when the conversation flagged, as though reluctant to leave us. We had liked his work enough to want to help him with it. I had seen the gratitude in others, but was not sure that was what I saw in him.

It was Judy who ended it. "Please forgive me," she said. "I've got to make a phone call."

If Meredith had been sitting down, he'd have sprung to his feet. "Sorry," he said. "I guess I'm like all writers at least in one respect. When the talk gets to me, I don't want it to end." He offered me his hand. "I like you, Silver. I'm glad you'll be representing me."

He turned toward their car. "Wait," I said, suddenly as loath to have the moment end as he was. "You going back to Long Island?"

"That's home, such as it is," said Anne, smiling. "Bayshore. We hope to come here some day. Permanently. Eric says it's where the action is. That you can't get attention unless you're part of the New York scene."

"He's wrong," I told her. "Eric could get attention if he were writing from Timbuktu."

"You *see*," Eric said, taking Anne's arm. "In his office he called it a fucking miracle."

She put her arm around his waist and squeezed.

"You'll start right in on the revisions?" I asked. "How long do you think they'll take?"

"No more than a week. I'll think over what you said. But I pretty much like the book as it is."

"Good. Meanwhile, I'll take Collins to lunch. Soften him up a bit."

Anne reached for my arms. I could feel her fingers through my coat sleeve. "Don't sell him cheap," she said, the tremor back in her voice. She's as hungry as he is, I thought. But for him or herself?

"I'll do my best," was all I said.

"We want to travel," she went on. "He needs the experience."

"You mean you haven't traveled?" Judy asked.

"Not east of Massachusetts or west of Chicago."

"But what about the Paris scenes in *Success*? When Ben and Alice spend the weekend at the Georges Cinq?"

"Research." She laughed, an enigmatic trill. "We wrote away for a price list; they sent us a brochure. And Eric has a vivid imagination."

"I'm fucking *cold*," Eric said suddenly, hating to be shown up. "And besides, we've taken too much of Judy's time." He shook hands with me and, impulsively, kissed Judy on the cheek, then held her by the shoulders, looking into her eyes. Anne smiled good-bye to both of us without touching. "You'll have the manuscript right away," Meredith said, "if only for Judy's sake. She inspired me." He took his wife's hand, letting go to open the passenger door for her. She got in the car, but he did not follow. Rather, he ran back to me and hugged me, his head nestled in my shoulder. "I've never been so happy in my life," he breathed, as though we were lovers. Then he turned and lumbered away, got into the car, and started the motor. It was Anne who waved, not he, as they drove down the street.

Judy moved to my side, putting her cheek against my shoulder, where Eric's had been. "Don't fall in love," she said, her voice muffled.

I hugged her as hard as I could. "What are you talking about?"

"With him. He's scarily seductive."

My hand cupped her breast. "I can only be seduced by girls," I said.

two

SUCCESS IS A STORY OF SIN AND REDEMPTION. BEN-
jamin, its hero, is the son of Arthur Holmes, an Episcopal minister
working among the poor of Wilkes-Barre, Pennsylvania, who is in
many ways a saint. Unwilling to judge anyone as unredeemable,
devoting his life to his congregation, Arthur is unable to form
any relationship to his son, whose mother died when Ben was
seven.

And so Ben turns wild as an adolescent. Promiscuous and per-
verse, he indulges in petty theft—first candlesticks from his father's
church, later holdups, minor forgeries, and embezzlements. A brilliant, handsome boy, he affects an intense shyness that masks both
his rapacity and his despair. He fakes his high school records in
order to get a scholarship to college, but once there he finds himself torn between drugs, sex, liquor, and his own intelligence,
which, almost by accident, enables him to discover that it is all
right to work and to think and to feel.

By this time Ben has married. Paula is a pathetic local girl,
sensuous but without depth. They have a child. She supports all
three of them in their off-campus apartment. Then he meets Alice,
the daughter of a city councilman, and the marriage is destroyed.

The central part of *Success* is the story of their passionate love.

20

It is an affair that lasts for years, through Ben's initial triumphs in business, through his rise to power, then the eventual collapse of everything he's built, both personally and professionally, to the great disaster—the death of his child—which leads to the accusation of murder. I won't tell you the outcome of the trial; those few of you who missed the movie version, where the revelation is held to the end, should have that shocking discovery for yourselves. But you can see, I hope, from this bald synopsis, that like most great books the story is not new. There are touches of *Crime and Punishment* here, of *An American Tragedy*—yes, of soap opera too. The book is made magnificent through the realization of its two main characters. It has suspense, a twisting and believable plot; these are what draw us along. But more important it has two people—"They're me, you know; both of them"—who are sympathetic and alive, American, not only facets of Eric Meredith, but of all of us.

The revised manuscript arrived a week and a half after our meeting. Eric had indeed made changes, minor ones, but not to accommodate my suggestions. The trial stayed where it was at the beginning, and Alice's parents remained remote. On second reading, I saw why he had not chosen to revise. I had wanted him to follow the form of a thriller; he wanted to eliminate artificial suspense, preferring to concentrate on the lovers—and he was right. He was interested in soul, not pyrotechnics.

Judy and I read the manuscript in bed together that night, I passing her a new page as soon as I'd finished. We read in silence, pausing only to go to the bathroom or to exchange a look when we'd completed a chapter. Even when we had stopped reading, we were silent. Judy snuggled against my side. I could feel how tense she was; the excitement that filled me filled her.

"This book," I said at last, "is going to make me the most famous agent in New York."

She moved slightly away and looked at me. Her eyes were grave. "*That's* what you're thinking."

"Yes."

"About yourself?"

"Yes. I have been since the book arrived the first time. What's the matter with that?"

She sighed. "I'd think you'd have realized it's *his* book, not yours."

I resented the rebuke but smiled despite myself. Her ardor was a manifestation of a selflessness that was one of her most beguiling characteristics. "I know it's his book," I said. "But my God, Judy! Books like *Success*—think what it could mean for us!"

She wriggled closer. My hand found a nipple. "It excites you, doesn't it?" she asked. "Thinking about your success."

The nipple hardened. "Seems to me you're the excited one," I said, reaching for her.

She moved away. "I'm serious. Talk to me for a moment. You're more interested in what the book will do for you than what the book *is*."

"What the book will do for *us*. I love you more than anything else in the world. We're about to get married. So yes, I want money, I'm scared now that we don't have any. I want to be able to move out of this apartment, I want to buy you things, I want to have children and not worry about how much it costs to send them to school."

"Those will come," she said, "and I don't care when."

"They're *here*." I tapped the manuscript by my side. "That's the point. I knew what a risk it was to leave Oliver; so did you. A salary's a salary and Oliver paid pretty well. But the authors who came with me, particularly Lustig and Monroe—loyal as they are and skilled as they are—aren't going to be big time. *Meredith has it*. A million-dollar author. *You* figure the ten percent." I paused, annoyed that she had made me feel guilty. "And if we got lucky, if the break happened sooner rather than later, then isn't that terrific? There's no law that says *agents* have to suffer, only writers."

She put my hand back on her breast. "I kind of liked the idea of struggling with you. You're adorable when you suffer."

Once more my hand touched her nipple. "You see," I said, "one big author leads to another. It isn't just Meredith. If I'm right, if he really is a million-dollar writer, then others will follow."

"Pinch it."

I obeyed. "And of course the book matters," I went on. "Isn't it wonderful to think that we're dealing with a great book, not just commercial shit?"

Her breathing grew rapid. "Now the other one." She squirmed on top of me and lay full length, letting me feel all of her body. We kissed.

"I've heard," she said, "that after marriage sex loses its novelty."

"Then let's not get married."

"No. Let's try to think of fifteen thousand novel ways to make love."

"Why fifteen thousand?"

"Three hundred times a year for fifty years."

"And after that?"

She giggled. "We'll write a book about it and become rich and famous."

She felt soft and strong against me. "What does this count as?" I asked. "A kind of spring training?"

Her hand reached down. "Yes," she said. "I think you're ready for the majors."

It was too late to laugh. We had shucked our clothes.

The phone rang.

"Don't answer it," Judy said.

Annoyed, disrupted, vaguely guilty, excitement ebbing, I sat up. "I always answer after midnight," I said. "Nobody calls unless it's an emergency."

She sighed. "To be continued . . ."

It was Meredith. He did not bother with hellos or apologies. "Have you finished it?"

"Good Christ!" I said. "It's almost one o'clock."

"I couldn't sleep. I had to know."

He deserved a little torture; it would serve him right. "What if I haven't finished? The manuscript only got here this afternoon."

"You've read it," he said.

"Yes."

"And?"

"You've done it," I said, my voice flat. "It's perfect."

"What does Judy think?" His voice was as noncommittal as mine.

I laughed. "How do you know she's read it again?"

"You want it, and you want her. I saw your eyes."

I wasn't sure of the logic, but I answered his question. "She loves it." I winked at her. "We were just now celebrating."

"I thought she would," he said. "Anne thinks it's better, too. Thanks for your suggestions. They were an enormous help."

He sounded sincere. My suggestions had clearly meant little, yet I was as pleased by his generosity as I would have been had I actually helped. "But you didn't take any of them," I said.

"That's not important. You made me *think*. And from thought came the changes I did make. I thought the book was ready to go. Obviously, it wasn't."

I had helped! I had a part in it! "Tomorrow morning, I'll call Arthur. I'll take him for a drink, hand him the manuscript, and make him read it fast."

"You talked to him about it before, didn't you? You said you would."

"Yes, talked to him. I promised you I'd take him to lunch and I did. I told him it was the best book I'd ever represented."

There was a moment of silence. "No shit. The best?"

"I don't have many clients."

His hurt was palpable; I regretted the tease. "It's better than anything Oliver Bishop's represented, too," I said. "And he has over a hundred writers."

The sound from Long Island was a sigh.

"I'm going to ask Arthur for thirty thousand dollars," I went on.

"If he doesn't give me that, I'll try Simon and Schuster or Random House."

There are qualities of silence. This was the second different one in a minute.

"Does the price seem right?" I asked.

"I got twenty-five hundred dollars for *Anderson's Luck*," he said. "Thirty thousand's a number I can't deal with."

"Too high or too low?" I was momentarily fearful he would think I had undervalued him.

"I'm not sure. I have to leave it up to you. Of course I think the book is worth immeasurably more, but I do realize, Tony, I really do, that the marketplace doesn't worry about quality, only about projected sales. Thrillers sell, romances sell, movie tie-ins sell, shit sells."

"Right," I said, relieved. Many authors don't know these truths; one of the most difficult parts of my job is to convince them that the literary merit of their books, or the emotional or physical effort they cost, has nothing to do with the eventual publisher's price.

"When I started *Success*," Meredith said, "I thought, if I can get ten thousand dollars I'll be the happiest man alive. Ten thousand dollars for a masochistic act that is my only pleasure. And now you say thirty thousand."

"That's why you need an agent," I said, not sure where he was going.

"When I finished, when I sent you the first draft, I thought it was worth millions. So thirty thousand's an insult."

"It *is* worth millions." His fantasy was interwoven with mine. "Only we're not talking about what it'll earn, only what one publisher is likely to pay in advance. There are foreign sales to go, a paperback sale, a movie sale. And it's only your second book."

He groaned. "I don't want to write more. I can't do better."

"That's what Beethoven said when he finished the Third Symphony."

He laughed. "I'm drained, Tony. Exhausted. I can't see starting again."

I had heard this sort of complaint before and had no sympathy with it. "If you continue to breathe, you'll continue to write."

"You're ruthless."

"I need the money."

"Three thousand dollars won't pay the rent."

I felt my agitation rise. "I told you, thirty thousand's for openers."

"Then you think it'll do better? Make a million? Be a best-seller?"

"Please stop pushing," I said, fighting for control. "I told you when we met, and I'm telling you now, that I think the book will sell. How many times do you have to hear it?"

I could sense his tension. "I can't hear it enough."

"But I'm only an agent, not an oracle. I've said it to you before: I don't want to get your hopes up."

There was a long pause. When he spoke again his voice was low. "What the fuck else do I have to live on?" he asked. "Money? Love? Talent? I'd rather live on hope."

"Yes." I sighed. "I was right. You'll go on writing, no matter what."

His voice rose. "Do you think I *like* it?"

"I think you eat it up."

There was another pause. Then he laughed again. "Holy shit. I do."

As promised, I called Arthur the next morning, met him for drinks that afternoon, and gave him the manuscript of *Success*. Three days later he called me back, agreeing to pay the forty thousand dollars I had requested.

three

"*FORTY?*"

"That's what the man said."

"Oh, you sweet man. You sweet, sweet man."

"Thought you'd approve."

"I'm in ecstasy. I can't believe it. Why did you tell me thirty?"

" 'Cause I was sure of it. And"—I laughed—"I didn't want to get your hopes up."

He must have put his hand over the mouthpiece or taken the phone away from his lips, for his shouted "Anne! Forty thousand!" was muffled. "She's coming to the phone," he said. "Wants to thank you personally."

I felt embarrassed, suddenly unclean. "There's nothing to thank me for. She should thank you."

"Still," he said, "here she is."

"I love you." Her voice was music. "You and your sweet Judy. My God, what you've meant to us."

"Eric's special," I said. "He deserves it. You both deserve it."

"Deserve . . ."

There was silence. The next voice was Meredith's.

"My God," he said, "she's crying."

Next, I called Judy with the news. We decided to go out to

celebrate. She worked three days a week for an interior decorator, her plan eventually to go into business for herself, and this was a workday for her. A New Jersey girl, daughter of Dr. Harry and Mrs. Harriet Solomon, she had gone to Connecticut College as an arts major and had moved into Manhattan immediately after she graduated five years ago. I used to tease her by naming her Queen of the Tri-State Area.

We had first come to know each other when Oliver Bishop decided to remodel his office. The job had been too small for Quentin Fielding, Judy's boss, even though Oliver represented Fielding for his book projects. So Fielding's "executive assistant" (apprentice seemed a better definition) was assigned the job. Two years ago, we met over a couch and some weeks later moved onto it.

Fancy dining meant little to me—agents, even impecunious ones, are taken to elaborate lunches several times a month—but to Judy eating out was special. The restaurant was L'Auberge, a favorite of ours, where one could sometimes discern the meat under the sauce. We talked about the wedding. Judy is level-headed, and so was not unduly excited, but her mother was frantic; Judy aped her misplaced hysteria over hors d'oeuvres, napkins, and match-books. While she talked, an idea was forming in my head, and when there was a pause I sprang it on her.

"Let's postpone the honeymoon."

She looked at me in astonishment. We had planned to go to an inn in New Hampshire, spend the week antiquing, playing tennis, and making love.

"*Why?*"

" 'Cause you deserve a proper honeymoon, a lavish one. Not just a week in New Hampshire. A month in France." France was our dream. Neither of us had been there.

But the code word offered no solace. Her eyes were disappointed. "Can't we have both?"

"Sure," I said, my voice hearty. "But let's cut New Hampshire to a weekend, save the rest of the money for France." I looked at her closely, trying to gauge the reaction.

Laughter. "Oh, Tony, you're so transparent!"

Guilty, I smiled at her. "What do you mean?"

"You don't *want* to spend a week in New Hampshire. You'd rather be here. With *Success*."

"I swear that's not it." I may actually have thought I was telling the truth, but she had an aptitude for seeing into my subconscious. "It's a fact that, thanks to the book, we'll be able to afford France. We'll put aside the four thousand we get from Diadem. And there'll be foreign sales, a paperback. Who knows how much it may mean."

Her look combined affection and irony. "And meanwhile, you can't stand being away from it. *Success*. Or maybe Eric."

"Not Eric," I said quickly.

"Then the book." She laughed again. "All right. But the full weekend. Okay?"

"You're not angry?"

"My ambitious darling, of course not."

"The south of France in a year," I said, relieved. "Next spring."

She took a sip of wine. Her eyes twinkled. "It's a deal. Besides, I like a man who puts his job ahead of his wife. It shows dedication. And how important *is* the little woman? She gives good head, but she can do *that* in New York. Books are important. Books and money and—"

Gloriously happy, I threw a roll at her.

❈

The love we made that night could have stood as a chapter all by itself in our book on the fifteen thousand varieties. Afterward we lay, as we often do, I lying on my back, she with her head nestled in my shoulder; and in that manner she fell asleep.

I was too euphoric to sleep. I wanted to call up Eric, tell him that my love for Judy was even more profound, even more moving, than Ben's for Alice. I felt more mature than he, and I wanted to assure him that as he grew older, experienced more, his books would be better, too. Mine was a contentment I've known too rarely; fulfilled in my personal life and my professional one, I could condescend to genius.

With such happy thoughts, I finally fell asleep. It must have been deep, for I did not hear the phone ring and woke only because Judy was shaking me.

"It's Anne Meredith," she said, handing me the phone.

"What time is it?" I shook my head, vainly trying to clear it.

"Two thirty."

"They're crazy! What's she want?"

"I don't know. She says it's urgent."

I sat up, terrified, and took the phone. "Yes, Anne."

Her voice trembled. "I'm sorry to wake you."

"It's okay."

"I just didn't know where to turn."

"Really. It's okay."

"Eric's gone."

"*What*? He's left you?"

"No. Gone. Disappeared."

Acid exploded in my stomach. "Disappeared? I don't understand."

She started to cry. "He went out for a drink. Said he'd be back to celebrate with me, but wanted time alone to digest the news. He was *wild* with happiness."

I guessed the rest easily. "And he hasn't come home?"

"No."

"Nor called?"

"No, of course not."

"Does he have a favorite bar?"

"O'Rourke's. I called it. He was there, left around ten."

"Drunk?"

"They didn't think so."

"*Does* he drink?"

She hesitated. "Sometimes."

"Did you call the police?"

"Yes. They said it's too soon to put out a missing person's alert, that he'll probably just show up."

"They're almost surely right." I waited a moment. "Did you call the hospitals?"

"What do you think I've been *doing*? I called both here and in New York. Every one I could think of."

"And?"

Her voice, still edged with tears, became flat, official. "Nobody of his description has been admitted."

"That's a relief!"

She began to cry again. "Not really. He could be in a ditch somewhere, run over. They wouldn't find the body until morning."

"Or," I said, trying to tamp down her hysteria, "he could have gone to another bar, then another." *Or found a woman.* The thought was inadvertent. "Forty thousand's pretty good for a second novel. Wild happiness has its side effects."

There was silence for a moment. Then: "I'm frightened."

"Don't be. It's too soon. Really. Has he ever done anything like this before?"

"No. I don't think *he's* done anything."

Another silence. I finally gave her what she wanted. "Do you want me to come out? Keep you company till he gets back?"

"Oh would you?" The words were out so quickly it was obvious she had anticipated the offer.

"Sure."

"It's not too late?"

"What the hell," I said. "I was getting up anyway."

"Bless you," she said. "I'll never forget this."

She gave me driving instructions and we hung up. I crept out of bed and began a groggy search for underwear and socks.

"You're really going?" Judy's muffled voice told me she hadn't fallen back asleep.

32

I switched on the light. "I have to."

"Be careful," she said.

"Don't worry. There won't be any traffic and I won't speed, I promise."

"I'm not talking about driving. I mean them. The Merediths."

I turned to look at her. She was sitting up and staring at me. One shoulder strap of her nightgown had slipped down, exposing a breast. I walked to her side of the bed and kissed her. "They won't eat me."

Her eyes were sad. "They're eating you now."

I went to wash and brush my teeth. When I came back, she was dressed.

"Protection," she said, trying and failing to make the word a joke. "I'm coming with you."

"That's crazy."

"No," she said, "essential. If you think I'm going to let you alone in a house with a beautiful blonde, you're nuts!" Again, the joke failed, and she realized it. "Besides," she went on, "you'll need me."

I held her. "I always do," I said.

Judy fell asleep almost as soon as we got into the car, and I drove across the Triborough Bridge and along the Grand Central Parkway listening to the news. The reports were full of the venalities of Richard Nixon, and I remember my pride in an America able to expose even its highest officer as corrupt. *Writers*, in this case journalists, had nailed him; the power of the written word had grown through the centuries and was at its most potent now, even as we relied on television for our entertainment and much of our news.

My elation made me dizzy. I was on a mission, out in deepest night to save a beautiful woman (I was convinced that nothing serious had happened to Eric—how could it when no accident had been reported, and when he had barely begun to exercise his talent?), another beautiful woman, the one I loved, sleeping securely beside me in the car. Yes, *we* would comfort Anne Meredith and win the respect of her genius husband—we, a civil servant's son now a force in American publishing, and his wife-to-be, queen of the tri-state area. Amazing!

There were few cars on the parkway, and I drove rapidly and with confidence—A.J. Foyt in a 1968 Oldsmobile. Judy stretched, smiled at me, put her head on my shoulder, and once more fell asleep. To my astonishment, I found myself thinking of what it would be like to have children.

On weekends, the drive to Bayshore takes over an hour. This night, I made it in fifty minutes. Anne's directions were easy to follow, and I found the house effortlessly, parked behind the Merediths' Ford in the driveway, and shook Judy awake.

The house was tiny, not much bigger than a mobile home, shielded but not hidden from its slightly grander neighbors by a few scraggly trees and a hedge still suffering from winter. From the outside, it seemed the home of a blue collar worker, and my heart ached that so great a writer should still be in such circumstances. It wouldn't last, I told myself. He deserved, and would earn, far better.

Anne must have been waiting by the front door, for it opened before we had a chance to ring the bell. "Thank God you're here," she said. "He hasn't gotten back yet. I'm frantic."

She did not look frantic. She was dressed in jeans and a turtleneck sweater, wore no makeup and no shoes or socks. Far from the regal beauty she had seemed in New York, she was now a younger, less glamorous woman, and, to me, far more attractive.

Her eyes, for all the crying she must have done, were clear. Her hand, when I shook it, was cool but not clammy, her cheek, when I kissed it, dry. I could not hold back the suspicion that she had napped, and napped well, between the time of her call and our arrival.

"No word from the police?" I asked.

"From nobody."

"A good sign," Judy said, kissing her too. "Tony can tell you—can't you, darling?—that authors act weirdly when tremendous things happen. There was a client of Tony's when he was with Oliver Bishop who flew to Bermuda when he won the Edgar (that's the award mystery writers get, sort of like the Oscar only named after Poe) without telling his wife where he was off to. He called her the next morning, said he had no idea how he had gotten to Bermuda, and invited her to join him. They spent a sensational week. He had truly blacked out from joy."

Her words seemed to have no effect, for all Anne said was, "Eric's not like that," and turned her attention back to me. "Would you like a drink?"

"Just coffee."

"Judy?"

"Coffee's fine."

"I know," Anne said, smiling. "It's breakfast for you, isn't it?" She walked to the bar, poured herself a Scotch, and downed half of it in a gulp. "For me, it's still the shank of the evening."

Judy and I stood silently, watching her, unable to fathom her nonchalance. "I'll get the coffee," she said, and disappeared toward the kitchen.

I sat in the room's only easy chair—the "master's chair," I supposed, when he was home—put my feet on its ottoman, and surveyed the room.

Despite her efforts, Anne had done little to hide its drabness, and once again I was dismayed to think that so fine a writer should inhabit so threadbare a house. The furnishings were sparse—a dun-colored couch with three red throw pillows, a coffee table that might have been bought at a tag sale, two high-backed wooden chairs, cushioned with the same color pillows that sprawled on the couch, the bar, and, at the far end of the room, a dining table beneath a hanging lamp from, as Judy described it later, the Grand Rapids school of Danish design. There was another lamp at the end of the couch, one more behind the easy chair. All three had been turned on, creating pockets of light and shadow throughout the room.

There were posters on the wall, advertising shows of modern art from museums as disparate as the Fondation Maeght and the Whitney, by artists as different as Milton Avery and Fernand Léger. And there were bookcases, stacked bricks and boards along each of the walls, containing at least two hundred volumes. Yet they were not crammed together; rather, there were spaces between clusters, filled with Anne's ceramics—animals, all of them, elephants, giraffes, zebras, monkeys, varieties of dogs and cats. To my non-trained eyes, they seemed delightful; at least their colors, standing out sharply from the dull cloth bindings, lent the only warmth to the room.

So their artistic lives did merge, I thought, watching Anne to turn and for the first time feeling admiration for her. She was bearing a tray on which rode a teakettle, two cups, a bowl of sugar, a pitcher of milk, and a jar of Nescafé. "Make your own," she said. "I'm afraid I'm too upset to have prepared regular."

Neither her voice nor her manner seemed upset at all. "None for you?" I asked.

She walked to the bar and poured another drink. "I'll stick to this."

"You must be exhausted," Judy said. "Come sit by me."

Anne joined her on the couch. "Actually, I'm not tired," she said. "I was—God knows. When I called you I thought I was losing my *mind*. But even though nothing's changed, I feel better." She smiled at me. "You came."

"I'm glad," I said, not sure that I was, feeling uncomfortable and superfluous.

"He'll come home, you know," Judy told her.

"Part of me says so," she admitted, sighing. "I love him so."

Judy looked at her sharply. "Even though he pulls this kind of shit?"

I froze, waiting for the reaction. There was none.

"Even so," Anne said emotionlessly. "He's never done this before, but he's done other things."

"Like what?"

"Forgetting birthdays, anniversaries."

Judy laughed. "Hardly in the same league. Tony does that to me, and we're not even married yet. I fully expect him to forget our wedding day."

"It's some time in June," I said, rubbing my chin. "But just what day . . ."

"See what I mean? Disappearing's different."

Standing, I walked to the nearest bookcase and studied its contents. Fiction only—Dostoevski, Tolstoy, Joyce, Proust, Mann. In the next shelf Dickens, Trollope, Austen, Fielding; and in the next, Melville, Hawthorne, Crane, Whitman, Dreiser. I wanted to ask if Eric read any of his contemporaries, but Anne and Judy were already oblivious to me. Judy, I realized, was the one Anne really wanted, not me, her husband's ally.

"It's my fault he's gone," Anne was saying.

"Why?" Judy asked. "Did you have a fight?"

"No. I'm not a fighting kind of person."

"But you *wanted* to fight. He could sense it?"

"No. I was thrilled for him, as thrilled as he was. It's not anything I did. It's *me*."

Now, at last, she seemed genuinely upset. Judy took her hand and held it. "I don't understand."

"Sometimes, at big times, I don't know what to say to him. I'm not happy enough for him, or not sympathetic enough. Today, I should have been laughing with joy, not crying; but when he sold *Anderson's Luck*—and until today that was the best news he had ever heard—when I tried to celebrate with him, tell him how happy I was, he said the book *deserved* to be sold, and why was I making such a big thing of it?" She paused, near tears. When she spoke again, it was as though I were not in the room. She was confiding in Judy alone. "It's that way in everything. When he buys me a present, it's the perfect present, just what I wanted;

when I buy him something, it's slightly off the mark. He returns it and comes back with something like it, only in a different color or a different size. Even when we make love"—there was only the slightest hesitation—"when we make love, he knows just where to touch me, where to kiss me, when to go slowly, and when to go fast. But I always feel so clumsy, as though I'm doing it wrong. I want it to be perfect for him. I want to show him that way how much I love him. I want to *will* my love into him, through his body. Still, he seems restless so often, unsatisfied. There are times I wonder—"

She broke off suddenly, her eyes horror-filled, looking toward the hall that led to the kitchen. I turned to follow her stare, hairs rising at the back of my neck, feeling a presence.

A boy of about six stood in the doorway to the room, rubbing his eyes. He was an amazingly frail child, almost emaciated, pajamas not concealing his ribs or concave stomach. He had pale gray eyes and a shock of black hair—in that respect, at least, his father's child. But his mouth was twisted down at the corners, into a sneer, as though he had just smelled something awful.

"David! Darling!" His mother, on her feet the moment he appeared, rushed to embrace him. She was smiling, a false spring to her step.

"I heard you talking," the boy said. "I didn't know who was here."

"Meet Mr. Silver and Judy," Anne said, obviously having forgotten Judy's last name. "Mr. Silver's Daddy's agent, the one who got him all that money for the book. He and Judy are going to be married soon. Isn't that wonderful?"

If he thought so, David did not divulge his opinion. He simply shook hands with us gravely, first Judy's, then mine, his direct stare—he made no effort to avert his eyes—vacant, emotionless. I had seen pictures of autistic children with eyes like David's, and I felt a tremor of sorrow for the boy.

"Where's Daddy?"

"Gone out for a while," his mother told him. "He was so excited by the good news he wanted to celebrate." Her voice went up an octave when she talked to him. I found it saccharine, as though she were talking to a pet dog.

"You had to stay home to take care of me," the boy said. It was a flat statement, not a question; I wondered if he were simply parroting his mother's words on other occasions.

"It's what I *wanted* to do!" Her voice rose still higher in protest. "We could have gotten a sitter. Besides, if I had gone out, I wouldn't have been here for Tony and Judy."

David digested this information silently; he and Anne sat down on the couch. "Five minutes," his mother said. "Then back to bed. It's a school day tomorrow, and you don't want to be exhausted."

"Orange juice."

"If you promise to go to bed, I'll get it." Her voice pleaded.

"Sure," he said.

I looked at Judy. She was watching David thoughtfully, and I wondered if, seeing what I saw, she was as disturbed by it as I was. Anne left to get the juice and I got up to pour myself a second cup of coffee.

"Don't sit back down," David told me.

"Why not?" I asked, playing along.

"I've wired the chair. There's an electric current running through it now. If you sit down, you'll die."

"My goodness," I said, smiling, not sure what the game was. "I don't want that. Where is it safe for me to sit?"

"Nowhere."

"But you're sitting," I argued. "You and Judy both."

"The couch is safe."

"Then I'll sit by you."

"You can't!" It was the first time the inflection of his voice changed. He was commanding now; his tone was stronger. I found myself momentarily unnerved.

"But I've got to sit down," I said, moving toward the couch. "Otherwise I'll spill the coffee."

"No! It's Mommy's place!" He was truly excited now, his mouth ugly with intensity. I was suddenly angry with him, and annoyed at myself for letting him get to me.

I moved back toward my chair. "Coffee's the antidote," I told him. "If you hold a cup of coffee in your hand, it works like a lightning rod and the electric current can't hurt you."

"Don't sit!" he screamed. "Don't sit!"

"David, honey, it's all right." Anne had returned, proffering orange juice. He took it meekly, calm again, and began to drink. Anne sat by him and caressed him, drawing him close. "Sorry about that," she said to me. "Little boys have immense imaginations."

Calm had returned to me as well. "He's amazing," I said, and sat down.

"You're lucky," David muttered. "I turned off the current." He lay down on the couch, his head on his mother's lap, and regarded me with his scowl and vacant stare.

We talked desultorily for a while. I gave a standard, simplified lecture on publishing in response to a question of Anne's; Judy chatted about the wedding. At length, Anne took David off to bed. He went willingly, shaking hands with us again in his grave manner, and taking his mother's hand as she led him down the hall.

Anne returned quickly and we talked some more. I nodded off briefly and I could see Judy fighting sleep, too. Only Anne seemed alert, operating, I supposed, on nervous energy. Twice she excused herself to "freshen up," and both times did indeed look refreshed when she came back. She gave no blatant sign of tension, but she smoked nearly continuously and, when not smoking, kept her hands tightly locked together on her lap.

Eventually, all talk stopped and we merely sat. I was reminded of train terminals or hospital waiting rooms. Outside, it had begun to grow light. My God, I thought, it's almost six o'clock in the morning.

And then David screamed, "Mah-meeee!"

Anne was on her feet in an instant, rushing toward the hall;

but David appeared before she could go far. He hid himself against her, trembling but not crying, his arms around her leg as if it would save her from collapsing.

"David! My God, what is it?"

"It's Daddy," the boy cried. "Coming home. Covered in blood!"

Anne gasped and rushed to the window, David hanging on to her leg, and looked outside. Judy and I, unable to stop ourselves, followed her and looked too.

It was indeed Eric coming toward us, but what David took for blood was nothing more than a red shirt, made vivid by the rising sun. He was about fifty yards from the house, his stride jaunty and unwavering. If he was hurt, there was no sign of it; if drunk, no indication.

"See, darling, it's just his red shirt. Daddy's not bleeding. He's coming home, just like he said he would."

There was hysteria in her voice, barely covered by the monotone she adopted, but made manifest by the rapidity with which she spoke. Whatever her inner turmoil, if David picked it up, all he said was, "Oh." No smile—no expression of any kind—appeared on his face. He watched impassively as his father approached.

For the first time, it seemed, she realized the implications of our being there, for she suddenly said, "Good Christ, what do I tell him about you?" as though we were her dirty secret.

"Tell him the truth," Judy suggested. "The son of a bitch—forgive me, Anne—has it coming to him."

"Oh," she said, pouring herself a drink and lighting a cigarette, "I don't want him to think I was worried."

Judy snorted. "What would he *expect* you to be—sleeping serenely?"

"That's what I've done the other times."

"What other times?" I asked. "You told me this was the first time he had disappeared."

Her shoulders sagged; she had forgotten. "I needed company," she said in a little girl voice. "I didn't think you'd come if you knew he had done it before."

"Of course I'd have come. He's my *author*!" I was yelling now, furious at myself as much as at her. I had allowed us to become part of their marital convolutions.

She stared at me uncomprehendingly. The door flew open. Eric stood there, eyes savage, God of wrath. He looked at Anne only, and when he spoke, I felt her fear.

"Why the fuck are you awake?" he said. "And what the fuck are these people doing here?"

Somehow, we got through it. Alternately abandoned child and seductress, Anne explained that this time she was really worried; he had never come back so late before. He growled that he did not have to account for his whereabouts—she knew how he was affected by big news, good or bad. They sparred with each other, she the aggressor, trying to get placating hands on him, he the defensive specialist, slipping her advances as though the thought of her conciliatory touch was repugnant. They paid virtually no attention to us, nor to David, who, an ineffectual referee, kept getting underfoot in his attempts to cling. I wondered whether they would fight when we were gone, or make love.

We left awkwardly, no more than fifteen minutes after Eric came home. Only Anne made an attempt to be cordial, her thank-yous mocked by the contempt in Eric's smile—only fools, it seemed to imply, go on fool's errands.

"Promise me something," Judy said when we were safely in the car and on our way home.

"What?"

"That our children won't be like David."

I looked at her sharply. So she had seen it too; the boy was bizarre. "We'll be better parents," I told her.

"I've never been through anything so weird in my life," she said, laughing. "The wife's a hysteric, the husband's a prick, the child's a dingbat. Just your ordinary Bayshore family." She couldn't seem to stem her giggles, so she moved closer to kiss my cheek. I put my arm around her and squeezed, trying to assure myself of her solidity. "Ain't it nice to be normal," she breathed.

My relief rose with hers. "I love you," I said.

She began to tremble. For a moment, I thought she was pretending, but she gave a little whimper and put her arms around me, holding on for comfort, her head against my chest.

"What's the matter?" I asked.

Her reply was muffled. "I'm scared."

"Of what?" I knew the answer.

"Of them."

"Nonsense," I lied.

"He's in our bloodstream," she insisted quietly. "They all are."

Her trembling increased and, watching the miles pass by, I kissed her hair, chasing her fears, exultant, rejoicing in the Merediths' vulnerability, and in hers.

four

WHEN A MANUSCRIPT IS APPROVED BY ITS EDITOR, as Eric's was by Arthur, two things happen to it immediately. First, it is "put into production," which means it is given to a copy editor who will check it for facts, spelling, grammar, and consistency before final review by the author and journey to the printer. Second, it is sent to the two major book clubs—the Book of the Month Club and the Literary Guild—in hopes that one will wish to sell the book to its members, and in the process pay the publisher for the right to do so, payment the publisher splits with the author.

Publishers value the sale not only for the income they receive, but also because free advertising is generated (a person not a member of the club sees the book on a member's table and goes out to buy his own copy at a bookstore), and because it is the first indication to the publisher that an outside, objective, commercial force —not the author, the agent, or the editor's in-house colleagues— has said, "Yes, this is a good book; we think our subscribers will want to buy it." If both major clubs like the book (there are many minor clubs as well, but I don't want to confuse you with technicalities), they will bid for it, since neither club will share with the other. The auction, conducted very much like an auction for antiques or cattle, can drive the price to one hundred thousand dollars or higher.

In the case of *Success*, both the clubs wanted the book as their main selection for the following March. The Book of the Month Club won the auction by agreeing to pay Diadem one hundred and fifty thousand dollars, half of which would go to Eric.

I had not spoken to Eric since the awful night at his house some two weeks ago, and it was with appreciable apprehension that I picked up the phone. Still, the news was so good I felt it would overcome any remaining anger he had toward us.

Indeed, he was calm, affable, friendly. To my astonishment, there were no triumphant whoops, no excited yells to Anne.

"Blasé so soon?" I asked.

"As a matter of fact, I already knew."

I felt a jealous pang. "Who told you? You got connections at the Book of the Month?"

"Collins called just before you did."

It was something I should have thought of. Editors love to call authors with good news; so often they have to call with bad. "Of course," I said, a bit ashamed of myself.

"He tells me it's significant."

I'd have suspected him of feigning ingenuousness, but he had no reason to do so. "Well, for one thing it means about one hundred thousand readers, right off the bat."

For the first time, I heard some pleasure in his tone. "Oho!" He laughed. "That's more than read *Anderson's Luck*."

"About fifty thousand times more," I said. "Besides, think of the company you're in. Steinbeck, Marquand, Shirer—they all had full selections."

"I've never read Shirer," he said, giving me the impression the others were beneath contempt.

"What does Anne say? She must be thrilled."

"I haven't told her."

"Good God! Why not?"

He pitched his voice low. "It's all that money. I don't want her to know I have it."

Nonplussed, I searched for words. "It's not so much money when you boil it down. They'll subtract the advance from your share—that's forty from seventy-five, leaving thirty-five—and even then you don't get it until your first royalty statement, a year or a year and a half from now."

"Collins explained all that. I still don't want her to know."

I had barely enough sense not to ask the reason for his secrecy; he volunteered it. "She's obsessed with money," he told me, his voice still low. "Jesus, she's practically spent the forty thousand already."

"Oh what?"

"Things for the house, mostly. I told her she should start thinking about a different house, not this one."

"What did she say to that?"

"That when we got the new house, we'd need stuff for it. So why not start now?"

"Forgive me," I said, "but your house doesn't look as if it could hold forty thousand dollars' worth of anything."

"I said 'mostly.' There are other things."

"Like what?"

He sounded suddenly tired. "Oh. Things."

We were silent for a moment. Then he said, his tone chipper, "At least I get a chance to meet Collins."

"You mean you haven't before?"

"No. I've spoken to him, of course. And I got two letters from him. The first told me how much he liked the book. The second, just a few days later, listed some editorial changes he wanted me to make."

I remembered our first conversation and smiled. "Good suggestions?"

"Minor. I incorporated a few of them. It took me one day, that's all."

I laughed. "The book really must be good. Arthur usually demands rewrites."

"*Success* isn't *Blood Lust*," he said coldly. "Besides, the good suggestions came from you."

I felt a sudden surge of pleasure. "That makes me feel good," I said.

"I mean it." He chuckled. "I was terrified when I sent you the book. Your reaction gave me confidence."

My face burned. All I could manage was, "And now you'll meet?"

"Next Thursday. To discuss promotion." I detected mockery in his tone. "Collins suggested you might like to join us."

Yes. How *right* of Arthur. "I'll come. I'll come."

"Good. I don't know anything about promotion."

"They have money for ads now," I explained. "The Book of the Month sale guarantees the book will be a leader for them; they'll want to push it hard."

He sighed. "So it's no longer a book. It's a leader."

"You complaining?"

His tone grew serious. "A little. Of course I want my book to make money, and of course I want people to read it. But I have the feeling that Collins doesn't care about the book, about Ben and Alice. That *Success* is the same to him as *Blood Lust*."

"I doubt it. I know how much he loves the book. But his *job* is to make it sell, not to cuddle it. Think how you'd feel if he did nothing. Remember Doubleday."

"Right. And most of me appreciates that. Anne, God knows, wants to be married to a millionaire. Still, Ben and Alice are mine, and part of me says they should be shared only with friends, not be felt up by strangers."

I had heard this before, from other authors. But if their books actually didn't sell, not one of them failed to scream. It was their way of assuaging the guilt that comes from baring one's soul— flashing, if you like—for money. "If you don't like it now, what will you do when the book comes out in paperback?"

He caught his breath. "Paperback? You think it will?"

I was astonished at his naiveté. "There'll be a sale, yes. B.O.M. full selections earn paperback sales. I don't know how much money's involved; that depends on the paperback houses' estimates of their eventual sales to the mass market, and how many companies will bid for the book. The rights are auctioned, you know. There's a kind of hysteria that sometimes builds up among the houses. Occasionally, the bidding goes out of control. Then paperback executives wake up the next morning thinking, 'Did I really pay *that* much? How can I get my money back?' "

He thought this over. "Let's hope the bidding goes *haywire*."

"Berserk."

"How much do you think I'll get?"

I laughed. "You know I'm not going to tell you."

"You don't want to get my hopes up." He imitated my tone. "But give me a range."

"No less than twenty-five thousand dollars. No more than two hundred and fifty."

"Two hundred and fifty!"

I laughed. "See what I mean? Strange that that's the number which sticks. And remember, you only get half. It could be minuscule."

"Listen, even twelve five's better than nothing. Found income."

I sighed. "Maybe you won't get anything after all. Nothing's guaranteed."

"Except *Success*," he said quietly. "The book itself. Let's not forget it."

"How could I?" My heart was beating rapidly. Not for the first time I was caught up in the fantasy I was trying to talk him out of. Two hundred and fifty thousand dollars. Ten percent of that, added to my percentage of the money he already had coming, would be more than I had made in a year's salary from Bishop. *And* there were foreign sales to go. A movie. Magazine serialization. Jesus—T-shirt rights!

He said something, but I was so carried away with my own

thoughts I did not hear him. "I missed that," I told him. "I was trying to figure out where we should have lunch."

His tone grew cold. "It wasn't important."

"No, tell me."

"I said I had an idea for a new book."

I thought my chest would explode. "Already? That's fabulous!"

"I think you'll like it when it's finished. There's nothing fancy in it, but it'll have everything. Sex. Violence. Slapstick. Tragedy. Characters larger than life."

"What's it about? That is, if you don't mind telling me."

"Oh, I don't mind. It's about my usual subjects—Anne and me."

As I laughed, for I was expected to, he hung up.

Editors have different restaurants for different authors. The first-time, small-time novelist gets the quaint restaurant near the office where the editor is known but the vegetables are overcooked. The nonfiction writer, whose book might sell better than the novelist's, gets seafood. And the author whose book is taken as a full Book of the Month Club selection gets one of the five or six fanciest places in town.

Arthur, Eric, and I had lunch on Thursday, April 17, at La Côte Basque. Walter Matthau sat at the table next to us with the most beautiful woman I had ever seen; Senator Moynihan was nearby. The men wore designer ties, the women designer scarves. The vegetables were tiny and firm.

I could see at once that Arthur and Eric did not really like each other. Oh, Arthur was expansive in praise of *Success* and Eric was at his most affable. Still, I could tell that the praise was for the book, not the man, and that the affability was forced, the bonhomie of a salesman, not a friend. It's not that there was hostility between them; that would be too strong a word. Yet neither man was at ease, and I was disturbed that my two most treasured professional friends, the oldest and the newest, seemed so remote from each other.

Arthur ordered a round of drinks, then quickly another, as though the alcohol would dispel the chill. Beyond the book, the only subject they had in common was me, and they spent a few moments teasing me about the wedding before falling into fits and spells of conversation, motors that failed to catch and turn over.

Even in their dress they were different. Eric wore a dark blue shapeless suit and nondescript tie; I was reminded again of a labor union official. Arthur was in his working clothes, an impeccable pinstriped suit, blue shirt, conservative tie. He might have been taken for a banker, except few bankers are homosexual, and Arthur obviously is. There is nothing mincing about him, nothing flamboyant, but a gesture here, a word there betrayed him, and as he talked I noticed Eric watching him suspiciously. (Later, he told me he was wondering whether a homosexual could really understand the love between Ben and Alice, but at the time I doubted whether Eric had ever knowingly been at a table with a homosexual before.)

Arthur forced a third round of drinks on us, only in Eric's case the "force" did not have to be excessive. He grew voluble at last, talking of his Wilkes-Barre boyhood, his strict, no-nonsense, minister father and his lean, tough, hardworking mother, who cared for her two men (Eric had no brothers or sisters) like a pioneer woman. Defiantly, he told us of the sins of his youth and young manhood, escapades already described in *Success* or *Anderson's Luck*. But mostly he talked about Anne.

"I can't live without her," he announced. "It's as simple as that. I need her. From the moment I saw her, I wanted her. When I won her, I won sanity. Salvation."

I thought of his behavior when the sale to Diadem was announced and could not reconcile it with his words. There would be a time in our relationship—a time not long in coming—when I would be able to catch him up on it, but this day I listened dumbly.

We had salmon mousse to start with; for a main course, Arthur and I shared a rack of lamb, Eric ate steak. Arthur insisted on a Bordeaux, so we drank more while we dined, our faces and voices flushed with the importance, if not the joy of this first collaborative meeting. Eric ordered a soufflé for dessert, and a double brandy. Arthur and I contented ourselves with coffee.

"To business!" Arthur cried when the coffee arrived. "We want you to go on tour."

Eric looked at him, baffled. "What's that?"

"A promotion tour. We'll send you around the country, get you on television and radio. Arrange newspaper interviews."

Comprehension, and with it horror, appeared in Eric's eyes. "You mean I'm to go from city to city, hawking my book?"

"Precisely."

"Oh, I can't do that. No way I can do that."

Arthur laughed nervously. "They all say that at first. Where's the ham in you?"

Eric glared at him. "I left it at the farm."

"No, really. It's the *way* to sell books. We know that. Newspaper advertising, by itself, doesn't work. People forget the ads by the time they've finished their morning coffee. We've found that only television's effective—that is, an author with an appealing personality gets on the tube, and the public responds to *him*. The next morning they go to the bookstore and tell the clerk they want the book by that 'nice young man on Johnny Carson last night.' They don't necessarily remember the name of the book, or even what it was about—but they buy it."

All Eric said was, "You want *me* to go on Johnny Carson?"

Arthur seemed oblivious to the scorn in his voice. "I'm not guaranteeing you Carson," he said, "or Donahue. But we'll try to get you on. And local shows, too."

"I thought you didn't send novelists on tour," I said, offering to protect my author but delighted they had such plans for him.

"We usually don't. Nobody wants to hear a novelist rave about his book. But Eric has a story to tell. Young novelist, first book does nothing, second becomes a full Book of the Month Club selection. Besides, *Success* is the story of Eric's life, and"—he smiled—"people like reformed hoodlums. They're better than reformed drug addicts."

"I wouldn't call him a hoodlum," I said.

Eric sighed. "You could." He ignored me now, concentrating on Arthur. Like a spark on tinder, the idea had caught. "When would this be?"

"Next March. When the book comes out."

"How long would I be gone?"

"I'm not sure. Two weeks or three, depending on how many shows we can get for you."

"Where would I go?"

"The book towns. New York, of course, Boston, Chicago, L.A., San Francisco. Maybe Cleveland, Philadelphia, Atlanta. Again, it depends on interest."

"And what does it entail?" he asked. "A city a day?"

"Sometimes two cities in one day, sometimes two days in one city. Very rarely more than that."

"Well," said Eric slowly, "I won't do it."

"It'll hurt the sale of the book," Arthur warned him. "We really need you."

"I don't want to make a horse's ass of myself. I've never been on television in my life. I wouldn't have the foggiest notion of what to say. I'd just sit there with my face hanging out. It's ridiculous."

"But we'd train you," Arthur said. "Gloria Pincus—she's our publicity director—can give you lessons, coach you." He mimed lighting a cigar and chomping on it. "Baby, we're gonna make you a star!"

"Would she come on tour with me?"

Arthur hesitated. "I suppose so, if you wanted. It's expensive."

"I couldn't go alone," Eric said. "Is she good-looking?"

Arthur laughed. "Not really. And she's married to an FBI agent."

"Shit." He paused, then brightened. "Can I take Anne?"

"Of course. Only you'll have to pay her way."

"Money's not the point. It's fear," he admitted. "But, fuck, taking Anne won't work. The tour's in March, you say?"

Arthur nodded.

"David's in school then. She'll have to stay with him." A sneer, much like his son's, appeared at his lips. "To sum up: the book will sell better if I go on tour; but I'm scared shitless to do it, know that it'll take me away from my next book—rip a month from it at least, by the time I get ready, then recover—and absolutely don't wish to go."

"You'll have fun," Arthur pleaded. "Lots of authors feel the way you do before they start out. Most of them end up enjoying themselves."

"We'll leave it up to Tony," Eric said, looking at me for the first time in several minutes.

Startled, I answered without reflection. "Don't go."

They both looked at me, astonished. "Traitor," Arthur muttered; Eric merely asked, "Why?"

"Because your new book will suffer. You said so yourself. You have no idea how draining a trip like that is. It'll be more than a month that you'll lose." I managed a grin. "Besides, I don't want you out of my sight."

Eric pushed his chair away from the table and crossed his legs, considering. "I'll go," he said, "if Tony goes with me."

"Done!" Arthur triumphant. "Of course he'll go with you."

"Now just a second," I said, heart pounding. Go with him! An easy lay, for the moment I played the flirt. "A lot depends on Judy."

"Fuck Judy." Meredith twitched with excitement. "You'll have been married forever by that time. If you're not boss by then, you'll never be."

"And I don't know how much work I'll have by then."

"*I'm* your work," he said, voice rising. He smiled at me. "True?"

"Yes."

"Then what more important work do you have to do?"

I had nothing. I kept silent.

"I'll pay," he offered, "if that's what's bothering you."

Nothing was bothering me. "I can afford it," I said stiffly. "I'll take my ten percent from you, nothing more."

"Then it's agreed." He practically slapped me on the back. "Do we have to work nights, too?" he asked Arthur.

"Rarely. Most of the tapings are done during the day, even if it's a night show. You'll have most nights free."

"Ah," he said, drawing out the word into a sigh of satisfaction. He pivoted in his chair, regarding me with satanic eyes, so intense they made my scalp crawl. "Arthur's right. We'll have fun."

As we were leaving the restaurant, I reminded Arthur of the wedding, and invited Eric.

"I don't think I can make it," Arthur said. "I'm scheduled to be in the Bahamas. I can't change it."

Eric, however, drew me to him in a hug. "Thought you'd never ask," he said.

five

WE WERE MARRIED AT THE HAMPSHIRE HOUSE. THE ceremony was performed by a rabbi, not because Judy and I had any religious feelings, but because her grandparents were Orthodox Jews. Infirm, they would nevertheless come up from Florida to attend the ceremony.

Since Judy and I had been living together for almost a year, I did not think the wedding would mean much to me. But my excitement began at the rehearsal, grew that night, and blossomed during the ceremony itself. It wasn't the solemn rite nor the joyous party which followed that accounted for the exhilaration; it was, simply and sentimentally, love.

The Merediths came early. During the initial crush of the reception I could not pay much attention to them, but I greeted them warmly and introduced them to several of my friends. They made no effort to be sociable, but instead talked to each other, or stood a little apart from the crowd, regarding me silently.

On the reception line, Anne kissed me lavishly and mumbled a few words about how lucky I was. Eric merely shook my hand and said congratulations, avoiding eye contact. Since they seemed to be making no effort to enjoy themselves, I was sure they would leave early, but instead they stayed, drinking and dancing with each other, while the crowd thinned. I was drinking a bit myself. Alan Davidson, my friend since childhood, was my best man, and we spent thirty laughing minutes while he regaled me with the joys of married life—at thirty-three he was negotiating his second divorce.

I met Eric at the bar. We had decided simultaneously that the champagne served by cruising waiters was not powerful enough for our needs and had gravitated toward Scotch and soda. When he saw me he grinned and put a boozy arm around my shoulder.

"So pleased for you," he said. "I really am. I only hope you're as happy as me and Anne." There was no irony in his voice, though I searched for it.

"I can't tell you how terrific this is," I told him. "I have the horrible feeling I'm monogamous. Judy's all I want and all I'll ever want."

"You're a declining breed," he agreed, putting his face to mine. "I don't envy you, but I'm proud of you, and truly happy that my friend has what he wants. Judy's a marvelous girl, and you alone deserve her."

I knew he was sincere, but the fulsomeness of it made me uncomfortable. "I should do one more mingle," I said.

"You go ahead." He was all magnanimity, "We're leaving now anyway. Anne dragged me into town early this morning so she could do some shopping, and I haven't had a chance to do any work."

"Work," I cried. "On my wedding day?"

"Shit, I worked on mine." His face came closer again, and our eyes locked. "There's nothing more important. Don't you forget that."

"Nothing more important for me than your work?"

"Okay, I'll grant you Judy on your wedding day," he said, smiling. He turned, then stopped and turned back. "I love you, Tony." He winked. "And as for Judy, don't let her out of your sight."

He moved away before I had a chance to answer, leaving me happy but wondering precisely what he meant. Judy approached, shepherding a stout, middle-aged woman with blue hair. "Darling, wonderful news. Sally's getting married, too."

"You inspired me," the woman said. "You two sweethearts look so blissful I got up the nerve to ask."

Dimly, the information penetrated. Sally was Judy's aunt from Minnesota. Max was her live-in. Their relationship was the family scandal before Judy took up with me.

"Max said yes!" Sally went on. "After fifteen years of asking."

"It must be the New York water," I said. "Don't blame it on us."

Judy glared at me, but Sally had turned away, having spotted someone else to buttonhole. "What's the matter?" Judy asked.

"Nothing."

"You sound angry."

"I'm annoyed at Eric," I admitted. "Sometimes I don't understand him."

"Neither does Anne," she said. "Look at that." She pointed to the far side of the room. Anne and Eric must have quarreled, for he was walking rapidly away from her, his face red, while she looked after him with palpable rage. She stared at him until he reached the door and disappeared. I watched Anne's shoulders sag; then she straightened and headed toward us.

No, toward the bar. She ordered a Scotch and only when she had it in hand did she approach us. "Eric's had to leave," she said. "He wants to work." She forced a smile. "I'm having such a good time I told him to go on without me."

"How will you get home?" Judy asked.

"Eric's left the car. Said he could begin work on the train. He writes in longhand," she added, as though letting us into secrets of the Cabala.

"I'm delighted you could stay," Judy said, kissing her and then going off to talk to her mother. Anne had already finished her Scotch, so I got us both another. She looked forlorn, distinctly unhappy, and she sniffled as though she had been crying. "You don't have to take care of me," she said. "I'm perfectly happy here by the bar."

"But you're the most interesting person in the room," I said, "new bride excepted. If I don't talk to you, I'll have to talk to her relatives."

"Good!" she said. "Then by all means talk to me."

"No." I smiled. "You talk to me. It's my wedding day so you can't deny me."

Flustered, she took a sip of her Scotch. "What do you want me to talk about?"

"Tell me about yourself. What does your father do, for example."

She grimaced. "Did. He died a few years ago."

Ashamed of my gaffe, I tried to cover it with a wave of my arms. "Sorry."

"We weren't particularly close. He was a late-night talk show host in Wilkes-Barre. Radio, not television. It should have given us a lot of time together during the day, but he was always off to some luncheon or ceremony." She sighed. "It's the old story. Local celebrity. Beloved by everyone except his family. My mother died before he did. My brother—he's six years older than I am—never came back after college. Which left the two of us, but even then he was too busy for me."

"You must have been lonely."

"Only for a short time. I had my friends in school, of course. But ten years ago I met Eric." Her hand trembled as she lifted her Scotch. "Still, it must account for how scared I get when he disappears. Like he did that night, or even now—there's no guarantee that when I get home he'll be there." She looked at me with mournful eyes. "Sometimes I wonder if there's another woman. But I don't think so. I—I think he needs solitude, not somebody else."

All the alcohol left me less tactful than I might have been. "What would you do if there were another woman?"

Her eyes flashed. "What would Judy do?"

I shrugged; the question had no relevance. "Kill me."

"That's what I'd do to him." She paused. "Or kill myself."

We stood in awkward silence until I said, "Well, I for one have no intention of being unfaithful. And neither, I'm sure, does Eric."

She seemed not to have heard me, for when she spoke again it was in response to an inner thought, not mine. "There are times I want to leave him. Times when I wish I had married a normal man. A businessman, even a coal miner. Half the time I can't figure him out. Sometimes, not knowing what his mood will be, or what will make him change his mood, I'm too terrified to talk. Tonight, for example, I don't want to go home."

Her hand was shaking harder; she had trouble lifting her glass. "But there's David," I said.

"Yes, David. That's why I'll go home, want to or not."

"Is Eric a good father?"

She hesitated, reflecting. "Yes and no. There are days when he'll devote himself entirely to David—play with him, read to him, even sing to him. He'll let David get away with murder on those days. But when he's working, he can be fearsome. If David so much as peeps, Eric's all over him, screaming at him to keep quiet, to get out of the way. I can see David just shrink when he does that. It destroys him. I've begged Eric not to and each time he's agreed, but still he goes ahead and does it again—he says he can't help himself."

She shifted her weight nervously from one foot to the other, then reached out to take my arm. "He's . . . inconsistent. With me, too, only more so with David." Her eyes got teary. "And, oh, Tony, every book I've read says the worst thing for a child is inconsistency."

"I don't know about that," I said, vaguely remembering having read the same thing. "He doesn't beat him, does he?"

"Of course not. But it's small comfort. You saw David yourself. Can you tell me he's a normal child?"

"He seemed perfectly normal," I lied. "Imaginative, yes. But what child isn't?"

"Then why doesn't he smile?" Her voice rose. "*Why doesn't he smile?*"

There was a sudden silence in the room; I remembered there were others, honoring the newlyweds. Judy, talking to her mother about fifteen feet away, caught my eye with an "Is everything all right?" expression. I smiled reassuringly, at her and at the other faces turned toward us. The hum in the room returned; I could hear Judy laugh at something her mother said.

"If he makes life so difficult, why don't you take David and leave?" I asked Anne.

She had regained enough control of herself to smile at the question. "I've only been talking about the bad things. There are good."

"Such as?"

"He's got a wonderful mind. He makes me laugh. He sees things more deeply and interestingly than I do. And I think he loves me. In his own way, he loves both me and David. He's a sensational lover." She blushed.

"Where did you meet him?"

"In college."

"Where was that?"

She smiled ruefully. "We both went to Wilkes. It's the college in Wilkes-Barre. Eric's a little ashamed of it, I think. Ashamed of the school but proud of himself for having surmounted its mediocrity." She paused. "He went there 'cause his parents couldn't afford to send him away. I went because they accepted me."

Her good humor had returned. She was talking normally now, an anecdotalist animated by memory. "I met him in the craziest way—through a game called 'Secret Santa.' I think it started at Harvard, but it's played at lots of schools."

"I've never heard of it."

"It works like this. At the beginning of Christmas week, just before recess, every girl picks a boy's name out of a hat and every boy picks a girl's name out of a hat. The picker is Santa; the one picked is Santee. It's the Santa's responsibility to give a present to the Santee for seven straight days—and on the eighth day, to reveal her or his identity. Obviously, one is both Santa and Santee at the same time, so while I was giving presents to my Santee, a

Secret Santa was giving presents to me." She laughed, enjoying herself. "Clear so far?"

"Perfectly."

"Good. Well, the boy I picked was the biggest nerd in the school, the pimply, sweaty kind, so I got him a box of chocolates, a book, a tie—boring things like that. I didn't work very hard at it. The nerd wouldn't have recognized imagination if it had hit him in the face. But while I was spending almost no effort as his Santa, somebody was going to a lot of trouble as mine."

She paused, evidently searching for the right way to continue, and at last I sensed what had attracted her to Eric. Talking about her youth, she seemed young; in this, our third meeting, I finally detected her sexuality.

She took up her story. "The first night was simple. I came back from class to find a sprig of mistletoe hanging over my door. Before I had a chance to take it down, four boys appeared, each dressed in a suit and tie—unheard of for Wilkes—each carrying a bouquet of flowers. Each came to me, handed me the flowers, kissed me chastely under the mistletoe, and whispered that my Santa thought I was the most beautiful girl at college. Naturally they ran off before I could ask them who my Santa was, but it was a nice thing to hear—it did my freshman ego a world of good."

"Fascinating," I said. "What a terrific game. I gather Eric was your Santa?"

"Of course. But let me tell you what else he did. On the second night a young man dressed in evening clothes, a towel over his arm, came to escort me and my roommate to dinner. He led us to the dining room, a foul place at the best of times, where just this night a table for two had been set aside from the communal tables we usually ate at. It was covered with a tablecloth—again, unheard of—and a candle glowed on it as we entered. He helped us to our seats, disappeared, and returned in a few minutes with a steak dinner for each of us. Sirloin! While the rest of the kids ate dark and nebulous meat, my roommate and I were dining on steak!"

"Nice," I said. "Good for Eric."

"It got better. On the third day, the head of the drama society, the best actor in the school, took me aside and recited 'How do I love thee? Let me count the ways.' On the fourth, a certificate arrived, promising a tennis lesson with an instructor of my choice. I'm a passionate tennis player, it's really my only exercise, so my Santa must have done some research." She laughed again; I wanted to touch her. "Anyway, on the fifth day I got my chocolates—or, rather, chocolate. Singular. One twenty-five-pound Hershey bar. God knows where he got it, but it was enough to feed the dorm for a month."

"That's the least interesting so far," I said. "Even I might have thought of that one."

"More research. Chocolate's another passion." I could see the tip of her tongue through her parted lips. "On the sixth night, my roommate took me to a double feature. It was unusually generous of her, ordinarily we would have gone Dutch. But I naively didn't think it was a put-up job until we got back to the dorm. In my room—my roommate and I shared a suite, so I had a single bedroom—was a Christmas tree. It filled the room, I could hardly get to the bed, and it was decorated entirely in tinsel, lights, and miniature candy canes, dozens of them! It looked so beautiful. He and his pals must have spent the entire time we were at the movies setting it up. When I saw it, I understood what 'my heart leapt' means."

She sighed, an enigmatic sound. "Nothing happened until almost midnight on the seventh day. Then my roommate, acting, she said, on command, blindfolded me. She led me to the sink in our bathroom and made me sit on a stool in front of it. I heard the sound of tap water, and then hands—a man's hands—dipped my hair into the water and began to wash it. I wore my hair long in those days; it was my pride. And oh, how fine those hands, those fingers felt! I love washing my hair. Imagine how good it was to have someone else, a mysterious stranger, a man, wash it for me." She shivered.

I stared at her, oblivious to the room, the guests, Judy. "Did he reveal himself then?"

"No. That was against the rules. Besides, it was more exciting for me not to know who he was. I mean, that way he could still be a fantasy figure, as gorgeous as I wanted him to be. So he simply stole out of the room when he was finished, never saying a word. And my roommate never let on who it was."

"How did you find out?"

"On the eighth night, the night before vacation, there was a dance at the gym. For the first dance, the women Santas had to pick out their male Santees. For the second, the roles were reversed. So I dutifully danced with my nerd and then waited—heart thumping, I can tell you—for my Santa to appear."

Her expression was happy again. The cloud that marred it had vanished; this memory was serene. "It didn't take long," she continued. "Almost the second the music for the first dance stopped, this absolutely magnificent man, with dark, wild hair and light, wild eyes approached me. 'I'm Eric Meredith,' he said, 'a senior.' And immediately he did what I was longing for him to do: he took me in his arms. Granted we were only dancing, but I have the feeling we looked pornographic to outsiders. I could feel his whole body against mine. He was a marvelous dancer, just perfect. I can't remember anything so exciting. He was as gorgeous as I had fantasized, and he was real!"

Touched by her emotion, I watched her closely. Her lip trembled as she finished, and her eyes shone. She shook her head, as though to chase the reverie; her smile was rueful.

"There are still days when he's my dream man. Only I've grown up, and so has he, and we have a son who doesn't smile, and I don't fantasize as much as I used to." She sighed. "He told me it cost him twenty-five dollars to buy my name from the guy who actually drew it. The whole thing cost a fortune, and he couldn't afford it. But he said he had been attracted to me from my first day at college. Still, even though he was a senior and I a freshman, he didn't dare approach me. I had seemed remote, he said, and rich, and aristocratic." She took a sip of her drink, until then neglected as she spoke. "Well, it was true my father was richer than his—radio personalities make more than Episcopal ministers. But remote, never, and aristocratic—" Again, the shake of her head. "You know, Eric didn't tell me about buying my name, about being scared of me, until our wedding night. I thought that was wonderful of him."

We stood awkwardly together for a moment, then impulsively Anne kissed my cheek. "Don't stop loving Judy," she said. "Please. Whatever you do." She turned away. "And don't keep secrets from her."

In love with love, I took her hand. "Don't go," I said. "I want to hear more."

"I've got to get back to the genius," she said, pulling away. "Kiss Judy for me. This was the second nicest wedding I've ever been to. And bless you, Tony, not only for what you've done for Eric, but for listening to me." She raised both her arms and extended them toward the room, taking us all in her embrace. "May you be eternally happy. May your love endure." She kissed my cheek again, then ran from the room. I watched her go, got another drink, and stood by the bar, an objective observer at my own wedding.

How prosaic it all seemed! How many thousands had used this room before us? How many middle-class faces had exclaimed over the beauty of the bride? How many goblets had been smashed, rings exchanged, rabbis paid, aunts and uncles, mothers and fathers, best and casual friends shaken hands with or kissed? An ordinary Jewish boy had married a sweet Jewish girl; we were merely a part of the eternal river.

I shrugged off my mood and walked toward the bride, briefly, only briefly, resenting her in resenting myself.

Directly after the wedding, we caught the last shuttle to Boston, then drove to New Hampshire for our idyll. Yet despite the charm of the inn and the star-filled sky surrounding it, our lovemaking that first night was more from obligation and ritual than from passion, and it left us both unsatisfied.

"I'm mad at you," Judy explained as we lay side by side in bed. "Not very mad, but mad."

I sat up. "Why?"

"For spending all that time at the wedding with Anne."

I smiled. "You jealous?"

She snorted. "Of course not."

"Good. Then what's the matter?"

"You should have circulated more. Spent more time with my family."

"I spent an eternity with your family." I leaned over to kiss her, the conciliator. "I thought it was the nicest wedding I've ever attended."

"It was nice," she admitted. "Only I don't think you circulated enough, and my mother was a pain in the ass."

"Why?"

"She didn't like the flowers. She didn't like the matches. She didn't like the napkins." She smiled wanly. "That's what she gets for giving birth to an interior decorator."

"She would have done it differently?"

"She would have done it in pink. I should have let her. Weddings are, I suppose, a mother's prerogative."

"You'd have been a lot madder than you are now if she had done it. I thought everything was beautiful. The wedding was you, not her."

"I needed you to tell me that then."

"When?"

"When my mother was bawling me out. You were talking to Anne."

"I saw you. You were laughing."

"Like hell I was."

"But I saw you."

She glared at me. "You were too far away."

I swallowed my anger, shuddering at my own childishness. "I'm sorry," I said, holding her. "From now on I won't go any further away than this."

She snuggled into me. "Promise?"

"You bet." I felt her breasts against me. "It's an easy promise to keep."

"I love you," she said, "with all my heart and soul. It was a beautiful wedding. Perfect."

"Mmmmm."

"Was that for the wedding or for me?"

"For both," I said, moving against her.

This time, our lovemaking came from passion. I decided not to tell Judy what Anne had said to me, or my thoughts at the bar.

We drove back to New York on Sunday night and both went back to work on Monday morning. It turned out to be lucky we had postponed our honeymoon.

Judy left for her job early. It was the first time we would be separated since the wedding, and we used it as an excuse to linger over our kisses. But both of us, I think, parted cheerfully, grateful that the strain of the wedding was over, happy to see life not so radically changed after all.

I spent the morning catching up on correspondence and reading a few manuscripts from potential clients. One started interestingly, and I stayed with it through lunch, eating a sandwich at my desk, only to find that the book collapsed at its climax. Still, the work had promise, and I labored over a letter to the author, agreeing to represent him if he would make substantial changes in the final third of the book.

By midafternoon, I had finished and was just about to start another manuscript when the doorbell rang. Judy home early, I thought, heart racing with pleasure. But to my surprise it was Arthur Collins, natty as ever, standing in the brilliant afternoon sunlight.

"Arthur! What brings you here? I thought you were in the Bahamas."

He blushed. "Something came up. It's a beautiful day. Too nice to stay in a stuffy office. So I decided to take a little walk, found myself in your neighborhood, and thought I'd drop in."

"You're welcome, of course. But your office is on Nineteenth Street, this is Eighty-fourth. Isn't that a bit far for a stroll?"

He grinned. "I came most of the way by cab."

I led him to the office. "Then there's more to your coming than casual friendship?"

He nodded. "I've a piece of news."

His excitement was palpable; he was practically hugging himself with glee. "News?" I asked. "Too sensitive for the phone?"

"Too good for the phone," he said, eyes twinkling. "It's far too impersonal an instrument for news like this. I wanted to see your face"—he began to sing—"hear your voice, touch your hand—"

"For Christ's sake," I said, laughing. "Tell me."

"We auctioned *Success* to paperback today."

My heart jumped. Paperback auctions are held exactly like book club auctions, only there are many more paperback houses than book clubs. "Today!" I said. "Why didn't you tell me?"

"What with the marriage and all, I didn't want you preoccupied over the weekend."

"Come on," I said, joking. "Anybody can get married. You can only auction *Success* once."

"I'm sorry if I acted badly," he said, not sorry at all, "but the deed is done."

"I'll forgive you if the price is right. Who bought it?"

"Bantam."

"For how much?"

"I'd say sit down, only you're already sitting."

"Then it went well?"

"You could say that."

"Damn it, how much?"

"Six figures."

I looked at him searchingly. "Six figures takes in a lot of territory."

"Right. And this is toward the outskirts."

"Damn it," I cried again. "How much?"

He pitched his voice low. "Seven hundred and seventy-five thousand dollars."

The breath went out of me as though he had slammed me in the stomach. I could feel blood rush to my face. "Repeat the number."

He did.

"Collins," I said, amazed by my earlier miscalculation of the book's potential, "you are one fucking great editor."

He beamed. "Editor in chief."

It was wonderful news! "My congratulations," I said, warm with pleasure for him. "God knows, nobody deserves it more. But I thought White was going to keep the position open. Save the salary." Matthew White owned Diadem; it was one of the few privately owned houses remaining.

"I persuaded him to change his mind."

"By threatening to quit and take Eric with you?"

"Exactly." He grew serious. "Then you're not sorry I didn't tell you we were selling today?"

"Somehow, I don't think you needed my advice. Give me details."

"We sent the manuscript out to all the houses two weeks ago. They knew about the book club sale, of course, and they know how excited Diadem is about the book. By Wednesday, people started calling back, saying how much they liked it. And Dell gave us a quarter-of-a-million-dollar floor."

A floor allows the holder to step out of the auction until the end, at which time he can top the highest bid if he wants to, usually by ten percent. "Thanks for telling me about it," I said sarcastically.

"As I said, it was just before your wedding. You wouldn't have wanted to know."

"Wrong again," I said. "But no matter. So, Dell had the floor."

"Yup. They insisted we auction quickly, and for that kind of money we said sure. By nine thirty this morning, the bids started."

"Who bid first?"

"Warner, believe it or not. Then Avon, then Bantam—bless their hearts—then Fawcett, then Ballantine, then New American Library, then Pocket Books."

I felt pride rising, not so much for the money involved as for the book itself. "Then all the majors were in it," I said. "They all liked it."

"They all loved it. It's a remarkable book, Tony. I bless you for sending it to me first."

"Seems I picked the right editor," I said. "Go on. More details."

"By noon, the bidding was over four hundred and fifty thousand dollars. There, Avon, Fawcett, and Ballantine dropped out. NAL came back after lunch with a leap to five hundred. We figured that was their last gasp. It took Pocket less than a minute to top it."

"So Bantam and Pocket fought it out?"

"Right. With Dell as the floor holder. The bids kept going up and up and up. I couldn't believe how fast it was all happening."

I ached that I had not been there with him as the auction was going on. How exciting it must have been! "Time flies when you're having fun," I said.

"I've never seen anything like it. We made two hundred thousand dollars in half an hour."

"But finally the fun stopped."

"Pocket dropped out at seven seventy-five."

"What did Dell say? When you told them what they had to top?"

" 'Oh shit.' Their words exactly. I think they expected competition, but not like this. Anyway, they had an hour to come up with a final bid—at that level, it only had to be five percent more than

Bantam's offer—and there must have been a fight in the executive offices. They took the whole hour to make up their minds."

"And then they said no, more's the pity."

He laughed. "Don't be greedy."

"I'm an agent," I said. "It's my job." I still couldn't grasp the extent of it.

He stood. "Anyway, you see why I wanted to talk to you personally. It's my all-time auction record, you showed me and only me the book, and I did want to say how grateful I am."

We shook hands solemnly. "I'll call Eric," I said. "What did he say when you told him?"

"I haven't."

I glanced at him, astonished. "Why?"

"Because I think we should both tell him in person. This is too special for a mere phone call. Let me take you and him to dinner. We'll break the news then."

"I'll pay," I said, suddenly expansive, shock not yet faded enough to let me consider the ramifications to the Merediths. "Anne and Judy must come too. Anyone you want to bring?"

He fended off his embarrassment with a joke. "It's the first time in my life an agent's offered to pay for anything. But I'll save you the cost of the meal. Thanks to you, Diadem can afford it."

"When shall we go?"

"Tomorrow's clear for me. We'll want to tell him before it hits the press."

"If it's okay with the Merediths, tomorrow it'll be."

"The Four Seasons?" Arthur asked.

He had picked one of the most expensive restaurants in the city. I had eaten there many times for lunch, but never for dinner.

"It'll cost Diadem its share of the paperback rights."

"I don't care about money," he told me. "Only art."

Chastely, we hugged good-bye.

More professional news was to come. At nine thirty that night, Judy and I having dined and washed the dishes, the phone rang. I picked it up.

"Mr. Silver?" It was a man's voice, gruff, southern accent.

"Yes."

"My name's Philip Reed. Do you know it?"

"Sure do! You wrote *Blood Lust*."

"Right. Have you read it?"

I determined to read it the next day. "It's one of the great thrillers," I said.

He seemed to take that for granted, for he made no response. "I'm looking for new representation," he said. "Word around town is you did a super job for Eric Meredith."

My heart was sprinting now. "Meredith did the super job," I said, marveling how news of the paperback sale had traveled so fast. "He wrote a masterpiece. All I did was send the book to your editor."

"But you know other editors, don't you?"

"I know most of them. At least one at every major house."

"So if you were to represent me, you could send the book to a publisher which was not Diadem."

A curlicue of fear made its way through my body. "I suppose so." I paused. "Of course."

"Good. 'Cause I'm looking not only for a new agent, but a new editor."

"But Collins did a terrific job for you!" I burst out.

The voice at the other end of the phone grew cold. "That what he told you?"

"He didn't say anything at all. But the book's on the best-seller list, you got a great paperback sale, I gather the British edition's doing well—"

"Yeah, and Collins is taking credit for it."

"I don't believe that."

"Don't you read the *New York Times Book Review*?"

"Sure I do." I stopped. "Except last Sunday's. I was on my honeymoon last Sunday and missed it."

"Then you didn't see the piece on editors and their best-sellers?"

I felt suddenly nauseated. "No, I didn't see it. What did it say?"

"Lots of editors talked about their best-selling books. Here's what Collins said about mine: '*Blood Lust* is a remarkably professional thriller, and Philip Reed is a remarkably professional writer. He takes editing gorgeously.' "

I felt disoriented. "That's all?"

"Isn't that enough?" he exploded. "Fuck, he's practically shouting that he collaborated with me."

"I wouldn't say that," I muttered feebly, recognizing Arthur's compliment. We had often discussed the fact that the better the commercial writer, the easier he was to edit.

"No, you wouldn't," he shouted, misunderstanding. "You'd say about me what you said about Meredith. You don't take credit when it isn't deserved."

"Didn't Collins edit your book?" I asked.

"He changed a word here and there. It's *my* book. How dare he take credit for it?"

Word was that Arthur had worked for two and a half years with Reed before the book could be published. "He's hardly doing that, Mr. Reed."

"Okay," he said with a sigh. "Take his side. Throw away a hundred thousand dollars. Be like my ex-agent."

"Who was that?" I asked, stalling.

He named one of the most famous agents in New York—it isn't important who. "I fired him because he sided with Collins," Reed continued. "He said he didn't want to *try* to get me out of my option." His voice rose like a siren.

"Usually," I said quietly, "an agent wants to keep an author with one publisher. It's disrupting to the author to move. He might be going from an unsatisfactory relationship to a miserable one. Especially when the first publisher has done him no damage."

A pause. Then, "Collins has done me no damage?"

"Collins made *Blood Lust* a best-seller."

"*I* made *Blood Lust* a best-seller."

I felt my neck go hot and was glad we weren't talking face to face. "Yes of course," I said. "I only meant that the book was well published."

"So well published, in fact, that anybody can put out the next one and have a best-seller on his hands."

"It's true the second time is easier," I admitted. "You're a brand name now, Mr. Reed, and brand names sell."

"Then I want an agent who can break the option. I want out of Diadem; no way I'll write another book for them."

I thought of the mercurial nature of my profession. That afternoon, Meredith had become a million-dollar author. Tomorrow Arthur would lose one. It had happened before, at other houses, to different editors, and it would happen again. An imagined slight, even a typographical error, was enough to drive an author from one publisher to another. It was sometimes simple greed that made them change, one house literally buying the author away from another by offering an advance that could not be matched. But often a small incident, a misinterpreted remark, an unsent congratulatory telegram, a publication day not suitably acknowledged, was the trigger. Arthur was congratulating Reed through his *Times* statement, not claiming collaboration. And now there was nothing he could do to defend himself.

"You're adamant then?" I asked. "You've thought it through? Nothing Collins can do will make you change your mind?"

His voice was remorseless. "You got it. I'd stop writing before I gave another book of mine to that son of a bitch."

"Then tell me. Did you sign the normal Diadem contract?"

"So I'm told."

"Then assuming it has the boiler plate option clause, you can get out."

He chuckled with a repossessor's glee. "Excellent. Then you'll represent me?"

In my head, I saw a match igniting one hundred thousand dollars. The image itself made me warm. "No."

His voice squeaked. "But you just said—"

"That you could get out of your option. Not that I'd get you out."

There was amazement, even sadness, in his tone. "I don't understand. It doesn't seem very professional for you to—"

"Look," I cut him off. "Arthur Collins is my friend. My professional friend. I could no more call him to say that an ungrateful shit like you wanted out than I could leave my wife." I took a deep breath, fighting for calm. "It's egomaniacs like you who are destroying this business," I told him. "For some fantasy, some delusion, you spit on your allies and bend over for sycophants. You ought to be ashamed of yourself. I can just guess what Arthur did for your book. He probably worked harder at it than you did." I was shouting now, out of control, foolhardy. "What do you say to that?" I yelled.

He did not say anything. For at some moment in my diatribe, he had hung up.

I looked at the phone, startled, and began to laugh. "Judy!" I yelled. "Wait till you hear this." And went to tell her.

She listened gravely, told me how proud she was, kissed me, meaning it, for reward.

Later, though, when she reminded her of my heroism and self-sacrifice, she brought up a question I had not thought of at the time:

"Would you have turned Reed down," she asked, "if Eric's book hadn't sold to paperback?"

six

THE DINING ROOM OF THE FOUR SEASONS, DOMI-
nated by a large shallow pool in its center and the gently swaying
chain curtains over its windows, is one of the most beautiful rooms
in New York. At lunch, it is frequented by movie, advertising, and
publishing executives (although many of them prefer the less
ostentatious grill, separated from the main room); at night, while
some business still goes on, most of the customers are there on
their own money, and therefore the atmosphere is more festive, the
hum brighter in the room—the rich are playing, not working.

Judy and I had never been there at night before; indeed, Judy
had never been there at all. We were the first to arrive, and she
studied the room carefully with her designer's eye, pointing out
features—the shape of the silver, the way the leather chairs added
a feeling of comfort to the room—I had never noticed before.

I was in an expansive mood. For the first time my being here
felt natural to me, as though I had earned my way into it. Before,
I had always thought of myself as coming on somebody else's coat-
tails—because the Four Seasons was where publishers ate, I was
allowed to sit at the same tables. But now, with the enormous
prospects for *Success*, I considered it only a matter of chance that

Collins would be paying the check, not I. Judy, dressed in a sleeve-less print dress and jacket, seemed to me more desirable than any other woman in the room; next time the dress would be a Chanel original.

"Some day," I said, my gesture taking in the huge room, "this will all be cattleland."

Judy laughed. "You love it, don't you?"

"What?"

"This place. What it represents."

"It represents good food and publishing success. What's wrong with loving it?"

She looked at me intently. "It represents style," she said. "Style you have innately but haven't been able to afford. You look"— she hesitated over the word—"comfortable here."

Something in her tone made me glance at her sharply. She met my gaze with solemn eyes. "And you?" I asked.

"I haven't figured it out yet. I know it's a funny thing for a decorator to say, the room is so beautiful. But L'Auberge is beau-tiful too, in its own way."

"Isn't that being a bit romantic?"

"I am romantic. So are you, I think." She took my hand. "Let's not go too fast."

"It's one dinner at a fancy restaurant. Is that too fast?"

She sighed. "Lots has happened this week. God knows, you de-serve it, and God knows, I want it for you. Still . . ."

I felt a twinge of resentment. "Don't let it go to my head?"

She nodded.

"What about my stomach?" A busboy had arrived, bearing miniature croissants. We bit into them. "You can learn to like it here," I said, "but if you really can't take it, there's a Burger King at the corner."

She did not smile. "You know what I mean. Be careful, Tony."

"Hush," I said. "Here's Arthur."

He arrived imperiously, nodding to the captain, kissing Judy's hand and shaking mine. "The lucky couple not here yet?" He smiled. "It's funny. When an author's book's a flop, he's always at the table first. A hit, and they arrive after you do."

He signaled for a sommelier, who arrived at once. "We'll want a bottle of champagne," Collins told him. "Chill it now please, but don't serve it until dessert. For now, I'd like a vodka martini, straight up." Judy and I ordered Scotch and soda.

"So you don't plan to tell them until dessert?" I asked.

"I'm not sure," Arthur said. "Let's play it by ear. It depends on their mood when they come in. Bad, and we'll tell them right away, good and we wait until dessert."

I wasn't sure I followed this logic; still, it was Arthur's show, and I could see nothing wrong in his reasoning. But it was impossible to judge their mood when they arrived, twenty minutes late, murmuring excuses about the traffic.

Even though it was summer, Eric was wearing his gray suit, the one he had worn to my office in March. Anne, on the other hand, looked beautiful in a simple black dress, cut low in back, less so in front. She wore a single strand of pearls; I could not tell if they were real. Again I thought of her as glamorous and forbidding, a star remote and sexless. She sniffled as we embraced and complained of a head cold; yet while Eric was glum and taciturn, evidently uneasy amidst all this opulence, she was effervescent, her eyes sparkling, the words tumbling out.

"It's the most beautiful restaurant I've ever seen—isn't it, Eric? Sometimes we go to dinner at fancy places on Long Island, but compared to this they seem—tacky." She laughed, and I could see Arthur smile at her delight. "This is something special. I'm afraid I must seem terribly unsophisticated, a real small-town girl, to be dazzled by all this, but I'm not ashamed to admit it."

"It's a celebration," Arthur said. "I wouldn't take the best new writer and the most exciting woman in America to a dive."

"Celebration of what?" Eric asked suspiciously.

Arthur giggled, enamored of his own mischievousness. "You'll find out." He ordered drinks all around. Anne, I noticed, drank her straight Scotch in a gulp.

Eric turned to me. "Do you know what this is about?"

"Yes."

"But you're not telling either?"

I shrugged. "It's Arthur's dinner."

"Then I'll talk to you both when you're ready." He turned away from me, not attempting to hide his foul humor. "How are things with you, Judy?"

She told him, and they started a conversation which, though I was just across the table from them, I could not overhear. Menus came, orders were taken, more drinks appeared, lavish food arrived. We made the appropriate appreciative noises and three of us, at least, ate for the most part silently, our conversation desultory and uninteresting. Anne, who had been so ebullient at first, grew morose and, when she had finished the main course, disappeared to the ladies' room. For a considerable time, she did not return. In her absence, Arthur and I gossiped about publishing and publishers, about books that were supposed to sell and were not, about who had been fired and who was unhappy at his job, and finally, inevitably, about who was sleeping with whom. Through it all, Eric and Judy kept talking animatedly, their chairs turned toward each other's, their faces close, their voices low. I was grateful she had taken the conversational burden away from me and was cheering up the star.

They came back to the general conversation when Arthur and I began to talk about publishing sex. Rather, Eric joined in, though it was as if he were merely going on with what he was saying to Judy privately, only now with his voice raised.

"I was a bit of a womanizer myself," he informed us. "Started early—May twelfth, nineteen fifty-eight, to be exact. I was fifteen, she was a year older. Her name was Phyllis, she had acne and absolutely scrumptious baby fat. She was a contortionist, she was. Had to be, 'cause we could only do it in cars and hallways."

"Is she Mary in *Anderson's Luck?*" I asked.

He laughed. "Hell no. 'Mary' was next. Her real name was Ruth Bermajian. On our very first date we went to a horror movie, *The Thing*. It was a scary son of a bitch, what little I saw of it, all about a hideous creature in the Arctic attacking a group of soldiers stationed there. Bermajian announces she's frightened and asks me to put my arms around her. I can't believe my good fortune, but I'm either too slow or too tentative about it, for she takes my hands and puts them right on her breasts. I remember thinking, 'Hey, if *they're* scared, what about the rest of her,' and by the time the creature pops up, her hand is in my lap, working on the creature there, and mine's in hers. She has parents who both work nights, and before the movie's over, we're at her apartment, banging away. It's the only time in my life I got laid on a first date."

I couldn't quite tell what effect his vulgar talk had on the company. I was angered by it, offended for Judy and Arthur; I'd never seen this coarse side of him before, although one would know he had it if one had read his books. But my wife and Eric's editor both listened impassively, interested, seemingly neither embarrassed nor ashamed.

"That story's in the novel," I said.

"I know what's in the novel," he answered sharply. "The best part of the story came later. And what happened with Rita Kramer after that—" He whistled through his teeth. "Ruth and Rita and Robyn after that. My three Rs for after school. There was nothing like them until Anne came along."

"Talking about me?" Anne returned directly on cue, smiling. She had combed her hair and put on fresh makeup. Her eyes were shining again, and there was a bounce in her walk. "In a way," Judy said. "Eric's telling us about his sex life."

She seemed unrattled by the statement. "Oh, that. The three Rs. I wish you wouldn't tell those stories. Nobody cares about them."

Her vivacity had returned. It made me happy to see that she had recovered. The more facets I saw of Eric the more I admired her. Sensing my own luck, I winked at Judy. She blew me a kiss.

Eric looked at his wife with venom. "You do."

"Well of course I do," she answered, refusing to be provoked. "I'm interested in everything about you. You're my husband."

"Maybe you're just a wee bit jealous," he said. "Maybe you think I compare you to them. Maybe that's why you—"

"Eric!" she warned, provoked now. There was a threatening, almost melodramatic tone to his voice which made my stomach turn over, but her cry brought him up short and he did not finish. There was a *pop* next to my ear, and I wheeled toward the sound, startled.

It was the wine steward, uncorking the champagne. Arthur had summoned it when my attention was on Anne. We must have all been surprised by the sound, for we sat in total silence while a waiter handed each of us a glass and poured a bit of champagne for Arthur to taste. He nodded, the glasses were filled, and Arthur raised his high. It did little to alleviate the charged atmosphere at the table.

"To a great writer," Arthur said, saluting Eric, "and a very rich man."

Blood rushed to Eric's face as though his veins leaked. "What do you mean?"

Arthur preened. "We sold the paperback rights to *Success* for seven hundred and seventy-five thousand dollars."

No one spoke. Anne gave a little gasp and took a quick swallow of her champagne. She did not smile. As for Eric, I could see from his eyes many reactions: noncomprehension, gradations of joy, sudden fury.

And it was anger, I think, that he sought to control when he finally spoke. "You might have told me in private," he said, forcing a laugh. "Going public like this is enough to give a fellow a coronary." I suddenly remembered how insistent he was that Anne not learn about the amount of the Book of the Month Club sale; this money, infinitely greater, should almost surely have been kept secret too. It was, I realized, our egos, Arthur's and mine, that were being fulfilled by this dinner. Without the talent of creators, we needed material signs of our brilliance. Eric needed none of it, or rather would look on the money as a reinforcement of what he already knew—that the genius was his, not ours.

"You don't seem very pleased," Arthur said.

Eric said nothing. I was afraid his self-control would break.

"He's speechless," Anne said, tears at the corners of her eyes. "So am I. But I know my darling. When he's speechless he's at his happiest. This means a new life for him—space to work in, privacy. We'll buy a house somewhere, a house and a guesthouse. Eric can use the guesthouse as his office—as a suite of offices. We can build a library there—"

"Hold on," I interrupted. "It's a lot of money, sure, but it gets paid out over three years, and you only get half of it, minus my commission. It's great bucks, but you can't yet afford the Taj Mahal."

"Besides," Eric said softly, "we're not moving."

All of us stared at him. "But we've got to!" Anne wailed, her voice so loud that diners at other tables turned to look at us.

"We're not moving," Eric repeated. "At least not yet."

"Of course not yet," Anne said, relief in her voice and worry in her eyes. "We'll take our time finding the house. We won't move until we hit on the perfect place. But we can start looking now, darling, can't we?"

"In a year."

"A year? Why so long?"

"Because I need to be where we are now. I need it for the new book."

"Oh darling!" she said. "You can write anywhere, I know it! You don't have to stay."

He looked at her disdainfully, a teacher chiding a not-very-bright student. "Of course I can write anywhere. But the novel takes place in that house; I need its atmosphere. I can't leave it until the book is finished. Surely you can understand that."

"You can remember it," she said. "By the time we find a new

place and move in, it'll be six months at least. You can remember after six more months, can't you?"

"I need its smell, its feel, its *psychology*. I have to be in the house to write about it."

"But it's so small, Eric. So cramped. David gets in your way —you're always complaining about it. You even complain about me."

He contemplated her coldly, seriously, as he would study a menu. "I'd say you and David could move early," he said, "only I need you both there, too. You're part of the psychology."

She flushed, and I could see her hand tremble. Embarrassed, I turned my head away, to catch Judy's eye, then Arthur's. They were embarrassed too. Anne picked up her napkin and dabbed her nose with it.

Suddenly she stood. "Excuse me. I've got to go to the ladies' room."

"No!" Eric commanded.

"But Eric—"

"I said no. You just went. There's no need to go again. Sit down."

My heart went out to her. Me, defender of women's rights. Judy glared at Eric. "Well, I'm going, and I want company. You may be a great writer, Eric, but you don't know much about real life. You've upset Anne; she wants to freshen up. What in God's name is wrong with that?"

When he answered, his voice resonated with contempt. "You're blind. Goddamn blind. For Christ's sake, *look at her nose.*"

Despite myself, I looked. Under her nostrils, where she had dabbed with the napkin, ran a thin white line. We all saw it, and Anne knew we did. She stood sobbing, unable to look at any of us, least of all Eric, her humiliation total. Judy took her hand silently and led her toward the door. Eric had turned his back to them, but Arthur and I watched them go, Judy's arm around Anne's shoulder. The rest of the diners watched, too, then lost interest and went back to their food and their conversation. Arthur signaled the captain for the check; it was rushed to him and he signed for the meal. I thought I could see tears in his eyes, too.

"Shouldn't we follow them?" I asked.

Meekly, his anger drained away, Eric stood up. He shook Arthur's hand gravely and managed a thank-you. Then he took my hand in his and squeezed it, as though asking for solace—or reassurance. "She had promised me she wouldn't," he said, his voice neutral, quiet, introspective. "I was an idiot to believe her." He sighed and let go of my hand. When he spoke, his voice had the unnatural briskness of a visitor to a hospital. "Right," he said, "cocaine. And the good news is that even if she spends two hundred thousand on the house, she'll have close to that much left for more."

seven

THAT NIGHT, I COULD NOT SLEEP. THE REVELATION
of Anne's addiction explained many things: Eric's fear of too much
money; Anne's strange behavior the night of Eric's disappearance;
David's pain; Eric's fury with her at our wedding. I felt a deep
sadness for the writer who had become my friend.

What burdens he lives with, I thought. To me, it seemed mirac-
ulous that he would continue to want his wife and son with him
as he wrote, but they were the stuff of his books, and of course he
needed them, no matter what hardship they brought to his every-
day life.

These thoughts whirled and thundered in my stomach and in
my brain. I was bereft, hollow, even though Judy slept by my side.
I kissed her exposed shoulder for comfort, put my head on the
pillow, and eventually fell into that restless half-sleep when, even
though time passes in chunks, it seems you haven't slept at all.

I was therefore groggy the next morning. Over breakfast Judy
said, "Give him up."

"What do you mean? Give who up?"

"Eric."

"Eric! Why?"

"He'll destroy you."

I snorted. "Destroy me? Nonsense. How?"

She was silent for a moment. Her eyes were troubled. "I'm not sure how," she said at last, "but he's a destroyer, and I don't want you caught up in that. Look what he's done to Anne. To David."

"What *he's* done? Seems to me it's they who are destroying him."

She had gone to the stove to pour herself another cup of coffee. Now she set down her cup and turned to face me. "That may be the single stupidest thing you've ever said."

The intensity of her attack jolted me. It revealed, if nothing else, the depth of what she was feeling. "If my wife were a junkie and my son a nuthatch, I don't think I'd bear up as well as he has."

"But what *made* her take dope? What *made* him sick? Maybe it was living with a husband who shut her out or a father who screamed at him because he was acting like a normal boy. Maybe it's because Eric Meredith is an egomaniac of the highest degree who doesn't have one thought for another person in that thing in his skull others call a brain."

I could not believe we saw it so differently. "You've got him all wrong," I shouted, standing up, as angry as she was. "He's a writer, and you'll never understand writers."

"He's a person and I understand people." She brushed her hands against her bathrobe as though drying them. "I understand you."

"You don't. How could you? If you can't understand writers, you can't understand me."

She looked at me hard. "Maybe you don't understand yourself."

"Myself and I have been living together a long time. We've reached an accommodation."

My sarcasm left her unmoved. "I mean understand yourself when it comes to Eric. You've got too much invested in him."

"If you mean financially—"

She waved the words aside with a gesture. "Psychologically. I see the way you watch him, listen to him. You're identifying."

"Bullshit!"

She smiled, victorious. "Hit home, did I?"

"No. You're being glib."

The smile broadened. "Think about it."

The argument lasted some time longer, but eventually it petered out and later, after Judy had left for work, I did think about her words and wondered if she was right.

No. He was not an egomaniac. There was too much compassion in his books, and I remembered with satisfaction his interest in me. And yes, I identified. But why? What did Eric mean to me?

A meal ticket, certainly. He represented my independence and, it began to appear, a solid financial base. As he prospered, other writers would come. There would be more Philip Reeds, without the treason. But there *was* more. Was Judy right when she said my needs were psychological, not financial?

What would happen, I thought, if after the next book Eric chose a different agent? The loss of income would certainly be catastrophic; it would take twenty authors to fill the gap. But the real question was, what would my *life* be like if I lost him? Less exciting, less colorful, less fulfilled? All of these, but they were the obvious answers; they did not take into account the needs of my soul.

Since I did not have his talent, being with him was the only way to partake of it. I had read alone as a boy, the books my truest friends, and even then I was pushed by my father to emulate the masters. Now I had met one, represented one. I had made contact; in all my life, that was my greatest triumph. And if I lost it? . . .

I began to sweat. This is terror, I thought, never having experienced it to such a degree before. I am not a fearful person, and I did not like the feeling. Automatically, I reached for the phone, but remembered that Judy would be unavailable all day. So I sat for a moment, attempting to banish dread, then looked up Eric's number on the Rolodex, and dialed. The phone rang several times before he answered. *I've interrupted his writing.*

"Just want to know if you've recovered from last night," I said, my voice as cheerful as I could make it.

"Sure. Fine. It was a lovely dinner. And unimaginable good

news. I've already called Arthur to thank him." His voice was warm; he seemed pleased to hear from me. If he was upset about Anne's behavior or his own, it was not apparent in his tone. Some destroyer, I thought, smiling.

"Is Anne all right?"

"Couldn't be better. She apologizes for last night, says she was nervous and needed Dutch courage."

"Then you're not mad at us for going public about the money?"

"I was at dinner," he admitted. "But then I thought I was an ungrateful bastard. How can you *not* celebrate that kind of money? I say to you, Tony, what I said earlier to Arthur. The three of us make a great team."

I was sorry I could not record the conversation, play it back for Judy. "Have lunch with me." I said it casually.

He didn't answer for what seemed a minute. Finally he said, "I'd rather not. Forgive me."

Annoyed at my disappointment, at my need, I pressed on. "But I'd like to see you."

"Why?"

Oh. Good question. "I've come up with a strategy for foreign sales. I'd like to discuss it with you." A weak response, but not bad for spur of the moment.

"Let's postpone it," he said. "You don't need my advice on foreign sales. And right now I'm working. When I do, I can't think about business. Hell, I can't even think about breathing."

"I understand," I said, too proud to urge anymore.

"Besides," he said, his voice balm, "it won't be long until we'll be living together on the road. That's when I'll need your counsel. I'm terrified of the trip. I couldn't do it without you."

The publicity tour. I had momentarily forgotten. It was then I would get to know him, get to understand why I needed him so much. More important, he would get to know me. I would make *him* need *me*.

"You're right," I said. "As you say, we'll have some fun. I look forward to it."

"The new book should be well along by then. If I'm satisfied with it, I'll show it to you. I'll welcome your suggestions."

Would he? "Call me anytime before then," I told him. "Anytime you want advice or diversion. I worry that you're working too hard."

"Don't," he said, his voice suddenly flat, unfathomable. "There's nothing to worry about."

Worry, like an asp, struck at my heart.

eight

SUMMER AND FALL PASSED GLORIOUSLY. WITH OUR immediate financial future secure, I was able to devote more emotional time to Judy, as she could to me, and we found that the more we gave our marriage, the more it flourished. I hired a secretary, a Wesleyan graduate named Erika Eliasof who believed in Literature but whose efficiency matched Judy's, even surpassed it. Her arrival freed Judy completely and, able to spend full time on her decorating clients, she prospered to the extent that she could rent office space and hire a secretary herself, one Charles Peters, marshmallow of face and always smiling, but a man, Judy assured me, with taste.

Masters, then, of our own schedules, we were able to take long weekends for short vacations, exploring each other in New England inns. We scheduled a movie or play a week, improved our tennis, made new friends and kept old ones. Indeed, I felt we were oversocializing, and our infrequent fights mostly concerned my desire for privacy, hers for the companionship of others. Everyone told us how happy we seemed. When we arrived at dinner parties, our friends smiled with the condescension one reserves for newlyweds.

Through these months I did not see Eric, but I met often with Arthur and kept up with the progress of *Success*. Arthur, naturally, was giving the book star treatment. Milton Charles, perhaps the best artist in the business, designed the jacket—bold black type against a scarlet background with an insert drawing of the two lovers, Ben and Alice, embracing. The interior typeface was lovingly chosen; the part titles and title page were both elegant and eye catching; the all-cloth binding had Eric's initials discreetly blind-stamped into it; the book had a "best-seller look," as we call it in the trade, a quality rare for publishing and flattering to the writer and the house that produces it. I had never been associated with a book so lovingly made, and it thrilled me just to hold it when it came off press in the first week of January 1976.

Even then, though, I did not call Eric but simply wrote him a note expressing my pleasure. It hurt, but I was determined not to call him unless he called first. Arthur had spoken to him and told me how delighted he was with the book and with the other events that had happened to it; but something held me back from calling him myself. I felt I had been told by him that *he* would call *me* when the time came, and that time would be in March, just before the tour.

The "other events" surrounding *Success* included sales to England, France, Germany, Italy, Japan, Spain, Finland, and the Scandinavian countries. I had made the sale to England myself, simply by sending a copy of the manuscript to an editor friend at Thrush Press and asking for fifty thousand pounds. An okay arrived within the week. The other rights were sold by subagents and came to an additional two hundred and fifty thousand dollars. It was virtually certain that Eric personally would earn over a million dollars from the book. It would go higher if a movie sale was negotiated.

And, just before Christmas, the deal was made. The price was three hundred thousand dollars, with additional moneys to be paid if the movie was a financial success. As you know, the film was marvelous, giving both Brenda Marsh and Tom Dunne the best roles of their illustrious careers. But, like many movies from serious novels, it was not a money-maker, at least by Hollywood book-keeping standards. When this sale was made, I did call Eric—it seemed important enough to do so—but Anne answered the phone and told me Eric was incommunicado. Everything was fine, she assured me; Eric was working well; David had learned to read and was thriving at school; she had devised a new ceramic technique and was, in her few minutes of spare time, perfecting it. She was cordial but remote in manner—taking her cue, I imagined, from her husband's performance of months before. Nothing, after all, had happened to change his attitude.

※

Also in December, advance reviews appeared. The Kirkus Service, *Publishers Weekly*, and *Library Journal* all run short reviews of most books to be published in the next two or three months. The reviews are mostly for libraries, but they can also be extremely important to the publisher. Beyond the knowledge they give of what the library position will probably be, they are the first indication of what newspaper and magazine critics are likely to say after the book is officially published. Thus publishers turn anxiously to the reviews when they arrive, and if they're extraordinarily good, an editor will often call a literary agent to crow.

Arthur called me on December 29.

"Your *Publishers Weekly* come yet?"

"Not yet. You folks in the business district get yours on Friday. I'm in the provinces. Mine doesn't generally come till Monday."

"Then let me read you this." His voice told me nothing.

"Good?"

"Judge for yourself." He cleared his throat in the manner of an orator. " 'Eric Meredith's *Success* is a minor masterpiece. Nothing in the author's first novel, *Anderson's Luck*, prepared one for the power, profundity, or passion of this story. Meredith has created two unforgettable characters, Ben Riley and Alice Latham, and set their love against a background of nothing less than contemporary America revealed. The book follows Ben through a crime-filled adolescence to an adulthood filled with power and fame; yet, Meredith seems to be saying, all else pales before love. If only love is important, then in Ben and Alice Meredith has given us people whose love matters, whom you love yourself, and the tragedy of their lives—for, its moments of high comedy and continuous wit notwithstanding, this is a deeply moving tale—will, we suspect, be remembered for decades to come, and not by any means because of its intense eroticism alone, although the prudish will want to run for the hills. It is quite possible that Ben and Alice will become classic lovers, like Heloise and Abelard, or Anna and Vronsky. True, in a way, this is an old story, and occasionally Meredith makes his characters too obviously symbols of America itself. But taken with all its flaws, *Success* shows us a new and commanding voice, a young talent ablaze. Book of the Month Club full selection. Seventy-five thousand first printing. Fifty thousand dollar advertising guarantee. Author tour."

I could feel my joy and laughter rising. "Okay," I said. "You wrote that. But what does *PW* say?"

"Have you *ever* read a review like that?"

"Never. Congratulations, Arthur. You've just become editor of the successor to Faulkner."

"Let's not go too fast," he said. "It's only *PW*. The real reviews haven't appeared yet."

"True. But this is quite a start. An omen. You read it to Eric?"

"First thing."

"What did he say?"

There was a pause. "You're not going to believe this."

"With writers, I'll believe anything."

"He asked if I thought it was a good review."

I laughed. "He couldn't figure it out for himself?"

"No. Really. He was serious. He was troubled that it was only a 'minor' masterpiece. That the reviewer found flaws."

I had experienced this kind of reaction before. Few authors can have their books praised enough.

"So he wasn't happy?" I asked.

"I left him contented. No more. And even that took some doing." He hesitated. "It scared me, Tony."

"What did?"

"His reaction. Anyone with that immense an ego scares me. Holy shit, he isn't Faulkner, let alone Tolstoy. And even they got some rotten reviews."

I remembered Judy's accusations. "Don't be afraid. He's just another author."

"Not quite," Arthur said, then dropped it. "You all set to go?"

"On tour? Sure. But I haven't spoken to Eric. I told you the conditions. Do you know if he still wants me to come?"

"He's counting on it. Told me so today."

Relief sang in my brain. "I could use an itinerary."

"The normal tour. New York, of course—that doesn't concern you. Boston, Washington, Philadelphia, Chicago, Cleveland, Detroit, L.A.—that's where it starts—San Francisco. Probably Atlanta. Maybe Seattle. Maybe St. Louis. Three weeks. First-class tickets. Limos. The best hotels. We spare nothing for your happiness, Tony."

"*My* happiness?"

"Sure. We've decided to pick up your tab. And fuck Eric. He doesn't even know a good review when he hears one." He laughed at his own lame wit. "I'll send you the exact schedule when I have it."

He hung up. I sat for a moment, looking at the phone, and then I began to whistle.

Gloria Pincus, Diadem's director of publicity, made all the arrangements for the tour. It was she I spoke to, not Eric, who, true to his word, did not contact me at all. He would, Gloria told me, meet me at the plane—she had reserved first-class seats to Los Angeles, our most important stop.

We had been booked on the noon flight on Sunday, and as is

my nature, I arrived early, barely past eleven, unable to contain my agitation, and sat doing a crossword puzzle, waiting for the flight to be called. I remember still how nervous I was, an unease exacerbated the night before by Judy's asking me whether I didn't think a certain degree of humiliation was involved in all this—after all, I was nothing but an all-expenses-paid chaperon.

"But he asked me to come as a friend," I protested.

She wrinkled her nose. "Some friend. He hasn't spoken to you in months."

Was she right? I wondered. Was I merely being used? And if so, why? What reason would Eric have to humiliate me? Why would he want me along, if not for friendship or at least companionship?

"Tony!"

His roar came from yards away and was so loud that the other passengers turned to look. He had spied me from the check-in counter and now bounded toward me, unkempt as usual, larger than ever. I was reminded of a sheep dog some friends of ours had whose every muscle shook with what seemed like pleasure each time she took a step.

I rose to greet him and found myself in a bear hug that took the breath from me. "Free at last!" he said. "Great God a'mighty, free at last!"

My head on his shoulder, I found myself hugging back. "It's been a long time," I said, stifling resentment, pleasure suffusing me like a blush.

"Ah, but I haven't been idle."

I felt a flash of vicarious excitement. "The book's coming well?"

"Came, m'boy. Came. A first draft's complete."

I had to fight for breath, as though I'd been running. "Eric, that's marvelous! When do I get to see it?"

He stepped back and looked at me as though the question were an impertinence. He had obviously forgotten his wish to have me read it. "In good time."

"But you're pleased with it?"

"I don't know," he said, his voice suddenly serious. "I haven't really read it through yet—just kept writing. I tell you, I've been a madman these past months. A madman kept hostage by demons."

Our plane was announced before I could ask him more. He put his arm around my shoulder and steered me toward the gate. "Tell me about Judy."

I got the sense he would rather be squeezing her. "She sends her love."

"And I reciprocate. You're a lucky man, Tony. I envy you."

"But you have Anne," I said.

He grinned. "Free at last. Damn it, Tony, the draft's finished. I'm unchained. This trip's going to be fun!"

We boarded; in time, the flight took off. I found myself shy with him, a boy with a baseball star, but he seemed not to notice. He talked nonstop, his mood as sunny as an MC's.

"You're going to be fine on those talk shows," I told him.

"You have the schedule? I seem to have lost mine."

I produced the one Gloria had sent me. He studied it for a few moments, then grinned again. "Three nights free in L.A. What an opportunity, Tony."

Yes. My time with him, to get to know him. During the day, he would be in the studios or conducting newspaper interviews while I, his trusted liege, waited outside. "Opportunity for what?" I asked, knowing.

He paused a moment. "For friendship."

Unbelieving, I said, "I'll drink to that," for the stewardess had come to take our order.

He stared at her. "Ain't first-class grand?" he asked. I had to agree.

❈

After a while, he began to talk about sex. "I think about it all the time," he confided. "Can't look at a woman without wondering how she is in bed, how her areolae pucker when her nipples go hard, how much hair she's got in her bush."

I smiled at him, uncomfortable at his confession. "Maybe that's why you write so well about it," I told him.

He shrugged off the compliment. "To me, it's the most important thing in the world," he said seriously. "Even more than writing—and writing is in some ways a sexual act. But it's masturbatory. I like sex with a partner." He paused to take a swallow of Scotch. "Is Judy good in bed?"

The question was so sudden and good-natured that I did not have a chance to be offended by it. "Terrific."

He looked at me and smiled, filing away the information. "Anne's good too," he said matter-of-factly. "She's a real screamer. I like screamers. I can play her like a mandolin."

I tried to picture regal, cold Anne singing as she was strummed, but the effort failed. "Still," Eric went on, "I could never be faithful to her. Good God! The idea of sleeping with only one woman for the rest of my life is appalling." He leaned toward me, about to confide some earth-shattering secret. "Every cunt is different," he said. "The man who doesn't sample as many as he can is the man who has no interest in staying alive."

I knew how silly he sounded, yet his talk excited me. "Why the obsession?" I asked. "Have you figured it out?"

He thought for a moment. "Inherited. As near as I can figure, my mother was a lusty woman, enjoyed her sex and wanted it frequently. I could hear them often at night; my room was next to my parents'." He frowned. "But I think her passion scared her. She wouldn't talk to me about sex—at least not the pleasure of it. All she did was warn me about the clap and insist I respect the girls I went out with."

"And your father?"

"The minister? He told me the facts of life as though they were part of a sermon, and once, when he caught me masturbating, nearly tore my cock off. Otherwise he stayed away from the subject as though it didn't exist." He sighed. "He was a tough man, my father. He rarely hit me, but he never touched me with love. I always felt there was a pulpit between him and me."

I digested this, knowing much of it from *Anderson's Luck*. "So sex was hidden from you?"

"Until I lost my cherry. And then it consumed me." He paused. "I suppose it's unusual, this obsession, and I don't think my parents' attitude or behavior is enough to explain it. I mean, everyone likes to get his rocks off, but for me there's more to it, more than the pleasure of the act itself. I *must* have it, in profusion and variety. It sustains me."

He spoke with such intensity that I was startled. "Does Anne know any of this?"

"Not a jot of it. You see, I love her and wouldn't want to hurt her. Her middle name is Jealousy. There's no reason she should know."

If there was logic, it evaded me. "You love her, but you'll cheat on her?"

"Of course. One has nothing to do with the other, don't you see?"

I didn't, so was silent.

"Sex sustains me. Anne defines me. I need both."

I remembered what Anne had said to me at the wedding and my sense then of how much she loved him, and I felt a rush of sorrow for her. Maybe she did know. Maybe that explained the drinking and the drugs. "The night you stayed away, when I sold *Success* to Diadem, were you with a woman?"

He looked at me sharply, and I regretted the question, but he answered without rancor. "Her name was Helen. I met her at O'Rourke's. For what it's worth, I haven't seen her since that night."

The answer sickened me. How could he not have celebrated with the wife he professed to love? "You're shocked?" he asked.

"Not at all."

"Then distressed. Ashamed of me?"

"I don't make moral judgments," I said, lying.

"But you wouldn't have acted the way I did?"

"No."

"Why?"

"Because Anne needed you that night," I blurted. "Don't you realize that?"

He looked at me, baffled. "She did?" he asked. "Why should she have needed me? She was safe. It was *my* book you sold."

❃

There are old and new wings to the Beverly Wilshire Hotel. As I understand it (Hollywood niceties are for the most part blessedly distant from me), the favored guests stay in the old part, the first-timers in the new. In any event, Eric and I were shown to our room in the new wing and, neither of us accustomed to such luxury, had no complaints.

Eric was in a manic mood. He whistled as he unpacked and virtually danced back and forth to the closet to hang up his clothes. He had not brought much—two suits, one the inevitable gray, the slacks and jacket he was wearing. I had brought more, even though I knew that while he was being interviewed, I could walk around in jeans and a sports shirt. Still, I had made some appointments in L.A. for my free time.

We established quickly that neither of us snored and neither cared if the other kept his bedside light on for late-night reading. I had not shared a room with a male since college; neither had he. But we both looked on the prospect with equanimity. Indeed, I fantasized talking to him with the lights off, sharing confidences like adolescents.

"Thirsty?" he asked when we had finished unpacking.

"Parched."

"Good. I suspect they have a bar in this place. Let's go ogle the stars."

"Let's let the stars ogle us," I said.

He did a short tap dance by the door. "Holly-wood," he sang, looked at me over his shoulder. "I'm glad you're here to share this, Tony."

So was I. So was I.

❄

We went to El Padrino, a restaurant in the old wing of the hotel. Dark and leathery, its long bar was almost deserted, since it was midafternoon, but many of the tables in the adjacent dining room were filled, mostly with women finishing coffee and dessert.

"Where are the stars?" I whispered. "You promised me there'd be stars."

"That's Janet Leigh," he whispered back, pointing to a table obscured by shadows. "That good enough for you?"

I craned to look. A beautiful, busty blonde was sipping coffee while her companion, busty and brunette, talked; but I couldn't be sure who she was. "How do you know it's Janet Leigh?"

"I've always loved her. Ever since she took that shower. It's *got* to be Janet Leigh."

"Then it is," I affirmed. "And that man at the farthest table, with his back to us, is Robert Mitchum."

We sat at the bar and ordered Scotch. "You see," Eric said, laughing, "I told you I'd produce stars."

"And look," I said, "we *are* being ogled."

Two women, both in their late twenties, tanned and expensively dressed, watched us from a nearby table. They had come in after us, and were just now starting on drinks—screwdrivers or plain orange juice. Each wore slacks and a silk blouse; each sported large rings, though not on the fourth finger of the left hand. I could not overhear their conversation, but their movements were graceful and they looked at us discreetly, sizing us up not as potential customers, I judged, but as potential companions.

Eric turned, not so discreetly, to stare at them. "Not bad for starters," he said. "I'll take the brunette."

I smiled. "Thank God we have different tastes. I like the blonde."

But it wouldn't, it seemed, be a matter of choice, for as soon as they caught Eric's stare, the women stopped looking and turned to each other, suddenly deep in conversation.

What if they hadn't looked away? I wondered. What if they had approached us? Would I, newly married and deeply in love, have allowed myself to—

No, I told myself resolutely. Before marriage, before I met Judy, I would have been excited by the notion. Casual sex was something I had not partaken of in New York (I had slept with four women before Judy, but had wooed and won each over months of effort); California was the place for it—it seemed to go with the territory. But now the idea was repugnant, and I was delighted with my own aversion. I was *not* Eric; he had not persuaded me with his talk on the plane. I smiled and shook my head.

"It's only starters," Eric said, misinterpreting. "We'll find others if you prefer."

"You could find me Raquel Welch, it wouldn't mean a thing."

He raised his eyebrows. "But you've been married for *months*."

"Perfect months. Sublime months."

He grunted. "Remember what I told you on the plane. Just because you love her doesn't mean you shouldn't fuck around."

"Then maybe love doesn't mean the same thing to you," I said.

Color rose in his face. "Pipsqueak," he said, his voice quavering. "Anne and I had the most passionate love affair the world has ever seen. Hell, you read about it in *Success*, and I underplayed it there because readers wouldn't have believed it if I had told them all." He clutched my arm, his eyes forcing mine to meet them. "Nobody —*nobody*—loves the way Anne and I love."

I removed my arm and took a sip of my drink, trying to lower the heat. "Would you kill for her?" I asked softly.

He considered. "I'd kill anyone who tried to hurt her."

"That's not my question."

"Then no, I don't think I'd kill *for* her—to get her."

"Would she kill to win you?"

"Today?"

"Yes."

"Then yes, on the days she wouldn't want to kill me." He laughed. "But you'd have to ask her yourself." He leaned toward me. "You see, Tony, Anne and I are different from you and Judy. I know it's presumptuous of me, particularly since I haven't seen you for months and I barely knew Judy; but Anne's and my love *is* different. Yours is so—tame. I didn't see thunderbolts at your wedding."

I felt my anger soar. "Perhaps you left before they got there."

If he heard my resentment, he didn't show it. "You don't produce lightning, not you two. Oh, it's clear you love each other; it's fun to see you together. But tell me"—again he leaned forward—"have you ever had a fight?"

"Of course. We fight all the time."

"Ever throw things at her?"

"No. Jesus, Eric, we're civilized—"

"She ever throw things at you?"

"No."

"Ever hit her? She ever hit you?"

"No. We fight with words."

"Exactly." He sat back, as though he had won a crucial debating point. "But only last week I slugged Anne, and she threw a cabinet full of dishes at me."

I looked at him in amazement. "Passion means throwing dishes?"

"It's symptomatic, yes. And it's a lot easier to talk about than what goes on in bed."

I thought of Judy and me making love; I would match our passion with anybody's. "This isn't a competition," I said, trying to defuse my own irritation. "But I can't believe that love doesn't extend to fidelity."

His look was condescending. "No need to get antagonistic. Anne is my one and only love. I literally couldn't live without her. Maybe

I wouldn't kill for her because I've already got her, but she is life to me, she and my work. She is my support and my sanity."

"But still," I protested, "that doesn't explain—"

He waved his hand, cutting off the question. "I have appetites," he said. "I told you. Needs. Beyond Anne. But now that I think of it, if she did know about the others, jealous as she is, in the long run she wouldn't blame me."

"She *wouldn't*?"

"No. And, if you were me, neither would Judy."

"If I were *you*?"

"Yes. I'm special, Tony. I've a special talent. God knows it isn't anything to crow about—I didn't earn it, I was born with it. But it exists, it's part of me."

"And it gives you special privileges?"

"In a way, yes."

I couldn't believe what I was hearing. "Beware of arrogance," I said.

"Why, if the arrogance is only the truth?" He drew nearer. I felt smothered. "Creative people are privileged," he went on, "and they deserve to be." He looked at me gravely and spoke in utmost seriousness. "Let me tell you about writers. Our job—our mission, if you will—is to reveal. What we want to set down is truth, not usually scientific truth, although that's part of it, but psychological truth, the truth of the soul. And psychological truth is mostly painful, or embarrassing, or despicable. Truth enlightens, but it hurts.

"Our primary resource for truth is, of course, ourselves, or the people we are closest to, love most. It's not easy to find. We have to dig for it mercilessly. And sometimes when we think we've discovered it, we find out later—even after the book is finished and published—that there is truth still deeper and more painful as yet unrevealed, and the only way to unearth it is to write another book, become tougher, drive ourselves harder, dig and dig and dig until our brains bleed."

He sighed, as though reliving recent pain. "But—and here's

the tricky part—once we've revealed it to ourselves by stripping ourselves bare, we immediately set about concealing ourselves. Novelists do nothing more profound than manufacture disguises. We invent characters and situations to assure our readers that it's not ourselves we're writing about—we don't want the truth known about our*selves*. If we wrote it straight out, it would be unbearable. So we hide behind our words, but at the identical moment use words to make sure truth is unhidden.

"I told you when we met, for example, that Ben and Alice were me, but I was lying to you. Ben and Alice are Ben and Alice. I am their inventor, they speak for me, but I created them specifically so that you *wouldn't* know me, so that I could hide, so that I could fool you, and indeed myself, into believing I was at most a small part of them. *I* would never think that way, behave that way, hurt that way. Ben and Alice would, but they're *characters.*"

He had neglected his Scotch, though he held the glass. I watched a drop of water slide onto his palm. He did not seem to notice. "Hence the name," he went on, smiling wryly. "Fiction. As differentiated from fact. Even the word is a disguise."

He leaned toward me. "Now two things happen when we write. The first is that we fall in love with our books. We at least know they are a disguise, one that lets us love ourselves, for what they disguise is us. We become attached to them just as we become attached to our wives and children, who always protect and reveal us too.

"The second thing is that we get scared. Not for ourselves, or for ourselves only secondhand, but for them. The books. The terror of publication is the triple terror of not having reached the truth, of someone seeing beneath the disguises, of seeing *us*, and of watching our loved ones being killed. By critics, by readers, by silence. We writers have ripped ourselves open, experienced agony and exorcised it—and then we expose all that, no matter how artfully disguised, to strangers. There is no terror like it, I promise you."

He sat back, exhausted. "Exposed to me, you mean?" I asked him.

"Yes, and from you to Arthur. You are both strangers in a way, but you at least are on my side, not because of my talent, necessarily, not because you understand or share the terror, but, to put it baldly, because I mean money to you."

"That's not fair," I said, hurt but grudgingly aware of some truth in his words.

"Maybe not. But as good a reader as you are, and Arthur is, you can't feel the terror the way I do, and God knows you don't take the risk. Your work represents energy and dedication; it's certainly an expression of yourself. But it's not the same thing as exposing yourself. You can hide your soul any time you want, without the need for penetrable disguises, and people won't think the less of you—quite the contrary. If you exposed it, you'd be sent to a nuthouse. Whereas I—" He shrugged. "You see what I mean."

"So the fact that you're a creative writer lets you cheat on Anne?"

He burst out laughing. "Still harping on that? It isn't the point. The point is that Anne has chosen to live with me—I'd venture to think she would say she was privileged. And by so choosing she has to take me as I am, without the cover-ups and controls of—"

He stopped. "Mere mortals?" I finished for him.

"Average people," he amended. "And of course there are times, dozens of them, when I hate my talent and wish I didn't write. For the disguising gets more essential when it comes to people even more removed from me than you. Christ, don't you see why I didn't want to make this trip? I'm exposing my *face*. And people will read my books and think, 'That man did those things, thought those things, that monster.' Hell, I'm not a monster. I just have monstrous feelings and thoughts, like anybody. Only I look at them square—all the time; every day—and I show them off no matter how disguised to strangers as though I'm proud of them. Do you wonder that I cherish anonymity? That I've hated myself ever since I agreed to do this, to throw anonymity away for fame?"

For the first time that day, I felt sympathy for him. "I can understand why you wouldn't want to do this," I said. His words buzzed in my head. "But go back a step. If you're privileged to do things we average folk aren't, where does that stop? Can an artist commit murder?"

"We do it all the time," he said softly. "And yes, we're permitted. They're psychic murders, of course, but name me one artist who hasn't committed one."

I thought of his son David, and my mouth went dry.

He must have guessed my thoughts for he said, "But not Anne. I pray to God, not Anne."

At that moment, I sensed two shadows behind us, and a woman's voice said, "You two seem to be having an interesting discussion. Mind if we join in?"

It was the blonde and the brunette from the nearby table.

Eric looked at them, blinking as though coming out of a sleep. Then he grinned and waved to the seats on either side of us. "God no," he exulted. "You're just what we need. Things were getting heavy around here. Let us buy you a drink."

nine

THEIR NAMES WERE CONSTANCE AND KITTY, THEY were production assistants on afternoon game shows, and they were overwhelmed with pleasure to meet a real novelist from New York. Eric, it seemed, was overwhelmed to meet two PAs from Los Angeles, for he was as expansive and affable as a conventioneer. Constance was the brunette and Eric paid particular attention to her, but I found myself tongue-tied with the luscious Kitty, awkward and ashamed, so she turned her attention to Eric as well, and he magnanimously included her in his realm. The velocity of our drinking picked up, the women staying even, and until Eric corrected course, even pulling slightly ahead. I found myself less tongue-tied and began to enjoy myself.

It turned out that while the women loved literature, they hadn't actually heard of *Success*, although it was by now stacked high in all Los Angeles bookstores. I assured them grandly that it was the equivalent of *An American Tragedy*, but they had not heard of that book either. Their favorite novel, they agreed, was *The Valley of the Dolls*. Winking at me, Eric told them he had not read it, but loved the movie.

An hour passed. We moved from barstools to a booth in the back, Kitty sitting next to me, Constance next to Eric. An imagist would highlight loosened ties and bright red fingernails, mouths open in laughter, a glimpse of bra, and above all the yellow of screwdrivers and the gold of Scotch.

El Padrino began to fill up. The new arrivals were fresh and elegant, about to start on their first drink of the day, not their tenth. They looked at us suspiciously; we were the unpleasant drunks at a refined party. But their disapproval struck us as funny, and the more venomous their glances, the more decibels to our glee. We must have been obnoxious, but at the time I rationalized that all Hollywood people were uninhibited free spirits, and I figured, when in El Padrino, do as the El Padrinans. Indeed, at one point a man in a white jumpsuit, covered with sequins, arrived at the entrance with a loud "Ta-da!" then, like a gymnast, did a series of spangled cartwheels till he reached an unoccupied table. There, sitting and smiling, he searched for applause, but not one person in the restaurant, besides the four of us, paid any attention. We cheered him, pounding on the table with the cutlery; but he looked at us, realized we were drunken nobodies, and sullenly departed, probably to ply his trade at the equally fashionable Polo Lounge in the Beverly Hills Hotel nearby.

It was at this point or thereabouts—my memory is somewhat fuzzy—that Kitty put a hand on my thigh. It was a discreet hand, neither lascivious nor aggressive, and it paused when it landed, unsure of its territory. Meeting no resistance, it started moving slowly uphill.

Itsy-bitsy spider, I thought, and felt pleasurable stirrings in its vicinity. My own hand reached down and captured hers. I gave a little squeeze, but made no effort to remove it. For the first time in aeons our eyes met, and I saw lust in a stranger, lust for a stranger.

I glanced at her breasts and she, noticing, smiled. She had good breasts and I remembered good hips and legs. I released her hand; it once again climbed higher.

Suddenly I stood; I had had a vision of the future. We were in bed together, in her frilly bedroom, spasmed out; there would be cats. And I, now bored with her fatuity and longing to leave, would have to stay for a while out of politeness, listening as I had just listened to her descriptions of a single woman's life in Hollywood. But I would not want to listen—consumed with guilt, I would be thinking only of Judy and how I had betrayed her, and for what? A spasm. The fantasy of great, faceless fucking, an anonymous body available for unimaginable acts, faded in the certainty of guilt and depression. Monogamous, I thought, and wished for a second that I wasn't. But it was only a second.

"I've got to leave," I said. "Sorry to break up the party."

Kitty pouted; there was no more reaction than that. I had taken away her toy, but she would find another. Constance didn't seem to have heard me. But Eric said, "Why? The evening's just beginning. Where the hell are you going?"

"To the room. I promised an author I'd read his manuscript and call him tomorrow."

"Read it later," Eric said. "You can't desert us like this."

"No, really." Sober, I feigned drunkenness. I could mumble with the best of them. "I'm afraid I had a bit too much. Not feeling well." I staggered toward the exit.

Eric excused himself to follow me. He caught up to me in the lobby. "You really sick," he asked, "or true to your word?"

"I'm fine," I said. "I just don't feel like it." Somehow, it was I who was embarrassed and apologetic.

"You're out of your mind. They're terrific. A strike on the first cast."

"They're both yours," I said. "You can take your pick."

"You're complicating things."

"Sorry." My stomach twisted. I was angry at him not so much for his adolescent joy at the adventure—after all, I had almost fallen prey to it myself—as for the pressure he was putting on me now.

He reached into his pocket, pulled out a ten-dollar bill, and handed it to me. I didn't take it. "What's that for?"

"Movie money. I'll need privacy in the room."

"Well, fuck you!" I said.

He seemed genuinely puzzled. "What the hell's wrong with you?"

"I'm not your flunkey. And I don't take bribes."

"I'm sorry," he said. "I'm not trying to bribe you. And I know you're not my flunkey."

"But," I said, still angry, "you want to get me out of the room."

"Not permanently. Just for a couple of hours." He paused. "Or join us."

"Why not go to Constance's house?"

"Maybe we will. I just want to keep my options open." He looked at me pleadingly. My God, I thought, he's a baby. He might have the talent; I was the man.

My anger evaporated. "Shit," I said, "I'll find a double feature."

The sun came out in his smile. "Bless you," he said. "I'll never forget this."

It was his wife's phrase; meaningless.

"Only I'll pay," I went on. "And you can pay me back in kind."

He was laughing now, edging back toward the entrance of the restaurant, anxious to have me disappear. "Anything. Anything." And he was gone.

Nothing, I thought. Not even a backward glance.

Feeling depressed, frustrated, angry, and superior, I bought a paper, found a double feature, and got into a cab.

❧

I still remember the movies—revivals of Marlon Brando in *Viva Zapata* and *The Men*. I admired the actor, Mexican or paraplegic, and without being consciously aware of it, my good humor returned to such an extent that, on leaving, I decided to be so benign that I would have a late solitary dinner before returning to the hotel. Thus it was not until after midnight that I got back to the Beverly Wilshire and made my way to our room on the fifth floor.

Scotch-taped to the door was a manila envelope with my name scrawled on it in large lipsticked letters. With a combination of amusement and irritation, I opened it. The note itself was written in regular black ink:

My dearest and best companion, Tony:

In this envelope you will find a key. It is to a room on the eighth floor. Much as I wanted your nocturnal company, I could sense when we unpacked your urgent desire for privacy. So out of the goodness of my heart, I persuaded the management of this mag-nanimous establishment to allow me to rent a room in your name —but on my check (neither you nor Arthur need worry!). Your toiletries and a change of clothes have been transported thither. Sleep well, my guardian agent. But do try to wake me in the morning. The pressures of this trip have already begun to weigh on me, and I might not be able to get to sleep until late.
Thanks for being so considerate. Yours for Success!

Love
E.

There was indeed a key. But before using it, I put my head against his door. The Beverly Wilshire is well built, however, and the faint sounds I thought I heard—giggles? cries of passion?—were, I'm convinced, imaginary.

Now more amused than annoyed, and, I'll confess, more than a little bit jealous, I made my way to the eighth floor, let myself into the room, and turned on the light.

I, who had had enough surprises for the day, had another. Eric had rented me the honeymoon suite.

It was, of course, I who did not sleep well. A combination of the strain of being with Eric, sexual frustration, and a vague guilt, as though I had actually been unfaithful or was responsible for Eric's infidelities, kept me tossing uncomfortably on perhaps the world's most comfortable bed.

When my wake-up call came at six o'clock (Eric had a pre-interview at the "Tonight Show" at nine, and had to arrive early for makeup; it was my job to shepherd him there), I rose quickly, showered and shaved, then called Eric.

The phone rang twelve times before it was answered.

" 'Lo?"

"Rise and shine," I said in a drill sergeant's voice. "We cannot be late for Johnny's minions."

"Sick," he announced.

"I'm sure," I said coldly, suddenly repelled by him. "Read hung over. But so what?"

"Postpone," he commanded.

"Impossible."

"Essential," he said, obviously reviving despite himself.

"If you don't get up," I warned him, "I'll call Arthur, tell him you're not cooperating, and ask him to call you every five minutes until you get up. Do you want that?"

"Fuck you."

"Good. Do you want to have breakfast in your room, or shall we meet downstairs?"

"Room," he mumbled.

I hesitated, then plunged ahead. "The car's coming at seven thirty. Are the girls still with you?"

There was a pause, as though he were looking for them, but all he said was, "What girls?"

"Constance and Kitty, or did one leave?"

"Shit. Both of them left ten minutes after you did."

There wasn't a chance he was telling the truth. "Then why the honeymoon suite?"

He chuckled. "You like it?"

"It's gorgeous. But lonely. Why would you move me out if it weren't for the girls?"

"Didn't you get my note?"

"Somehow, I didn't believe it. You've never shown such altruism before."

"It's the spirit of Hollywood. Besides, you've been good to me. I took your moral lesson to heart."

"Bullshit."

He chuckled again. "Is that any way to talk to the star of the 'Tonight Show'?"

"Then you'll come after all. What a relief!" I had never doubted it.

"Ol' reliable."

"To what do you refer," I asked, suddenly daring, feeling more free with him than I ever had, "yourself or your cock?"

This time, he roared. "Myself, of course. I told you, there was no hanky-panky. Chaste is my middle name."

"As it will be tonight?" With a shock I realized we had two more nights in Los Angeles before going to San Francisco.

"Naturally."

"But I'm to stay here for the next two nights?"

"It would be ungenerous of me to ask your return."

"I appreciate it," I said, putting as much sarcasm as I could into the words. "And in San Francisco? At the Stratford Court?"

"We must wait and see," he said. "In all probability, we rejoin forces. After all, while you've made me a wealthy man, Anne has done all in her power to disperse that wealth. Still, who knows what adventures lurk ahead? It may be that you'll pay for your own room for your own reasons."

"Indeed," I answered, catching a hint of reproof in his tone. "It's you, after all, who has made me rich, not vice versa. But Judy, on a smaller scale, does what she can to unload the riches." Forgive me, Judy, I thought, feeling mean. She was in fact the most frugal of wives, spending almost nothing on herself, and I regretted sucking up to Eric at her expense.

"You might thank me," he said, bringing me back with a start. "You haven't, you know."

"In fact," I said, meaning it, "I love the suite, lonely as it is. I do want the privacy, as you say. So I do thank you, Eric. You've made me a happy man."

"In your happiness lies mine." He was practically humming with goodwill. "See you in the lobby at seven thirty."

"Promptly," I said, feeling he was never on time.

"On the dot." He hung up.

I went downstairs for coffee—the room was far too grand to eat in alone—then came back and called Judy. She had not left for work; she rarely did before ten, and the sound of her voice was welcome as sunrise. I told her of last evening's episode, heard her voice go cold when I described Kitty and Constance, but soon had her reassured and laughing. I promised that when we finally went on our true honeymoon we would have a room even more sump-tuous than this one, told her that *any* room with her in it was more beautiful than this one was without her, and both of us believed it.

I yearned for her; it was the first time we had been apart since our marriage. But there was plenty to do that day. Besides shep-herding Eric I had made appointments to see three movie produc-ers in an effort to place some of the other properties I represented. (Eric was to be picked up at NBC after the test by Diadem's sales representative, who would accompany him for the rest of this day and the next, so I was free.) Work, in other words, dimmed the longing for Judy, and I went downstairs feeling important and adult, an established figure rather than a ripening one.

Eric was in the lobby with Constance and Kitty, dressed in their clothes of the day before. I was not overly surprised to see them. In their defense, the women had the grace to blush when I ap-peared, but Eric was all bonhomie.

"You remember Constance and Kitty," he said. "Seems they often breakfast here before going to work, and I ran into them. Decided not to eat in the room after all—it's depressing when you're alone—and a lucky thing I didn't. Imagine: two days in Los Angeles and we meet on both days."

"I can't think of anything as fortunate," I said, controlling the irony. "I'm only sorry I had to leave so early last night."

"We're sorry too," said Kitty, no irony in her tone either.

"But we had fun without you. Didn't we, Eric?" Constance asked.

He smirked.

We stood awkwardly for a moment, the three of them obviously morning strangers after the intimacy of the night before, I feeling as though I had intruded on a party to which I had not been invited. Rescue came in the form of our chauffeur, a dazzlingly handsome young man, an unemployed actor, I guessed, scrounging for living money, who bounded through the lobby calling Eric's name. We flagged him down and he skidded to a stop, all patronizing subservience, ours to command.

" 'Til tonight," Constance said.

"Will you be joining us?" Kitty asked, relentless.

"I'm afraid Tony's busy tonight, too," Eric answered for me.

"Yes, busy," I said.

"So it's the old familiar drill," Eric said gaily, edging toward the exit. "Let's meet at El Padrino's at—" He looked at me.

"Your last interview's at six," I said. "You'll be back by seven, latest."

"Seven," Eric said. He took their hands in turn and kissed them gallantly. We walked toward the door, the women staying behind. "Free at last!" Eric said under his breath.

I turned to look back at Kitty and Constance. They were staring at him, smitten. An attack of jealousy, worse than last night's, assaulted me.

"What's it like?" I asked him, curiosity conquering decorum, marveling at his power.

He looked at me and licked his chops. "With one," he said, grinning, "man knows heaven." The grin grew. "With two, paradise."

We got into the car.

❊

Constance and Kitty followed us to San Francisco, but then left the tour; perhaps coincidentally, a renowned playwright had newly arrived in Los Angeles.

It was just as well. I was tired of being alone in the evening, of eating by myself, of buying single tickets to double features. True, I got a lot of reading done and caught up on my sleep; but I wasn't enjoying myself. I thought of the work piling up back home, and of the fact that this present work—the wooing of Eric Meredith—had been sidetracked, a victim of sexual excess.

It was just as well for Eric, too. He was marvelous in his interviews in Los Angeles, and even good in San Francisco. But he was operating on sexual energy, and when we left San Francisco and headed north toward Seattle, he collapsed in the plane and I had to wake him when it touched ground. For the next three days, in Seattle, Cleveland, and Detroit, his performance was at best adequate. There is a sameness and a tedium about repeating oneself show after show, interview after interview, that exhausts even professional performers who have written books. For the amateur, for the *writer*, it is debilitating.

Eric had fallen into a depression, not serious enough to prevent him from functioning (only I was aware how much worse his performance was in the midwest than on the Coast), but severe enough so that when we were alone together, mostly at night (we had gone back to sharing a room) and on the weekend, he spoke barely at all, and then in the distracted fashion of one who has grave problems on his mind.

I tried to draw him out, to entertain him—he actually accompanied me once to the movies; but his silence and his depression grew.

"Why don't you ask him what's bothering him," Judy said one night, when I had called to discuss my difficulty, "or find him two more girls?" Obvious advice. But something prevented me from doing either, at least temporarily. I pretended there was nothing wrong, acted reassured when he told me he had spoken to Anne and all was well at home, and endured his silences as though they were what I wanted from him.

I worried about him. Eric subdued made me more nervous than Eric grandiloquent. The explosion came in Chicago.

Eric had woken up on that Monday morning more fatigued than usual, even though we had not worked on the weekend. He ate no breakfast; on previous days, he had had eggs and toast and bacon. He dressed carelessly; usually, for television, he made an attempt at nattiness. And, before leaving, he sat so silently and still that I thought clinical depression had at last overtaken him.

Yet when I told him it was time to leave for the studio, he went willingly enough, never losing his self-engrossed manner, but walking with firm step to the limousine. The show was live, from nine to ten, and Eric was the last of the participants.

From the moment he got on camera, it was apparent to me— and surely to Eric—that the host had not read *Success*.

They talked generally about Eric's childhood, about his life with David and Anne, about coal mining, petty crime (this was the "subject" for the whole show, the excuse for Eric's being on at all), about prison conditions (a subject on which Eric had little to contribute), and, of course, about sex. But all that was a prelude to the host's real interest: money.

Q: Is it true, Mr. Meredith, that paperback rights to your book were sold for over one million dollars?

A: No.

Q: But it was a large sum?

A: Yes.

Q: Can you tell us how much?

A: Does it matter?

Q: I think our viewers would be interested. Many of them are aspiring writers and they'd like to know, I'm sure, what the rewards might be.

A: As I understand it, most novels don't sell to paperback at all. So I don't see how my case can mean very much.

Q (*Laughing*): I respectfully disagree. We all have fantasies. Tell us about the up side, please.

A: Seven hundred and seventy-five thousand dollars.

Q (*Whistles*): And there are book club and a motion picture sale, too?

A: Yes.

Q: So it can reasonably be said that the book has earned more than one million dollars.

A: Yes. Of course, I don't get all of it—

Q: One million dollars. (*Pause*) Do you think that's fair?

A: I'm afraid I don't understand.

Q: I've always had the impression that authors have the world's easiest job. I mean, there's no physical labor involved.

A (*Ominously*): What physical labor do you do?

Q: That's not the point. (*Laughs*) Besides, who said that talk show hosts deserve their rewards? We're talking about writers in general and you in particular. I want to know if you think you earned the money you made.

A (*One can see Eric's anger mounting. The goad is beginning to work*): How much is suffering worth? Of course I think I earned it.

Q: Don't you think that's a little pretentious? Suffering? I mean, you sit in a comfortable room, can take a break any time you want —do you have a word processor?

A (*nonplussed*): No.

Q: An electric typewriter?

A: Yes, as a matter of fact. I write first in longhand, then retype. But what has that to do—

Q (*Triumphant*): Then it isn't even hard work striking the keys! So really, there's no hassle. On days you don't want to work, you don't have to. If you want to take a coffee break, you can. If you want to go for a walk, or go to the movies in the afternoon, there's nothing to stop you. You can stare out the window, take a nap, grab a snack, watch television—work at your own pace and to your own schedule. Now really, Mr. Meredith, can you honestly say that's suffering?

A: I don't think you understand what a writer does—

Q: Is any of what I've said untrue?

A: No, but—

Q: Then please answer the question.

A (*In despair*): I've forgotten what the question was.

Q: Did you earn the money you made? Did you earn one million dollars?

A (*Resigned and quiet*): Yes.

Q: Well, I contend you didn't. I contend that writers—successful writers—are among the most overpaid people in the world.

A: I don't agree. Obviously, you've never—

Q (*On a soapbox*): Further, I'm sick of the talk about how artists suffer. As if you're special, as if other people—ordinary people—don't feel just as much pain. I contend that writers are mostly a self-pitying lot, filled with grandiose ideas of their own importance, thinking that somehow they're put upon when in fact they've got the cushiest of lives. Now how do you respond, Mr. Meredith?

Eric said nothing. Rather he picked up the microphone and hurled it at his host. Since it was connected to a wire attached to the floor, it did not travel far, but crashed loudly on the table, the noise of impact amplified a thousandfold before the microphone went dead. The host screamed; the screen went blank. The final picture was of two station guards taking hold of a maddened author and, with difficulty, subduing him.

※

Years later, watching the tape (Eric gave it to me shortly after we got back to New York; it is one of my prize trophies), I find it all terrifically funny. Lord knows the host deserved his comeuppance; Eric was justified; the Chicago audience got more entertainment than it anticipated. And at this remove it is difficult to remember just how upset I was at the time. But upset I was.

I watched the show from the hotel room. After California, I had made no business appointments, but confined myself to accompanying Eric when he wished it (he did not in Chicago; here again Diadem's salesman performed the service) and to reading or sightseeing when he did not. That morning I had not even dressed, but lounged in bed, happily private, reading the *Sun-Times* and drinking room-service coffee until the show went on. The only interruption was a call from Anne sounding upset, asking for Eric. I told her where he was; she assured me there was nothing I could do for her; she needed Eric himself.

Like Eric, I was horrified by the questions. The host was a clod, as ignorant about the nature of writing—of all artistic endeavor—as he was about the canons of politeness and good taste. But after all, he was not unique; we had encountered hosts almost as bad, and just as unread, in every city we visited. So patently something had set Eric off. It did not take me long to find out what it was.

Not five minutes after the screen had gone blank, Eric was on the phone.

"Did you watch it?" His voice was breathless.

"Best fight since Ali-Frazier," I said cheerfully.

"The fucker. I should have killed him."

"Agreed. But you should have committed murder in Seattle and Detroit."

"This guy was worse."

" 'This guy' will guarantee you never appear in Chicago again."

"Good. I'm through, anyway."

I had been afraid of that. "What do you mean?"

"The tour. Call Arthur. I'm canceling out."

"You can't do that."

He paused. "I can't go on."

"It's only a few more days."

"A few more minutes is too much."

Futilely, I tried to come up with a solution. After all, I had been brought along—with expenses paid—to keep Eric in line, and I had failed, both here and in Los Angeles.

"You can't do this to Arthur," I said, "or to me."

"I can't go on," he repeated.

"So the guy's an asshole. They're smarter on the East Coast. Why not just cancel today, then start again in Boston tomorrow?"

"Because I can't take one more minute," he roared. "Not one more mother-fucking second."

"Please," I said.

"Pretty-please," he mimicked. "No, Tony. Call Arthur or I will. I'm going home."

His voice cracked on "home"; I felt a chill. "Is something wrong there?" I asked, once again feeling that pang in my stomach when I asked him a question that might anger him.

"What do you mean, wrong? You saw the show." His voice was level; I could detect neither anger nor sorrow in it.

"Beyond the show."

"Nothing. The mother-fucker made me mad, is all."

"Other mother-fuckers made you mad."

He hesitated. "I don't know why I exploded." His voice softened. "I'm sorry, Tony, if I screwed things up."

"I'm your friend," I said, with a too-long-in-coming premonition. "You can tell me."

"It's David," he said.

"David!"

"Yes. Anne called me this morning at the studio. Got me just before I went on. David had just tried to kill another kid. A schoolmate."

I could feel the hairs rise on the back of my neck. "But he's only seven. An accident—"

"It was deliberate." Again, his voice cracked. "I don't have the details; Anne was near hysterical. But it seems he was with the kid in a classroom, just before school was supposed to start, and suddenly, for no reason that anybody knows, picked up a scissors and stabbed him with it. I mean, he *stabbed* him. A boy named Freddie

Stevens." He took a deep breath. "Freddie's been to our house. A blond kid. Sweet. Anne loves him."

"Maybe it *was* an accident," I said. "Maybe they were playing and the scissors slipped."

"Four times? Besides, a teacher saw them. He went for him with the scissors, no question of it." He paused. "My heart aches for him, but still more for Anne."

The words surprised me. I had not thought him capable of such empathy. "What about you?"

"No, Anne. She'll bear the brunt of it, whether she deserves to or not. She'll take the guilt on herself. But oh, Tony, if only I had been better with him. Paid more attention. Been a full-time father. Maybe then it wouldn't have happened." His suffering was genuine, and I wished I knew how to comfort him. No words came.

"Look," he said, in control again. "Please call Arthur, or Pincus if you can't get him. Tell them something's come up, but for God's sake don't tell them what it is. Ask them to cancel the rest of the tour. And"—here his voice broke; his sobs were remorseless—"tell them I'm sorry, really sorry. But there's nothing I can do."

"Don't be sorry," I said, feeling awkward. "I'll check us out, book us a flight, pack for you, and meet you in the lobby. You'll be home in a few hours."

His voice was low, a lover's. "Thank God you're here. I couldn't cope without you." He hung up.

I called Arthur, explained that something had come up with Anne and David that forced Eric home, countered his vociferous objections, then made the arrangements for departure, as I had promised. I'm generally good in an emergency. My emotions shut off and I act mechanically and competently. And here I was better than competent; I had accomplished everything in half an hour.

It made me feel good to handle things so well. At last I was of use to Eric, after what I believed to be my failure in Los Angeles. Yes, I was disappointed that the trip I had looked forward to so ardently since last spring was aborted—we had never come close to the intimacy I had fantasized. I still did not understand why he attracted me so strongly; I certainly had not made myself an essential part of his life. But the consolation was Judy, for I would see her this day. And at least—at least!—for this day Eric was right: he could not cope without me.

Traffic must have been terrible, for it took three-quarters of an hour for Eric to arrive. I had expected him to be distraught, but in fact he was in command, merely grim-faced and silent.

We bundled ourselves and our luggage into a limousine and set out for the airport. Eric sat at the edge of his seat, fidgeting, his face expressionless and his eyes sad. Mostly he stared out the window at the thruway-dominated landscape, but occasionally he would turn to me as though to ask a question, only to avert his face again.

I felt frustrated, unable to offer consolation. Now the fact that the trip was ruined, and with it my plans for mutual confidences, mutual discoveries, hit me with force, and depression settled over me like mist. Had I gotten to know him on this trip? Yes and no; better but not profoundly. Had he come to know me? No. I had not expressed any of my yearnings to him, though what they were I cannot articulate even now. Did I like what I knew? I wasn't sure. His amorality did not overshadow the humanity he had just now shown. They coexisted.

Despite the delay getting started we caught the noon flight without trouble. Eric had two double martinis on the plane and fell asleep before lunch was served. He waved off the stewardess who woke him with an offer of food, and slept soundly for more than an hour.

Meanwhile, I thought of Judy. I had not called her from Chicago, so she would be surprised by my early arrival. I had a fantasy about coming home to find her in the arms of a lover, but quickly dismissed it. Neither Eric nor I would return to that. Instead, we would be welcomed hungrily, although out of different needs. I too accepted a drink and refused lunch. I read *Time* and *Sports Illustrated* and then dozed off myself, thinking with pleasure of the night to come.

Eric awoke as we were nearing Kennedy; I had been awake for

a half an hour before. He asked the stewardess for a glass of orange juice, combed his hair without leaving his seat or looking in a mirror, and composed his face into pleasant, noncommittal blandness.

"I want to thank you," he said. "You put up with a lot from me." There was no animation in his tone.

"I enjoyed it," I told him. "Really. And you weren't difficult at all." I laughed. "Shit, I hardly saw you."

"Don't tell Judy about the girls."

I looked at him in surprise. "Don't you mean Anne?"

"No, I know you wouldn't do that. But I don't want Judy to know, either."

I misunderstood. "She'd keep your confidence." I did not tell him I had already described Constance and Kitty.

"Oh, of course she would. It's not that." He paused. "She was so enthusiastic about my novel. I don't want her to think badly of me."

I smiled. "She's a grown-up. I hardly think your sex life has anything to do with her feelings about your work."

"But she seems so innocent."

I thought again of our nights, past and future. " 'My lord, I know not seems.' Don't be fooled by appearances."

He sighed. "I've told you, you're a lucky man. There was a time when—" Abruptly, his eyes clouded and his face went red. "You know, Tony, it's hard being a writer and a family man." The plane landed smoothly. I was watching him so intently that I hardly noticed it. "I don't do it well," he said, suddenly bent in despair.

Anne was waiting for him when we arrived; she must have checked with the airline to find what flight we were on, then hired a baby-sitter for David. She wore sunglasses; evidently she had been crying. When Eric saw her, his face grew grave and he kissed her solemnly on the cheek. Both of them ignored me, and I stood awkwardly by their side, unsure of whether to call attention to my-self by moving out of earshot, or to remain still.

"David?" Eric said.

"Home. He didn't want to come to the airport. He asked if Carol could sit with him, and I got her." She sighed. "It's not clear what the school intends to do. We're to come see the principal tomor-row."

"What have you told David?"

"The truth."

His eyes blazed. "What? That he's a potential murderer?"

"That he did something very bad and has to be punished for it."

"Is keeping him out of school punishment?"

"I think so."

"That isn't the point. What does *he* think? Besides, just how bad a thing was it? Maybe the kid deserved a knifing."

"Eric!" Her voice, which she had kept carefully quiet, came out a scream.

"Sorry," he muttered.

The three of us walked toward the baggage claim area. It was my opportunity to fall behind, to let them suffer privately, but at that moment I was never conscious of the thought; I was, at least until the baggage arrived, part of the mere scenery of their lives, and I would not have wanted it otherwise.

"Don't be angry at him when you get home," Anne said. "Don't yell. He may not know precisely what's happened, but he's terribly upset. You don't want to upset him more."

His voice was a snarl. Gone were the guilt and the sympathy he had expressed earlier. "Jesus Christ! What do you expect me to do? Here I've called off my trip, the most important trip I'll ever make in my life, and I'm not supposed to upset him?"

"He needs help," she wailed.

He stopped so suddenly that I almost bumped into him. "What do you mean, help?"

"A psychiatrist."

"Never!"

She began to sob. "But I can't help him. I don't know how. And you won't. You're destroying him. You're destroying both of us!"

"You hear that?" he asked, turning to me, for the first time acknowledging he remembered my presence. "It's my fault. Not hers. Not God's. Mine!"

"Yes, yours," she said, as though he had not stopped speaking to her. "You're so fucking terrifying. Sweet one day, good one day, darling one day. And the next— It's unnatural. We can't figure you out. David gets praised for acting one way on Tuesday and screamed at for doing the same thing on Thursday. So do I. For God's sake, tell us how you want us to act."

She had turned to him, her face dark crimson, tears coursing down her cheeks, oblivious to the stares of the other passengers. Her fists were clenched and, as she had during the other fight I had witnessed, she waved them at him in a grotesque imitation of a prizefighter. Her hair was disheveled and there were black smudges under the glasses that hid her eyes. Anger had conquered misery and I silently cheered for her as she went on.

"I'm getting him help," she said, "like it or not. Let's spend some of that money you're so proud of."

There was a pause while he looked at her, revulsion in his gaze, then he said softly and ominously, "Okay, get help. Spend every cent. I don't give a flying fuck about the money. But if you do take him to a psychiatrist, if you humiliate me in that way, I'll want a return."

My God, I thought. Humiliate *him*. Couldn't he see the urgency?

She straightened herself defiantly and looked him square in the face. "Okay. What do you want? How much is the salvation of your son going to cost?"

The words hit him harder than her fists could ever have. He took a step backward and I heard a whoosh of air as the breath went out of him. Suddenly his face contorted, and he too began to cry; he jammed his fists against his eyes to stop the flow. I looked away, embarrassed, longing for the baggage to arrive to end the public pain. The passengers, curious at first, had by now moved away from them as though they were diseased; there was nobody except me within ten feet of where they were standing. At last he took his hands away from his face. He was sweaty and pale, and his eyes, no longer angry, were those of a supplicant. "Let me write," he said softly, standing tall and determined, as unafraid of her as she was of him. "Let me write in peace."

"Eric!" she cried. "Oh my God, we've tried!" Then she rushed into his embrace, and he held her. They stood with their arms around each other, he kissing her wild hair and smoothing it with his caresses. My vision blurred. The lights in the airport became stars, the people shadows. Finally I turned and walked away so that they could be alone.

❖

That night, as I lay with my head on Judy's breast, sated with lovemaking, the joy of our reunion tempered by the recollection of the scene at the airport, I told her about David and the fight between Eric and Anne.

"Now will you believe me?" she asked.

"About what?"

"That he's a destroyer."

"Eric was with me. *She* was with David."

She gently pushed my head away and sat up. "David needs a father, and Eric abandoned him."

I looked at her, annoyed. "Oh, for God's sake. Fathers go on business trips all the time."

"I don't mean now. Eric abandoned him years ago." She returned my gaze, serious and sad. "Don't take his side. He can destroy you, too."

"I'm not on cocaine," I told her. "I'm in control; I handled things well with him. He *needed* me."

"So do I," she cried, and hugged me. "That's why I'm so worried about you. Remember, he's promiscuous—"

"So would I be if you were an addict."

"—untrustworthy." She paused. "Did it ever occur to you to ask yourself why, knowing what trouble David was in, he nevertheless went on that show?"

It hadn't. "I suppose because he was already at the studio, because he had made a commitment."

"A commitment more powerful than his son? What would you have done?"

"Canceled," I admitted. "Come home immediately. But Jesus, Judy, you should have seen how upset he was."

Again, the serious, sad look. "You know," she said, "I've never put much stock in long distance grief."

She kissed me, then rolled on her side and turned off her light. I sat thinking for a long time, reliving the day. Judy was right in one respect: Eric's conflict and pain had become mine.

✛

Except for the arrival of the Chicago tape, I did not hear from Eric for seven weeks. This time, neither did Arthur. *Success* climbed on the best-seller lists until it reached number four. Gloria Pincus called the Meredith home every week to announce the position, but talked only to Anne. I wanted to call, to find out if everything had settled down with David, but my old shyness returned, and I did not try.

Arthur called several times, with no success. Anne simply told him that Eric did not wish to be disturbed. I told Arthur little of what happened on the trip, and nothing about Constance and Kitty or David. Those were Eric's secrets, I thought, and if perforce he had shared them with me, I would not break his trust.

We went on with our lives, Judy and I. My post-trip depression faded (giving Judy the opportunity to point out how much better life was without Eric intruding in it), and a new crafts-book client took our attention. She had written a book on home decorating, Judy had liked it, and so I had agreed to become the agent. Chuckling at my command of the jargon, I sold the book immediately to

Scribner's. In April, Central Park opened for tennis, and I played every morning. We spent several weekends in New England and on weeknights saw our friends. I cannot say this was a happy time for me; the shock of Eric was too real. But there was contentment in the days and nights. Our pace was nearly normal.

And then, in the last week of May, a package arrived, unheralded. It was the manuscript for Eric's new novel, *Flaws in Diamonds*.

Part

II

ten

THE OFFICES OF ANTHONY SILVER & ASSOCIATES, LIT-
erary agents, located on 64th Street between Fifth and Madison,
opened on January 20, 1977. The associates were Paul Kieling, a
young recruit out of the William Morris Agency, responsible pri-
marily for nonfiction; and Erika Eliasof, my secretary, a poet who
had taken the part of woman-of-all-work because she needed the
money, and stayed because she liked the job, even after her poems
began to be published and a play of hers opened to considerable
off-Broadway success. I suspect that Erika does her writing during
lunch hour (Paul and I are never in to check on her; she never
goes out with editors or authors), for she is immensely beautiful
and at five thirty there is invariably a young man at our door waiting to take her out.

The offices were lovely. We had furniture from Knoll; prints
picked up by Judy on First and Second Avenues adorned the walls.
The typewriters were electric and the three of us kept them humming. There was carpeting on the floor, wood paneling on the
walls, even a spare, brilliantly lit room for authors to work in or
for our free-lance accountant to use when he went over our bur-
geoning records and invested some of our excess in nonliterary
endeavors.

The money to pay for all this came mostly from *Success* and from *Flaws*. There were other successful authors working with me, other paperback and club sales, even other movie options. But without Eric, there would be no Silver & Associates, no suite of offices, no paneling—no coffee machine.

And how I loved those offices! I couldn't wait to get to them and was glad for the days when work kept me there until everybody else had gone home. Then I would prowl through the suite as though it were the King Ranch, lord of my acres, reveling in the view of similar offices from my windows, in the smell of new wood and new leather. The offices represented professional maturity to me, a step up in age and class. I even loved the pencils and the paper clips, for I had paid for them so that others might use them. I had a staff.

We gave a party commemorating the opening a week after we had settled in, inviting publishers, other agents, and of course all the authors I represented. It is famous still as one of the great disasters in the social history of publishing. Even thinking back on it from this ten-year perspective, I cannot shut out the trauma.

❧

But let me briefly take you back to the arrival of *Flaws in Diamonds*, when "office" still meant one room of a small apartment. It took me several hours to open it, so apprehensive was I that it would be a disappointment. I put it in the middle of my desk, its wrapping intact, and circled it warily. Indeed, I still hadn't opened it when Judy came home. I told her it had arrived and she, without my emotional investment, made a dash for it. I beat her to it, ripped it open, and side by side, still standing, we began to read.

From the first, we knew that Eric had not lost his power.

Flaws in Diamonds has the same intensity, the same eroticism, the same propulsive, action, the same psychological insight, the same capacity for bringing people alive, that made *Success* so remarkable. If anything the writing is more precise, the metaphors

more accurate; and Ben and Alice—for it is their story continued
—seem even more persuasive here, now that they have gotten
older.

Yet with it all, *Flaws* was a disappointment to me. Oh, I know
that several critics consider it Eric's best work, and the reviews
were, if possible, even more favorable than they were for *Success*.
But still, even as I passed Judy the pages as I finished them, in the
back of my mind buzzed the heretical thought that Eric was repeating himself, that he was saying what he had already said, that
it was the *same* strengths I was admiring. There are new adventures in *Flaws*, new conflicts and new characters. The atmosphere
of the claustrophobic home, wife, and child is magnificently realized. But, to me, the book is not much deeper than *Success*. It reveals, but it reveals only what we already knew Eric understood so
much better than we. It's as though Beethoven, having changed
music forever with his Third Symphony, decided to use the same
ideas in different forms in the successive works. We would have a
feast of marvelous music—but we would not have the Ninth or the
last quartets.

Naturally I said nothing of this to Arthur, to whom I sent the
manuscript the following day. He had been pressing me for it for
months, not because he thought I was keeping it from him, but
because he was as nervous about it as I, as eager and as apprehensive, and by calling me he did not have to call Eric.

He phoned the next morning. "What took you so long?" I asked.

But he was in no mood for jokes. "My God," he said, "it's better
than *Success*."

"Agreed!" There was no need to share my true feelings. "But I
should warn you that statements like that will cost you."

"I'll pay." He laughed. "I think it's worth a good five thousand."

This time, I didn't think it was funny. "Try multiplying by a
hundred," I told him. Given the sales of *Success* and the skill of
Flaws, it was not an outrageous demand.

Arthur groaned. "For that kind of money, I've got to ask management."

"I know," I said happily, aware that Diadem couldn't afford to lose an author like Meredith. "But you agree it's a fair price, don't you?" I didn't want him to think I was gouging him. He had done a lot for *Success*, published it as well as it could have been published and I had no desire to hold his company up for more than seemed appropriate. On the other hand, I didn't want Eric to feel he had been undersold.

"God pity me," Arthur said, "it's fair."

"And of course we'll want a sixty-forty split on all moneys received from the book club and paperback sales," I announced.

He had known it was coming; it had become customary in the business for the biggest names. "Of course," he said, defeated without a fight.

"Those are the parameters," I said, the tough professional. "We can work out the smaller points later."

"You're a hard man, Silver," Arthur said.

I took it as a compliment.

Two days later, Arthur called back, accepting all my terms. "The only thing we ask is that the five hundred thousand be paid slowly," he said. "Five payments each year of twenty-five thousand for four years."

I was sure I could do better. "I don't know about that."

"Frankly, there's a cash flow problem," Arthur explained. "This'll solve it."

"I'll have to discuss it with Eric," I informed him. "If he says no, if he needs the money more quickly, then it's no."

"Try hard," Arthur pleaded.

Actually, I didn't have to try at all. Eric was delighted with the arrangement. (On so important a business matter, I had no trepidation making the call.) He and Anne were now actively looking for a house; they would want to pay off the mortgage slowly, and the measured payments from Diadem would force them to spend the money on the mortgage and not, as Eric put it, "on Anne's frivolities."

Overall, I was saddened by the call. I remembered his joy at the forty thousand, and here, for more than ten times as much, he was as matter-of-fact as a banker making a new car loan. All we did was solemnly congratulate each other on our prosperity, and then hang up.

Other sales quickly followed. Since all have been reported in the papers (on the basis of *Success*, Eric was news), there's no need for me to repeat them here. All were higher than for *Success*: the paperback sale was over one million dollars; countries like Argentina and Iceland bought not only *Flaws*, but now, *Success* as well; and Universal Pictures bought the book outright (there was no option payment; I would not let them have one, though they tried) for a flat million. Even American Express called to see if Eric would appear for them in television commercials. Eric was not amused, though I was. He told me to tell them to take a flying fuck; I politely refused their offer.

And Meredith's agent? I acquired three new novelists, one of whose books I sold to Random House, which immediately sold the paperback rights to Fawcett for one hundred thousand dollars; a priest whose book on American Catholicism was nominated for the National Book Award; and a California guru whose treatise on meditation sold more than one hundred and fifty thousand copies at $9.95.

In short, we were rich. Judy and I debated moving to a larger, more fashionable apartment, but for sentimental reasons decided to stay where we were and rent offices instead. We decided, too, on our honeymoon at last. We would go to the South of France, to the hills above Nice, and we would eat ourselves silly, tour, and make love morning, afternoon, and evening. It seemed a good plan to both of us.

❧

And so, the party. It was scheduled from six P.M. to eight, cocktails and cheese; more than eighty people accepted. There's no reason for you to remember the night, but if you recall a large snowstorm in '77, it fell on our date. People, loyal friends all, arrived wet and dispirited, kicking so much snow off galoshes that soon puddles appeared on the floor outside our doorway. We had rented coatracks, but not enough, so the coats were bunched together and soon began to steam. For it was hot in the corridor, even warmer in the offices themselves; and the smells of sweat, perfume, and dank fur mingled in hallways and offices.

Generally, I like publishing parties. The people in the profession are, for the most part, committed to it—we love books and most authors. Too, on the whole we're a bright bunch—or if not bright, then at least articulate; the gossip has bite and the wisecracks are often funny. Thus it can be amusing to see one's colleagues performing, and the challenge to top them lends an edge to the group conversations that I find stimulating.

Maybe it was only that it was my party; maybe the anticipation and the symbolic significance made the fact that it was just another publishing party disappointing (though Lord knows what I had expected); maybe it was simply the bad weather and uncomfortable conditions; but to the host the party appeared tired, as though my publishing friends had come out of duty, not desire.

I accepted mechanical congratulations mechanically and watched the inevitable early leavers (the nondrinkers and those who came only for business purposes) go, taking their departure as a personal affront, although I knew better. Most of the guests stayed, however, uncomfortable as many of them appeared. They behaved as they often did at bad parties, with one eye on the person they were talking to, the other on the door to see if a more interesting friend was among the late arrivals.

Rushed as I was as host, and thinking more about my unease than the situation warranted, I came only slowly to the realization that what they were waiting for was Eric. Of course more of them would have gone home! It *was* a dull party. But he was a genuine, first magnitude star, and even those sophisticated people, many of them publishers of or agents for stars themselves, were curious to meet the new phenomenon. In a true sense it was Eric's party, not mine; he had paid for it and he was its main attraction. He had reached a point where book people came just because he was going to be there, and those book people could go home and tell their families that they had met him personally. Their children could boast that their parents knew him and "he was a very nice guy."

Saul Bellow, William Styron, Philip Roth, Norman Mailer were such authors, writers whose books not only sold in the millions but had literary cachet as well. Eric, with one "big" book out and one book pending, had become their equal.

It was hardly a profound revelation, but I was pleased to have seen it, and pleased too over my lack of resentment. I was delighted it was Eric's party, and that I was merely his surrogate until he arrived. I had placed the responsibility where it belonged and was now able to relax with the other guests, looking over the shoulder of one of my authors to see when my *author* arrived.

Eric did not disappoint. He entered hugely, noisily, feet clomping, shaking off snow from his boots and coat, tossing his wet and unruly hair; he had worn no hat. Even those unable to see his entrance must have sensed it, for there was a drop in the noise level in the suite.

He was dressed in jeans and a work shirt, and his fingernails were dirty. When he hugged me, I could smell stale sweat.

"Where's Anne?" I asked.

He frowned. "Isn't she here yet?"

"No, unless I missed her."

"We arranged to meet at the party," he told me. "I've been out working."

"I can see that. But aren't you a writer?"

"No!" He grinned triumphantly. "I've given it up. Master carpenter and electrician. Country homes fixed a specialty."

I stepped back to look at him. The grin broadened. "You've bought a house!"

"Not a house. A mansion. A palace."

"That's fabulous. Where?"

"Upstate New York. New Concord's the name of the town, but we're about ten miles from it. Near Chatham."

"When'd you buy it?"

"Three weeks ago. Anne's wild for it. It's got a great school nearby for David"—the grin faded—"a special school. And twenty-five acres. A stream. Apple trees. Butterflies. The works."

"What kind of house?"

"Who the fuck knows? Georgian? Anyway, old. Needs a lot of work. But it's huge, Tony. Baronial."

"Privacy at last," I said. "Maybe you'll go on writing after all."

He laughed. "There's so much work to be done on the house I don't see how I'll have the time."

"Make time." I smiled. "I need the money."

"You'll visit?"

My first invitation from him! "As soon as you'll have us."

"Good. Anne will call Judy." He paused, considering. "But it'll need a lot of fixing up. I've hired an architect to redo the ground floor—we'll want a porch, glass enclosed. And the place needs wallpaper, paint, a new kitchen. Besides, we don't really move in till June. Anne wants David to finish the semester"—again, there was a perceptible pause—"even though he's not happy there."

"But I'd love to see the place. It doesn't have to be finished," I persisted. "Besides, maybe we can help. Judy's a decorator—"

He beamed. "Of course. I'd forgotten. Let's plan it for the first nice day. Anne would love to have Judy along. She's got dozens of ideas herself, but another eye is always welcome."

He was so warm, so outgoing, even so intimate in the midst of the hubbub about us, that my depression lifted. He was *my* star. I loved him.

"Anne must be thrilled," I said.

"I've never seen her so happy."

"Sure. She wanted the house in the first place."

"We both wanted it, actually. And now that we have it, I think I'm more excited than she is."

Arthur came over to us, carrying two Scotches. He handed one to Eric and sipped at the other. "Instant relief," he said. "If you feel the way I do about parties, you'll need it."

"Actually," Eric said, "I'm having a marvelous time."

I looked victoriously at Arthur. "Eric's bought a house. Get him to tell you about it."

And I wandered off, at peace.

Cynthia Baum, a diminutive, feisty restaurant critic and the author of novels that verge on the autobiographically pornographic, stood alone in a far corner of my office; the other guests, many of whom had read her books, seemed to shun her as though they were afraid of being raped. I like Cynthia. She came on to me once, but I waved the name Judy in front of her like a Christian fending off a vampire, and she backed away into a serene friendship that lasts until this day.

I had decided to surprise Judy by carefully planning our trip to France, to take place in May, after I had fully settled into the new offices, but before the work brought in by the expanded staff would become overwhelming. So I was glad to see Cynthia standing alone. It would give me a chance to ask her advice about restaurants; she would know one-stars as good as, but less expensive than, the threes.

She greeted me with pleasure—to her, I was more a friend than her agent—and began rattling off a list of names which I dutifully wrote down on a piece of paper. But she never got to finish the list.

There was a scream from the outside corridor, then another. I heard a woman's voice shout "Cocksucker" in such fury that the incongruity and surprise of it were chilling, not funny. Cynthia and I both turned toward the noise, but stood immobile, for the sound was so alien it disoriented us both (I talked to her about it later and so can speak for her as well as myself), and it took a moment to realize that the noise applied to *us*, threatened *us*.

In another second, though, I ran toward the sound, pushing my way past stunned guests, my heart racing, thinking of how bad a party it had been—and now this!

A madwoman had entered the room and, still screaming, was fighting her way toward Eric. Her hair was tangled, her eyes wild with fury, her teeth bared. She almost howled as she reached her prey and began pummeling him with her fists. Then she opened her hands and went for his eyes, clawing at him as though she would destroy him.

He let her hit him, standing stunned and red-faced, the blows ineffectual, but when she attacked his face, he grabbed her hands and held her off; her nails missed his eyes by inches.

We formed a circle around him, spectators at a school-yard brawl. I remember Arthur's calling out "Stop it, Anne, for God's sake!" and my own shouts and those of others to break it up. But they stood oblivious, in place, he rigidly, she trembling as though invaded by cold. She had stopped screaming and eventually his tight grip took effect. Her trembling ceased and her body went soft, almost crumbling, and he was at last able to hold her gently against him.

He looked at us all, his eyes sad, perhaps apologetic. "She's had this problem," he began, but at the words she pushed herself away from him, her eyes again wild.

"It's not that," she hissed. "Not that. *This*!"

She reached into her coat pocket, took out a crumpled piece of paper, and flung it with all her force into his face. The paper struck him, then fell to the floor; he made no attempt to pick it up, but merely watched her gravely, with unnatural calm. They stood apart now; the only sound in the room was her gasps, her sobs.

"What is it?" he said. From ten feet away, I could feel his self-control.

"It's from your whore." Her voice was choked. "Don't you want to read it?"

"I don't know what you're talking about."

"Your whore!" she screamed. "Kitty."

Kitty. My breath stopped. I moved away from Eric, willing him not to look at me; I did not want to acknowledge complicity. So I stood now at the edge of the crowd around them, though I could still see them clearly.

Eric was a superb liar. "I still don't know what you're talking about," he said soothingly. "I don't know anybody named Kitty."

"How about Constance, then?" There was no lessening of Anne's fury.

Eric smiled. "Constance is the name of your cousin. And she's hardly a whore."

"Don't patronize me," she said, her voice suddenly quiet. "You know perfectly well I don't mean my cousin."

"But she's the only Constance I know."

"Liar!" The word exploded from her. She began to tremble again.

"I'm taking you home." He reached for her hands.

"I'd never go home with you. Never. Never again!"

"Yes, you are," he said sweetly. He had taken her hands, his touch surprisingly soft, and tried to draw her to him.

"I hate you!"

"And I love you." His voice had darkened momentarily—it was the only anger he showed—but his voice remained consoling. "Let's talk alone."

She began to cry. "You wouldn't have done it if you loved me. You *couldn't* have."

"Done what?"

She pointed at his shoe as though it had stepped in excrement. "That."

"Lies," he said, now able to bring her close. "I won't read it."

She put her face into his shoulder, hiding it. "Oh God, I wish I hadn't!" she said, her sobs muffled but her body calm.

"Come home," he repeated. "We'll talk there."

Without looking at anybody, he led her, unresisting, away, stopping only to get his coat from the rack in the corridor. A phalanx of subjects, we watched the regal pair depart in silence, and quickly thereafter the rest of the invitees left, like guests at a party where the host has received word of a death.

At last, only Arthur, Judy, and I remained; even my two assistants had gone home. But we had nothing to say to each other, beyond commonplaces. Arthur, the diplomat, tried to assure me that the party, despite its ending, was a success. It was so ludicrous a statement that I made no effort to refute it.

"What were they fighting about?" he asked me. "Do you have any idea?"

I did indeed, and so did Judy, but I did not wish to enlighten him, and Judy, taking her cue from me, kept silent too. All three of us engaged ourselves in cleaning up—the detritus of cheese and plastic cups, cigarettes and half-finished drinks that are the residue of any publishing party. The mood was somber; we did not look at each other as we worked.

Finally we finished and went downstairs together. The snow was falling as hard as ever but, sheltered from the wind in the doorway, we felt warm. The beauty of the night served as an antidote to the tawdry display of an hour ago; the air was cleansing. A solitary empty cab cruised up Madison and Arthur rushed from the doorway to hail it.

"You take it," he called. "I'm going downtown, and besides, I want to walk for a bit."

We gratefully accepted and settled into the backseat. Judy moved close to me, and I put my arm over her shoulder. She smiled and turned her face up to kiss me. Aroused, I kissed her back, but then a thought intruded, and I pulled away, shifting to look at her.

"The letter," I said. "We must have left it there, or did somebody pick it up?"

Judy's expression was full of love and concern. "I have it," she said, patting her pocketbook. "We'll read it when we get home."

eleven

"OH MY GOD."

Judy finished reading and handed me the letter, instinctively folding it. Her face was white. I opened it:

My darling, darling Eric:

I saw in Variety that you have finished a new book and that it was sold to the movies. I am very happy and proud that you are my friend—my more than friend! Constance and I tell all our friends we know you, and they are very impressed. They have all read Success and so have we, and we all think it is one of the best things we have ever read, as sad as Sophie's Choice.

I hope and hope (and so does Constance!) that you will come to Los Angeles to promote your new book (damn! I've forgotten its name although it was in Variety) because we are both horny for you and want to continue what we started last time. Do you remember when you lay between us upside down, so you could feel our breasts against you, front and back, and we could lick your cock and your ass? (Jesus, I'm getting turned on just thinking about it!) You seemed to like that a whole lot, and so did we, only Constance and I agree that we liked it better when you finger-fucked us both at the same time and then put your cock in

143

me and then in her and then in me and then in her, etc., etc., etc., etc.!!!!!!

We have thought of some new games to try—we spend a lot of time talking about it!—only I won't tell you what they are in this letter. You'll have to come to Los Angeles to find out, but we promise you won't be disappointed!

So please write and tell us you'll come (no pun intended!). My address is on the top of this letter—don't you think it's fancy? I can feel your mouth on my tits and your cock in my cunt as I write this, so please hurry to us 'cause it's much more fun when it's real! If Constance were here she'd say the same thing. She is just as horny as I am, and sometimes we make love to each other, thinking about you.

comecomecomecomecomecome.

Your hot
Pussy (Er, Kitty—heh, heh)

I stared at the paper dumbly, unable to decide what to do with it. Finally I walked to a table at the far end of the room and put it down. Judy remained standing all the time I was reading, but now, the act finished, she sat heavily on the couch.

"I'm sorry for Eric," I said.

Instantly, she was on her feet again, her face bright with fury. "*Eric*! That shit. What about Anne?"

"No, Eric," I repeated. "Those girls don't mean a thing to him. They're just star-fuckers and he knows it. They were a distraction, a relief from the tensions of the tour."

" 'A relief from the tensions of the tour,' " she mimicked. I had never seen her this angry at me before. "Jesus, Tony, try to look at it from Anne's point of view, or are you too egotistical, like your writer friend? Some relief, say I. How would you like it if I got the same relief from the tensions of being an interior decorator?"

"I'd hate it."

"And I'd kill you if you did it." She took both my hands in hers and looked closely into my eyes. "You didn't, did you?"

"What?"

"Kitty and Constance. There weren't four of you on that bed?"

I blessed my former restraint. I did not have to lie. "No."

"Swear it." I could feel sweat on her hands.

"As God is my witness."

"And you didn't help arrange it?"

I could feel blood race in my temples. "You mean pimp for him? Certainly not. I told you at the time, I didn't hammer down his door when he threw me out, but that's my only sin in all of this."

She continued to hold me tightly and to look in my eyes. I could see anger abate in hers. Then, suddenly, she released me. "I believe you," she said quietly. "For so help me, if you ever pulled anything like that, I'd leave you. With me, Tony, love is sacred—it means *everything*—and being faithful is part of it."

"For you, yes. And for me too. But Eric is different."

"Bullshit." She turned and began to pace.

"He *is*," I protested. "Artists are different."

"Romantic hogwash. You tell me that all the time, just as I suppose your father told it to you. But I say it's nonsense. It seems to me just an excuse to let writers get away with anything they want."

"Ah, Miss Perfect." I was angry myself now. "Divine judge. When have you taken risks anywhere near Eric's?"

"Maybe when I married you," she shouted, and she looked so fierce, so combative, that my anger broke.

"You warned me about Eric," I said. "Maybe you were right."

She looked at me, astonished. "What do you mean?"

"We're fighting now about *him*. About something *he's* done. I wasn't unfaithful, you don't take drugs, and we have no children. Yet here we are going at each other. He's invaded our house."

"And our lives," she agreed, calming noticeably.

"We don't want him entirely out of our lives," I reminded her. "He's a great writer."

"Yes, and he gives you something valuable. He fulfills you, hits some place I can't touch."

I put my arms around her. "My God, think of that household. There'll be an explosion. Imagine the pain for them all."

"And David, again, in the middle."

I thought for a moment. "Will she leave him?"

Her answer came quickly; she had thought of the question too. "No, if only for David's sake."

"But she'll torture him."

She smiled ruefully. "Can you say he doesn't deserve it?"

"What'll happen to his writing?"

She pulled away abruptly, anger returning. "That *is* what you care about, isn't it?"

"And you?"

"I care about his heart—and yours."

"My, my," I said.

She wheeled away from me. "I care about people, not fucking books."

I caught up to her. "What's that supposed to mean?"

"All you're worried about is his writing. Will the 'explosion,' as you call it, slow him down? Will you have to wait two years for the next book? Will you be able to pay for your precious new office?"

"That's not fair and you know it." I was shouting now, a step behind her as she walked the room. "I love him."

She stopped abruptly but kept her back to me. "He's not lovable," she said coldly. "What he did was vile and disgusting. He's impossible to love, and you of all people, my perceptive, darling Tony, should know it. You can't love people who only love themselves."

"But he's been generous to me. Warm and sweet and—"

"Going for months without speaking to you. Using you when he feels like it. Wanting to fuck me, not matter what he feels about you—"

"What?"

"You heard me."

"You're crazy!"

"No. You're blind." She shuddered. "You don't *look*," she said. "The touches, the soulful looks, the lingering hugs. Jesus, he gives me the creeps!"

"I'll kill him."

"Nonsense. It's harmless to me, for Christ's sake. I can fend him off. It's just an itch in him. Hence Kitty and Constance." She paused. "But that's what I mean, Tony. You don't see him for what he is, so you can't possibly love him. I think you love the idea of him, the fact that he's a truly great writer whom you discovered, and a truly great earner who's paying the bills."

I thought of the publicity trip, of the scene between him and Anne at the airport, of our first meeting and subsequent ones, of the way my heart reacted when I heard his voice—yes, like a lover's.

"It's more complicated than that," I said.

The phone rang.

"I'll get it," I told her, knowing instinctively who it was.

But she reached the doorway ahead of me. "No, let me."

I didn't follow Judy, but merely waited for her report.

"It was Anne," she said, returning. "She wants us to come out there."

My stomach lurched. "Why?"

"She didn't say."

"When?"

"Immediately."

"What did you tell her?"

She glanced at me quizzically. "Did I have a choice?"

"Of course."

Her voice was flat, ironical. "Oh, I didn't think I did. What with her being the empress and all, and we her loyal subjects. Anyway, I said we'd come. If you think that's wrong—"

"No, no," I said quickly. "We have to go. How does she sound?"

"Anne? Terrible."

"Upset?"

"Beaten. Her voice was dead."

"Was Eric with her?"

"I don't know," Judy said reflectively. "Funny, I didn't think to ask."

"I just want to know what to expect when we get there."

"Expect trouble," Judy said, laughing mirthlessly. "That way you can't go wrong."

⚜

This time I drove cautiously, even though the snow had stopped and the highway was clear, as though by putting time between the phone call and our arrival, Anne's pain would have lessened. We said little as I drove; neither of us knew what to anticipate. But I at least imagined horrors—physical violence, Eric's having stormed off forever, the joint announcement of a divorce, David in tears having heard it all. Or all of the above, I thought.

Judy sat calmly beside me, arms folded demurely in her lap, her breathing even and unexcited. If she was worried about the encounter, she gave no sign of it.

"What would a letter like that do to you?" I asked at last, as much to break the quiet as out of desire for information.

The question startled her; she looked at me sharply. "I don't know."

"You said you'd leave me."

"If you were unfaithful—I'd sure want to. But I'd probably wind up thinking it was my fault. Isn't that the standard reaction?"

"I'm not sure. It hasn't come up."

She patted my inner thigh. "It comes up all the time," she said, laughing at last. "Actually, the letter's so sick I'd probably learn to live with it. You couldn't *love* such a person."

"True."

"So at the worst it's a defiance. That is, if the letter's real."

"It's real all right."

"And it isn't the first time. Even if you hadn't told me about his affairs, I'd have known he'd had them. Just the way he looks at me makes me sure he's done it before. I'm not all that exceptional. He must have looked at many other women the same way."

"You *are* exceptional," I said. "But I take your point. Just think how upset she was the night he disappeared. I'll bet she suspected there was another woman, no matter what she says."

"But this was far more violent. She was trying to take out his eyes."

"The cocaine," I suggested.

"Umm. Or lack of it."

Unconsciously, my foot pressed on the gas pedal. Judy was right, I thought. Trouble either way.

Lights were on in every room of the house. So they're up and waiting for us, I reflected unhappily, knowing there could have been no alternative.

We walked slowly toward the door, holding hands tightly, Hansel and Gretel at the gingerbread house. The only sound was the hum of a car motor on a distant street.

"At least she's not murdering him," I whispered.

"Maybe she already has."

We reached the door but paused. "Frightened?" Judy asked.

"Scared shitless."

She squeezed my hand harder. "Me too."

At last I rang the bell. Somebody must have seen us coming or heard the car, for the door flew open instantly—only nobody was on the other side.

Puzzled, we stepped in cautiously. I could see both Anne and Eric seated in the living room, he on the sofa, she on the chair that had nearly electrocuted me on my first visit. Neither seemed to take account of our arrival; they sat motionless, staring at the floor.

"*Boo!*"

Beside me, Judy let out a little gasp, and I could sense her body stiffen.

David stepped from behind the door. He was wearing a fright mask, the fanged face of a gorilla, black unkempt hair streaming from its head, flecks of blood at its lips, the eye sockets cut out revealing David's own eyes, savage and full of such hate beneath their mischief that I felt my scalp tingle.

"You scared me," Judy said, recovering; her voice was one of mother-pretending-to-child.

"Me too," I said, taking her cue and keeping my voice light.

"I'm scary!" he announced. "I'm the fiercest, baddest, most scary animal in the jungle!"

"Oh no you're not." Judy laughed. "I recognize your voice, so I know who you are. You're David."

"Grrr," David growled, denying her.

She reached toward him. "I was scared, but I'm glad you're really David."

"No!" he shouted, shying away. "No!" He ran to his mother, who, without looking at him, opened her arms and hugged him, her head on his shoulder, his face on her breast.

Eric had remained slumped on the couch, an exhausted fighter resting between rounds, but now he got up and with a visible effort of will came toward us.

"Welcome," he said in an attempt at gaiety. "Welcome to the Meredith monkey house." He kissed Judy lightly on the cheek and shook hands with me. The joke had fallen flat, and the three of us stood together in silence, too embarrassed to speak.

Finally Anne gently lifted David from her embrace and got up to join us. She too kissed Judy and shook hands with me. She was unnaturally pale and there were dark gray circles under her eyes.

She had combed her hair and put on lipstick for our benefit, but that only intensified her aura of suffering. She reminded me of my mother, who, even in the last stages of cancer, would always make herself up before receiving me.

"It was good of you to come," she said in a bereaved voice.

"Our pleasure," I said, so clumsily that the words cast us into silence once more and we stood in freeze frame for what seemed like a minute.

"A drink?" Eric asked at last, and both Judy and I accepted, though I had little desire for one and I doubt she did either. Eric went off to fix them; for some reason, they had taken the bar out of the living room.

"I heard you bought a new house," Judy said in the same voice she had used with David. "You must be thrilled."

"Yes, isn't it wonderful," Anne said without emotion. I guessed she thought of the house as a symbol of permanence that might not exist.

When do you move in?" I asked, knowing the answer.

"I'm not sure *we're* moving anywhere," she said in a lugubrious voice. David must have overheard, for he gave a little whimper and caught hold of his mother's skirt.

"Of course you will," Judy said briskly, a hospital nurse at bedside.

"Did you read the letter?"

Judy and I looked at each other; she nodded slightly. "Yes," I said.

"And you'd live with somebody after that?"

"As a matter of fact, yes," Judy said, still brisk. "Oh, I'd be mad. Boiling, fucking mad. But I'd think to myself, what a sick mind must have written that letter. What a pathetic woman. Tony couldn't love her, I'd figure. He must love me."

Anne stared at her, thunderstruck. Perhaps she expected female unity, perhaps she had never really thought of what Judy was telling her. "But it's filth!" she cried. "He wallowed in it. With two of them!" She began to sob.

Judy put her arm around Anne's shoulder with a gentleness that made my heart ache. "Yes, it's filth," she said, "and he wallowed in it. I can understand why you're so unhappy, so repelled. I imagine it'll take weeks before you can go to bed with him again." She led Anne to the sofa and sat her down, all the time talking to her in a confidential, therapist's tone. "But it isn't fatal. It's not a love affair. Don't you see, it's a physical thing, a boy's night out. But it doesn't involve his heart. Nor his soul."

It's difficult to know just how much of this got through to Anne, but at least her sobbing stopped and her body relaxed.

"Think what a shock it was," she said. "The letter came with the rest of the mail this morning. I was going out shopping, so I put all the mail on the hall table, where I always do, and didn't look at it until I got back this afternoon. There were only bills and fliers—and this one letter, written by a woman, marked 'Strictly Personal,' addressed to Eric." She shook her head at the memory, and the tears flowed more quickly. "I don't open his mail, I really don't. I'm not that type of wife. I trust him, always have, even though I've been suspicious from time to time. And on that trip— well, he was with you, Tony, so when he was gone I didn't give it any thought." Judy handed her a Kleenex, and she used it to wipe her eyes. "I'm not the person to open other people's mail," she repeated, her voice rising in emphasis. "But 'Strictly Personal'—that bothered me. I figured it was a crank letter; he's gotten them from time to time after *Success* was published, and he's hated them. So I thought I'd spare him the pain of this one." She laughed. " 'Spare him the pain.' So I opened it and got—"

"Fantasy," Eric said. "Lies."

I had not heard him return, so he appeared simply to have materialized, carrying a tray with four drinks on it. His expression was sober and sympathetic. If he had heard any of Anne's story beyond the last, and if he was angry with her or upset, there was no way to tell. He was gentle and calm.

"I've been telling her that for hours," he said, looking at me.

"I don't know a Kitty and I don't know a Constance except for Anne's cousin. I've never made love to two women at once. I was not unfaithful during my publicity tour. I love Anne and only Anne—Anne and David," he amended with a glance at his son; David pressed himself against his mother's side, holding the fabric of her dress lightly between thumb and forefinger. "But I can't convince her; she won't believe me." He sighed. "That's why I asked her to ask you to trek all the way out here. I'm sorry to have put you to all this bother again. But"—he shrugged, exaggerating the gesture—"I need you."

Sweat stood out on my forehead, and I could feel bile rise in my throat. I knew what was coming.

"Tony," Eric said calmly. "Tell Anne that you were with me every night in Los Angeles. That we roomed together. That there were no Kittys and no Constances. That I behaved myself, that I was a good boy." He swung around to look at his wife. "Tell her please, Tony. Tell her the truth. She doesn't seem to believe me."

I dropped my drink. My hands had gone suddenly numb, and the glass simply fell from them, Scotch soaking the meager carpet.

"Clumsy," Judy said. I cannot even now figure out whether she meant something beyond the obvious by the word.

I leaned down to wipe it up with the flimsy napkin Eric had provided with the glass. "I'm sorry," I said, getting up. "I'll get some towels in the kitchen."

"It won't stain," Anne said sharply. "What *is* the truth, please."

There was to be no respite. I could feel Judy grow tense by my side and, head bowed, could nevertheless sense Eric's eyes and Anne's staring at me. There was no time to think through my answer. I knew immediately that whatever I said would be wrong and that I would regret it.

"I know who Constance and Kitty are," I said slowly, considering the words, my head still down.

"You *do?*" Eric's voice was a threat.

Carefully I raised my head to look at him—only at him. "Sure.

You remember, Eric, they were those two girls in the El Padrino, the ones who kept staring at us our first afternoon and then asked us to buy them a drink."

Eric's eyes were expressionless. "I don't remember," he said. "What did we do?"

"We beat it. Couldn't leave fast enough."

"Of course!" Eric slapped his forehead in a gesture I thought too theatrical. "You're right, Tony." He turned to Anne, humor lighting his eyes and condescension his tone. "Honey, they were two bimbos who tried to pick us up in California. I had forgotten completely about them. We were rude as hell to them, walked out when they pressed us. That letter was written in retaliation, not passion."

She ignored him and kept her eyes on me. "Is that true, Tony? You walked out on them?"

"Yes," I said, meeting her look.

"And you didn't come back to pick them up later?"

"No."

"Don't lie to me now," she said. "I don't believe Eric, but I'll believe you. Did you spend every night with him?"

"Of course."

"And there were no"—her voice caught on the word—"bimbos?"

I could feel Judy's hand on my leg, a gentle pressure. I did not know what it meant. "No bimbos." I smiled.

"You swear it?"

"Yes."

"No," she said sharply. "I want to hear you swear it."

"Anne," Eric said. "Stop it. You're making him angry."

"She's not," I said. "I swear it."

She gave me a long, searching look; I did not blink. And then, without warning, tears started to roll down her face, and she turned her back to me so I would not see her cry. "I'm sorry," she whispered. "Awfully, terribly sorry," and she walked slowly to Eric and put her arms around him. He hugged her gently and stroked her hair. David, who had sat motionless through all this, came to them, and Eric included him in his embrace. I caught his eye, seeking I'm not sure what—maybe gratitude—but he merely looked at me as though he were studying a not-too-interesting painting on the wall. Judy had moved away from me on the couch. I felt myself blush and once again stared at the floor, as ashamed of myself as I had ever been, thankful that Anne had her back to me and could not see that shame.

Eric reached behind him and unclasped Anne's arms. "I love you," he told her. "But now we've got to get Tony a drink."

　　　　　　　　　　　✖

"I had to do it," I said. We were in the car, going home.

"Yes, *you* did." Her emphasis startled me; I turned to look at her. She was staring out the window, face averted.

"What's that supposed to mean?"

"Just what you said. You had to do it. I was agreeing with you."

"But you wouldn't have done it?" My fingers tightened on the steering wheel.

She took the question seriously, pausing a long time before answering. "Probably not. I hate lying."

"Even for a friend?"

"A lie that large? Even for a friend."

"Do you think I enjoyed it?"

She must have sensed my pain, for her voice softened. "Why did you do it? Can you figure it out?"

It was the question I had been asking myself. I did not answer.

"Because he pays the rent?" she prodded.

"If so, it's the smallest part of the reason." I shook my head. "No, that's not it."

"It's nice, this life," she continued. "Material success, comfort, recognition. No money worries. Respect of your peers. Ease. Eric means all that, doesn't he?"

I could feel how tense she was. I wanted to look at her, convince her with my eyes as well as my words, but I had to watch the road. "It's precisely the opposite," I said. "It's not ease he gives me, but disquiet. Sure I like the material things and the recognition, but I could give them up in a second. I was happy before we met Eric, and I could be very happy going back to that kind of life. Eric's talented. Dangerous. Volatile. Those things I'm not."

"Thank God," Judy said.

"But that doesn't mean I can't be attracted by them."

Her voice turned cold again. "They hardly seem reasons for lying."

"Eric's my friend. He asked for help, and I helped him."

"You lied for him!" She was implacable.

"And maybe saved his marriage."

I heard her intake of breath. "Marriages get saved by lies?"

"Ours, never. Theirs, maybe. Damn it, Judy, Eric needs Anne. If you'd been with them at the airport, you'd know that. I did what I thought was right to keep her from walking out on him."

"And so you saved his books. The one he's writing. The ones to come."

"No. I saved him."

"By lying. And should I save Anne from him by telling the truth?"

I felt cold and turned up the heater. "Anne needs Eric as much as he needs her."

She reached out to hold my arm. I turned to her and saw how much I had hurt her.

"Nobody needs a relationship like theirs. When he needs an agent to do his lying for him."

Her words stung like hail. "Forgive me."

She considered it. "Yes and no. Yes, because I love you deeply and passionately, and what you did does not alter that love. You were, after all, being loyal in a fashion. No, because I saw a part of you tonight I don't like. I won't forgive that part. I want it to go away."

I was not fatuous; I did not promise that it would. I simply took her hand and kissed it. The car skidded on a patch of snow. "Careful," she said. "You are my life."

I kissed her hair. "You're my life too. You really are all I want and all I need."

That night, at that moment, I believed it.

twelve

THREE DAYS LATER, I MET ARTHUR FOR LUNCH. THE purpose was more social than business. We had made our subsidiary rights money on *Diamonds*, the book would be published in a few weeks, orders were cascading in. The question was not whether it would be a best-seller, but how many more copies it would sell than *Success*.

"It's the brand-name factor," Arthur told me over drinks. "Even if *Diamonds* was a lesser book, which it isn't, Meredith's a marketable name now—'the new Meredith' means something to bookstore owners. They'll sell the hell out of it."

I had seen the same phenomenon many times in the past. With Agatha Christie, for an obvious example, whose sales kept going up even as the quality of her books went down. Most hardcover novels, even literary ones like Eric's or Saul Bellow's, are given as presents, and it is therefore safer for a buyer to purchase a well-known author than an unknown. It's the reason why so many of the same names turn up over and over again on the best-seller lists.

"What else is selling for you?" I asked, not really wanting to discuss Eric. I had decided not to tell Arthur of our encounter, or the contents of the letter. I might have if I had been proud of the way I acted, but as it was I was ashamed of the whole incident, and it still made me queasy to think of it.

"Nothing's hot," Arthur said, his eyes sad. "Thank God for Meredith; he's saving our skins." He reflected. "I thought *Success* would attract new business, other authors who saw how good a job we'd done and want to be published by us. But it hasn't happened. All we've been sent are some of the most godawful 'literary' master-pieces you ever saw. Lots of adolescents with acne, scared of sex. Or even worse, housewife novels. There are hundreds of women, it seems, surrounded by diapers, longing to break free."

I had read dozens of books like that myself. "No kidding," I said, playing along. "What happens to them?"

"They find out affairs are unfulfilling and independence isn't what it's cracked up to be. But meanwhile their husbands realize they can't live wifeless. And both discover that the enduring value in life is love."

I shook my head. "I'd never have believed it."

"But that's all we get," he said, gloomy again. "If there's another Harold Robbins around, he ain't pointed in our direction."

"Which leaves you with Meredith."

"Meredith and a lot of books on knitting and crochet."

"I don't have much to offer you," I told him. "Nothing near as good as Meredith, anyway."

"I'm not asking anything from you," he said, smiling. "You've done enough for me. Besides, even if you had something terrific, I'm not sure it'd be a good idea for you to send it to me. You don't want to be a one-publisher agent any more than I want to be a one-author editor."

"True. But if you're in trouble—"

"Not as long as there's Eric," he answered, slightly embarrassed. "Trouble'll only come if he goes. That's why I hate to be so dependent on only one writer."

"But he won't leave. He thinks you're marvelous."

He seemed surprised. "Every writer leaves, sooner or later. You'll see. Even Eric, who thinks I'm marvelous."

A shot of adrenaline hit my stomach. "There'd be no reason for him to leave," I said.

"There's never a reason. Or there always is. It amounts to the same thing." He signaled for another round of drinks.

"It's a working day," I protested.

"You're working now." He laughed, and we branched off into other, less painful areas.

But when the meal was over, he brought up Eric again. "I want you to do me a favor," he said.

"Sure."

"I want you to get the rights back on *Anderson's Luck* and sell them to Diadem. To me."

I was astonished. "Doubleday'll never give them back. If I ask, they'll simply reissue the book themselves, or at least sell it to paperback. And you know full well that if it's in print in any edition, they don't have to revert rights to me or to anybody."

He waved his hand impatiently. "I know. And indeed, Doubleday's thought of reissuing, only Eric's forbidden it."

"He has?"

"Yup. Says that if they reprint in its present form, he'll disown it and sue them."

I felt a pang of jealousy that Arthur knew this and I didn't. "What does he want to do, revise?" The notion surprised me.

"Maybe. But he'd only do it for me. It's his gratitude present, he told me. What happened was that I finally got around to re-reading it—God, it's a talented work!—and I honestly thought it could be improved. So I called Eric, asking him if he'd be interested in revising, and he said yes, provided he liked my ideas for changes—"

"Did he?" I interrupted. "I'd go carefully with him, Arthur."

"I will. I haven't discussed the changes yet. First, you have to get the rights back."

"If Eric stays adamant there shouldn't be a problem."

"He's adamant. He says he only wants his books published by Diadem."

I smiled. "By Diadem or by you?"

His eyes twinkled ."Modesty forbids—"

I raised my coffee cup in salute. "Then who gives a shit whether or not you get another author. It's obscene to be greedy."

From a British publisher friend of mine I rented for the month of May a small farmhouse on the outskirts of a little town called Bar-sur-Loup in the mountains of southern France. Our plan was to use it as the base for our honeymoon-at-last, taking excursions to Lyons and Paris, but when we got there—at last—the place was so extraordinary, we decided to take no more than day trips away.

Bar-sur-Loup is only fifteen miles northwest of Nice, but our house, set in the hills outside the town proper, was as remote from the publishing world as an outpost in Antarctica. The house itself was unprepossessing. Built in the seventeenth century out of rough stone, it consisted of a living-room–kitchen–bedroom complex on the ground floor, two guest bedrooms on the second. There was a small garden in front, kept up by its owners, who used the place for long weekends except when they rented it to rich Americans; in back, the trees came to the edge of the house, a hammock the only sign of civilization.

If the house was crude, at least the plumbing worked, the beds in all three bedrooms were comfortable, and the solitude was absolute. Every day the sun shone, casting the house in soft, dappled light that turned my bones languid. Flowers grew everywhere, in the garden and in the woods, and the hammock swung easily in the soft winds that caressed us each afternoon—yes, we made love there, too. Every morning at about eleven, a truck rolled into Bar-sur-Loup's central square and parked. One side of it was hinged, opening to form a large window, the base of which served as a counter displaying the contents of the truck: over one hundred different kinds of cheese. We came upon the truck by chance on our second day, and every morning thereafter I was delegated to drive into town (we had rented a bright yellow Ford Fiesta for the month) and pick up two cheeses for lunch—no duplication allowed of the ones we had eaten the day before. The game was that if on any day I picked a cheese that displeased Judy, I would lose my job and Judy would take my place as provider. I never missed, nor did I fail with the peaches or wine or bread which accompanied the cheese. At least, Judy never complained.

Our days became deliciously routine. We would sleep late, often awakening to make love. In the morning, after I had completed my errands, we would go for a walk through the woods or up into the mountains behind the town. Around two, we would feast on the cheese and wine, and then I would retire to the hammock, Judy to a canvas chaise, and we would read through the late afternoons, maybe nap, and plan where we would go for dinner. Occasionally, we would travel to Nice or Cannes or Monte Carlo during the day, to swim or go to a museum, but the crowds displeased us; we guarded our isolation and the only intruders we welcomed into our lives were a waiter or sommelier.

Judy decided to read *Remembrance of Things Past* during those sunlit days; she told me that Proust's prose, soft and vivid, matched her surroundings and she could not imagine one without the other. I read more prosaic stuff, mysteries and best-sellers, catching up on the competition, but so content that I did not even fantasize about representing the authors—it was fine that they were with other agents; I had authors enough.

Of all the good times in our lives, this was the happiest. We had the comfort of youth and the deepening of a relationship in which we discovered that the better we knew each other, the more sure we were that our marriage was blessed. Professionally secure, needing only each other's company, richer by far than we thought we would be at this stage of our lives, we wanted nothing more than what we had. And all of this in honey-filled France, in exquisite spring, where the sun dazzled but was not too hot, and the breeze turned up the paler side of the leaves of the trees in the afternoons so that we might not become glutted with the deep green of the mornings.

For the last day of our third week, we took an excursion to a restaurant-hotel called Beaumanière, situated outside the remains of a medieval town, Les Baux, about sixty miles from Bar-sur-Loup. This was a three-star place recommended by two sets of our friends and Cynthia Baum as, simply, the most wonderful in the world, and for it we made an exception: we would stay overnight. I had reserved a room from New York and had been anticipating the trip ever since, for the proprietor had written to ask whether we wished a plum or lemon soufflé for dessert—since the preparation time was considerable, he explained, it was best to know our desires in advance of our arrival. I chose the lemon, immediately regretted I had not picked the plum, but was forgiven by Judy, who assured me we could always return if necessary.

Les Baux is hewn out of a white mountain. The drive to it takes you through fields filled with thousands of white flowers—a carpet of lilies—their fragrance almost as powerful as the smell of poppies that put Dorothy and her companions to sleep on the way to Oz. But there was no thought of sleep for us. Wide-eyed, enchanted, exhilarated by the wonders of things made by nature and by man, we felt ourselves in paradise, and the dinner of vegetable tartlets, rack of lamb, and the amazing soufflé, confirmed it.

We slept that night in beds as soft as a sultan's pillows, and woke to miniature croissants, still hot from the oven, served with butter, marmalade, and honey, all so fresh they must have been produced that morning. Languorously we made love, then took another walk through the old town, buying strawberries, as though they were needed, for the trip back to Bar-sur-Loup. We said little on that walk, each fulfilled by the possession of the other's hand and the private realization that life could get no better. But we knew that times like this, rare as they were, could be duplicated, would be duplicated, for us lucky ones—the very, very rich in all senses of that word—from time to time as we grew older.

"I feel sorry for the poor people," I told Judy.

"Hell," she said, "I'm always sorry for them. Today I feel sorry for the queen of England."

The morning light made the white town glow, and standing on its topmost walk we could see what seemed like an ocean of flowers, with only our hotel as a majestic ship in that sea. Like dancers long rehearsed, Judy and I turned our gaze away from the panorama, looked into each other's eyes, and kissed long and deeply, our arms about each other, urgent but secure, confident in our love and the power it gave us.

"I want you to know I've never been so happy in all my life," Judy said.

"It's the Beaumanière," I assured her. "After meals like those you'd say that to anybody."

"No, I'm serious." Her mouth smiled but her eyes didn't. "It's you, not the Beaumanière. I'm happy because I'm here with you. It wouldn't be the same with anybody else."

"How about President Carter? I know how sexy you think he is, how you lust after him in your heart—"

"Idiot."

We kissed again. I closed my eyes, but the sun left soft white circles around the lids. "Let's go back to the hotel," I said. "We just have time for a quicky before we have to check out."

She spun away from me, holding my hand. "What are we waiting for?"

We ran, as hungry for each other as if we'd been apart for months.

❧

"You know what we did that was clever?" Judy asked as we drove back to Bar-sur-Loup.

"What?"

"Saved a week in France. I don't think I could have stood going right home from the Beaumanière."

"Our house is a pretty nifty decompression chamber," I agreed. And indeed, it looked particularly gorgeous in the later afternoon light, a creation by Corot in an introspective but serene state of mind.

"Home." She smiled at me, gave me a quick hug, and waited while I unlocked the door.

"Look," she said, "somebody's left us a note."

Only our postman, who had a key to all the houses in the neighborhood, could have entered; the note must have been from him. I picked it up.

"S'il vous plaît, téléphonez à Monsieur Meredith à New York."

"Shit," I said.

She came to my side. "Trouble?" I handed her the note. "Maybe it's good news," she said.

"Fat chance. He's never called with good news in his life." I looked at my watch: four thirty. "If we hurry, we can get to the telephone office before it closes."

She stood at the door, barring it. "Wait till tomorrow."

I looked at her, astonished. "Why?"

"Because I don't want to spoil today. Yesterday and today. They're simply too precious, and I don't want to let them go."

"What if it's David?" I asked. "What if it's something serious?"

"If it is, what can you do about it in France?" She sighed and moved away from the door. "Oh fuck," she said. "That's what I mean. You should see your face. It's all screwed up and tense, your New York face—your Eric face." Her eyes were wet. "It took a week before it went away once we got here, and now it's come back. I *hate* him."

"He's paid for the house," I said coldly, already out the door and heading for the car. "Want to come along?"

"No."

"Okay. I'll be back as soon as I can. It's probably nothing."

"Shit," she said. "Fuck."

"You're eloquent when you're mad," I told her. I got into the car, started it, and drove off quickly, hoping the telephone office would still be open.

It was, and although I got a few furious looks for keeping the staff beyond five, I was able to request that a call be put through to America. I waited nervously while the operator got to work.

"Booth two," a voice called in accented English, and I went inside the hot, cramped space and picked up the phone.

"Eric?" I said.

"It's Anne," she announced. "Eric's on his way to the phone."

"Is he all right? Are you?"

"We're fine." Her voice was calm.

"David, then?" I could feel my heart dancing.

"Same as ever. This isn't a *physical* crisis, you understand."

I breathed more easily. "I didn't know what to think."

"Eric's upset, that's all. Here he is now. He'll tell you himself."

His voice was jovial, hail-fellow, the tone I liked least in him. It spelled unpleasantness. "Good of you to call," he said. "How are things in la belle France?"

"Gorgeous," I said. "It's paradise here."

"I hate to be your snake," he said, chuckling slightly, "but I need you back here."

"*Now?*" I imagined Judy's face and my heart flipped.

"I'm afraid so."

"Why?"

"I can't explain over the phone."

"Well, you'd better tell me something. Judy'll kill me."

There was a pause. "It's Arthur," he said finally. "He's betrayed me."

I could only stammer. "Arthur? Betrayed? How?"

"It's a long story. I really can't tell you over the phone."

"I can't believe it. Arthur's your friend. He—"

"I'm telling you he betrayed me." Eric's voice was cold. "You don't have to believe me."

"It must be a mistake," I said desperately. "A mix-up."

"It was a deliberate betrayal. I want you back here to fix it."

"Fix it? How?"

"I really haven't made up my mind," he said, his voice now steel. "That's why I want you back here—to help me."

I felt stifled in the little booth. "It can't wait a week?"

"For me, no. For you, it can wait forever."

A bead of sweat made its way from my scalp to my collar. "What's that supposed to mean?"

"That agents, like editors, are replaceable."

The threat buzzed in my ear like a wasp.

"Well?" he asked at last. I had not realized how long we had been silent.

I cleared my throat in an effort to clear my head. "There's an early morning flight from Nice to Paris. I suppose we could catch the noon plane for New York."

"We? Judy doesn't have to go with you."

"I think she'll want to."

"You could probably fly back in a day or two."

"We have only a few days left," I told him, some steel in my own tone now. "Besides, Eric, as your agent I get only ten percent. Frankly, I can't afford to fly back and forth."

"Without me, you couldn't fly at all," he said evenly. "Can we meet tomorrow night?"

"If I can book the plane."

"It's preseason. You'll get seats."

I knew he was right. "I'll call you from Kennedy."

He sighed, content. "Bless you. I'll never—"

I hung up.

❖

When Judy is particularly upset, the muscles in her face seem to lose their strength, and her mouth and jaw fall, like the mouth and jaw in a mask of tragedy. So it was this time after her rage had cooled and her disappointment, far worse to me than fury, replaced it. My own reactions passed from guilt to self-loathing. I became defensive.

"Look," I said, "if we were in government, and there was a crisis, I'd be called home. If we were in big business, I'd be called home. Shit, if I were a *publisher*, I'd be called home."

"Yes, *you* must get back." She used the same emphasis that had so chilled me the night of our fight in the car. "Only please remember that you're an 'independent literary agent,' and I don't see much independence."

"Then you please remember I'm a servant," I said hotly. "I serve my authors and, yes, their publishers if I think my authors are being unreasonable. I'm not creative, not even talented, except at being an agent."

Tears formed in her eyes. "And so you do what Eric commands. But oh, it hurts to see you bending over for him. Offering yourself time after time."

I stared at her. "Do you think I'm going back for *Eric*?"

"It sure sounds that way."

"No. For Arthur. What Eric said, that Arthur betrayed him, is impossible. But I seem to be the only one who can straighten it out."

Her tears stopped. She wiped at her nose with her sleeve. "I hadn't thought of that."

"Arthur's in trouble. Rationally or most probably irrationally, Eric's after him, and he won't be able to defend himself."

She sighed. "So off you go. And I go with you."

Touched, I kissed her. "We'll come back," I promised.

"No."

"Why not?" I asked, astonished.

"Because it's our honeymoon house," she said. "Ours for this special moment."

"What's the matter with a honeymoon every year?"

She took it seriously. "Because there's only one. For me, anyway. Only one, with you, here, now." She shrugged and headed briskly for the door. "And now it's over."

"But my love for you isn't over. Quite the contrary. And that's what matters."

"I know," she said cheerfully. "Indulge a romantic in a little romance."

"Where are you going?" I asked.

"To the phone. And you're coming with me."

For a moment, I thought she was going to call Eric herself, tell him we would not come. I felt both fear and a transcendent joy. "But the phone's closed," I told her. "I was the last one there. They could hardly wait for me to leave."

"Not that phone, silly." She laughed. "The local pay phone in the village. We're going to have to call some airlines if we want to get out of here tomorrow."

❧

The plane from Paris was late, so we did not arrive at Kennedy until a little before five o'clock. As soon as we had cleared customs, I called Eric, who told me to come over immediately, so I put Judy and the luggage in a cab and took a different taxi to the Merediths', planning to get back to New York by train once the discussion was over. By Paris time, it was around eleven P.M. when I got to their house, and I felt addled and disoriented, grimy from the trip, a bad taste in my mouth and a dread in my heart over the forthcoming interview.

Eric met me at the door, dressed in slacks and a polo shirt, looking unusually fresh and clean, as though he had just showered. We shook hands firmly, eyes on each other's; he was in his serious-but-friendly mood, a notch up from hail-fellow.

"Where's Anne?" I asked.

"She's taken David out for a pizza. A treat."

"How is he?"

His eyes darkened. "Not so good. Awfully quiet." He led me into the living room, talking all the while. "It's the most bizarre thing. He's taken to being very finicky about his food. He'll eat only the outside of things, potato peels, for example, or the skin of chicken. Anne served a steak the other day, and he ate only the fatty part, not the meat. He won't tell us why, won't discuss it with us at all. But when we try to make him eat—oh, vegetables, say—he just clamps his jaws shut and no power of mine can open them. Maybe pizza will help."

"That's weird," I said, sitting on the couch. "But kids go through strange patterns with food, don't they? My mother told me there was a time when I'd eat nothing but corn flakes and hot dogs."

He nodded briefly. "Maybe you're right. Only I'm worried about him and Anne's damn near frantic. Of course, he'll change schools next year and that might do some good. But it's a spooky thing living with him. I feel he's always *watching* me. It gives me the willies."

"It'll be much better in the new house," I assured him. "There'll be lots more room. You'll have your privacy."

"I know, but it's a little crazy, isn't it, for a father to want to hide from his son."

"I don't know. I've never been a father."

"Well, Anne tells me it's unnatural." He paused, then the words burst out. "But Jesus Christ, Tony, I can't work and have him watching. He fucking watches all the time!"

The vision of David's troubled face sprang up at me. "When do you move?" I asked. There could be no direct response to Eric's dilemma.

His voice was calmer. "In three weeks. The place is all set; we've only got to bring up our things, turn on the plumbing, and we're in business."

"It'll be a relief to get away from here." It was more a question than a statement.

"I don't know. I've written three good books here."

"You'll write greater ones upstate."

He took the obvious flattery seriously. "I'm not sure. I'm not comfortable with it yet. I don't think I'll be able to go on as well as I've started."

The news delighted me. So he had begun another novel! "I didn't know you were writing."

"This one wouldn't let me rest," he said. "I started it the night of your party."

As long as I live, I thought, I'll never understand writers. "Good God! With all the *sturm und drang*?"

"Because of it." He got up to pour himself a drink (the bar had returned to the living room), asking with a gesture if I would join him. Still groggy, I shook my head and he shrugged and doubled his own portion. "We're not here to talk about me," he said, "but about Arthur."

I had not forgotten. "You said he betrayed you?"

Eric sipped at his drink, then walked to the couch where he stood above me, fixing me with a look. "I want to sever relations with Diadem," he said without inflection.

I had sensed it coming, but nevertheless the shock made my heart lurch. I thought of Arthur and of our friendship; I thought of how I had tried to prevent Reed from leaving him; I remembered Arthur's own admission of how reliant he and Diadem were on Eric's work—and all the tales of how authors had deserted their publishers, for whatever reason, good or bad, came flooding into my head. "With Diadem?" I asked, stalling, "or just Arthur?"

"Isn't it the same thing?"

"Not really. You could be assigned another editor at Diadem, work with him or her."

"Wouldn't Arthur resent it?"

"Probably, but he's a pro. Obviously, he'd want you to stay with his house. You mean an enormous amount to Diadem, after all."

"Don't they have Philip Reed? They can get along without me."

"They lost Reed, too."

"An author of Arthur's?"

I almost lied, but he might easily have remembered. "Yes."

He pounded his right fist into his left palm. "You see? That son of a bitch!"

Sooner or later, I would have to ask about Arthur's sins, but for the moment I avoided it. My disgust with Eric was enormous; I fought to keep myself coherent. "You haven't answered my question about another editor."

"It wouldn't work. Every time I came into the office I'd see his face. His idiot face."

"Diadem might fold if you leave them."

He smiled. "I didn't know I had such power."

I couldn't tell if he relished the notion or was matter-of-fact about it. "Your next book will bring in over three million dollars. For a small house that's life. Losing it is death."

"I don't see that Diadem's my concern. If they hired better editors, they'd survive."

His callousness made my head throb. "Just telling you the facts, so you'll know before you decide."

"I've already made my decision." His tone was unemotional.

I had to resist. I felt shaky from fatigue and silent anger. I shook my head to clear it. No crime of Arthur's could be so heinous as to ruin him. Arthur worshiped Eric. He thought Eric was the greatest writer alive. If there was a crime, it had to be unintentional.

And where did my loyalty lie?

"I beg you not to do it," I said. "It'll hurt your next book."

He glanced at me, expression unfathomable. "Explain."

"The Diadem sales force is used to selling you. It'll hurt your continuity to have a new sales force handle your work."

The advice might have been sound for a not-yet-arrived writer, but for Eric it was ludicrous. Any sales force in the world would be thrilled to have him.

"Do you really mean that," he asked, "or are you just trying to protect Arthur?"

My stomach knotted. "Shit, all it takes to sell your books by now is a telephone. Even I could do it. I'd just announce the new Meredith and wait for the orders to flood in."

He went to the sideboard to pour himself another drink. "Then what you're really doing is shielding Arthur—or trying to."

"He's my friend, Eric." The words burst out hoarsely. "I've

known him for years. He bought the first book I ever represented. I love him."

He grinned cruelly. "I thought you were happily married."

"Not funny."

"He's a miserable little faggot. And I find it surprising, really, that you'd defend him at my expense."

I began to sweat. "I'm not defending him at your expense. I'm just defending him. There's a difference."

He looked at me disdainfully. "But you don't even know what his offense is yet."

I dreaded it. "Maybe you'd better tell me."

"Better still," he said, heading for the corridor, "I'll show you." And he disappeared.

I waited for him dully, my head aching, willing myself not to speculate. He returned carrying a piece of paper which he handed to me silently. I unfolded it, recognizing the Diadem colophon at its top. A letter.

Dear Eric:

As you know, I've been very anxious to publish a new edition of *Anderson's Luck*. It seems to me a public would exist for it now that was not at your disposal when the book first came out; like it or not, you've become a famous novelist—a fame much merited, I should add!—and I think people will want to read your first steps into the realm of literature.

But I think if you read the book again (*do* novelists reread their own work?), you'll find a few passages in it that will dissatisfy you, as they dissatisfy me. There are places where you can go deeper, plot devices that seem to be too predictable, motivations —particularly those of Anderson's parents—that are unclear.

What I've done is paid (yes, Diadem will not charge it to your royalty account) to have the entire book retyped onto manuscript pages (there's a switch!), and, as you'll see, I've then edited that manuscript, making marginal notes where I think changes would help, and recommending small cuts—I've the feeling that these are changes you'd make yourself these several years later, given the fact that you get smoother, sharper, more profound in each novel.

Obviously, you don't have to accept any of the suggested changes. They're meant as suggestions *only*, not dicta, and if you so choose, patently they can be disregarded. As you know, I have the firm theory that the author and the author alone is responsible for his books; the editor's function is to lend an objective eye to the material and to point out to the author those places where, in the editor's opinion, the book gets derailed.

Anyway, please look over the changes and tell me what you think. For what it's worth, the book will probably sell better if we do revise it than if we simply offset from the old edition, for I think the typeface in the old edition is ugly, and we'll want to give the book—the "new," "revised" book—the kind of promotion it deserves.

Meanwhile, sales continue to pile up on *Diamonds*. I suspect it'll stay on the best-seller lists—*high* on the best-seller lists—through the summer, and I'd guess (yes, I know we're not supposed to speculate like this, but I want to share my thoughts with you!) that the book will out-success *Success* by some 100,000 copies. As I've said before (and tell myself gleefully every night), the real pleasure in all this is not the money, not even seeing Diadem's name alongside yours on the best-seller list, but the fact that books of such quality—works of art; your works of art—can outsell all the dross, all the sensationalistic crap, that so often fills the top rungs of that list.

My hat's off to you!

I look forward to your reaction, and send love to Anne,

Best,
Arthur

I carefully read the letter twice, feeling panic rise in my throat. There had to be a trap somewhere. Was there something here I didn't see that had offended him enough to want to fire Arthur? I turned the paper over, looking for clues, but the reverse was blank.

"Well?" he asked, seeing I had finished, his gaze direct.

A man in a minefield, I chose my words slowly. "I'm not sure it's reason to fire him."

"You don't think so?"

"Frankly, no."

"If you were me, you wouldn't look for another editor?"

"No. I'd give him another chance."

He took the letter from me, then sat next to me on the couch, so close our bodies almost touched. I could feel his breath on my face, and I turned my eyes toward the floor, making myself sit still and not move away from him. His breath smelled of Scotch, but he was not drunk. *He's a monster*, I thought, and then remembered him in his human form, remembered the compassion he had shown in his writing; and so I sat silently, waiting for him to speak.

"I'm glad you're not me," he said finally. "You're too fucking nice."

From him, "nice" was a libel. "I don't understand."

"You'd have gotten a letter like this—this *excrescence*—and wanted to give the sender one more chance."

I kept my voice even. "What bothers you most about it?"

"Shit, Tony, do I have to analyze it for you? Can't you see for yourself?"

"I see things I don't like," I answered, hoping he would not ask me to be specific, "but I want to hear your version."

He sighed, a sorely put-upon author. "Okay then, let's take it paragraph by paragraph." He sipped at his Scotch, then opened the letter on his lap so we could both read it. "Item: 'I've been very anxious to publish a new edition.' Where the fuck does he get off saying *he's* anxious? Whose decision is it, anyway?"

"All he meant was—"

"Don't tell me what he meant! If you knew how to read, you'd *see* what he meant. But let me finish. It gets worse." His voice had grown louder; my head rang from it. "Item: Think of the presumption of telling me I'd find things in my own work which would dissatisfy me. I don't submit a book for publication *until* I'm satisfied. As a matter of fact, I reread *Anderson's Luck* just before I got his insane letter, and there's nothing I'd change. Nothing!"

I thought of our first meeting, of the writer who would "welcome" suggestions. "Hold on," I said. "Arthur told me you had agreed some changes were warranted."

His look was lethal. "Arthur lied."

"Then why didn't you let Doubleday republish?"

"I wanted to do a good turn for Arthur. And *this* is how he repays me. I told you, Tony, he's betrayed me."

"You don't remember his calling and asking if you wanted to revise?"

"I don't remember authorizing *him* to revise."

"He's not revising. He's suggesting changes."

"Predictable plot devices and unclear motivations are *not* flaws in *Anderson's Luck*."

I double-checked the letter. "But he says clearly you don't have to make any changes you don't want to."

He snorted. "Thanks. He asks me to rewrite the entire book, then says I don't have to. I'd rather write a new book, and his inconsistency is so gross it's nauseating."

"He's entitled to his opinion."

"Precisely. And so am I. My opinion is that he can't read, could never read, and will never be able to read. I'm only horrified that I didn't realize this earlier on. And frankly, Tony, I'm horrified that you sent *Success* to him in the first place."

My flesh froze. "I sent *Success* to him because I thought he could publish it better than anybody else. And he did. He published the hell out of it."

"It would have been a best-seller if it had been published by a vanity press," he said icily. "*Success* is a masterpiece."

"That may be. Nevertheless, Arthur published it beautifully."

"So beautifully that he now wants to be my collaborator."

He *was* mad. "What are you talking about? How could he possibly be your collaborator?" For a second, my thoughts went back to Philip Reed. He too had used the word unjustly.

He shook his head pityingly. "Seems you can't read either. Look at paragraph five. It's paragraph five that made me decide to ditch him."

I looked and yes, I saw it. My God! "You mean the line, 'if we do revise it'?"

"Hurrah! Yes, I mean precisely that line."

"But surely the 'we' means you as author and him as publisher."

"Surely it does not. He means me as author and *him* as author—a collaboration."

"You're crazy. Arthur would never presume—"

He had risen as I spoke, walked to the side table, and picked up a manuscript. I had not noticed it before; now he handed it to me as though it were contaminated. "Here's my proof."

It was the newly typed manuscript for *Anderson's Luck*. I thumbed through it. Arthur had made marginal notes on some of the pages, say a fifth of them, and made lightly penciled corrections of the text itself—minor stuff, I noted, a rearrangement of subordinate clauses, the elimination of a few adverbs, in one case the deletion of an entire paragraph starting a chapter. It was, from my experience, a light, even reverential editing job.

I glanced up at him—he was still standing—prepared to tell him so, but stopped when I saw his face. It was ashen, as though by looking at the manuscript he was looking at a corpse.

"I feel cheapened," he said. "He's shit all over it. I'd have thrown it away only I wanted you to see what he had done."

There was no irony in what he said; he genuinely believed that Arthur had desecrated his work.

"Let me put it this way," he went on, somewhat more calmly. "Suppose Beethoven—you like Beethoven—had sent the Ninth Symphony to his publisher, and his publisher had decided to make 'a few minor changes' in it. The publisher, of course, is no musician, and his changes make the music more ordinary, less idiosyncratic—the publisher's lesser voice, not the voice of Beethoven.

"What does Beethoven do in such a case?" He stopped for a moment, as though actually expecting an answer. "I'll tell you what he does—he gets himself a new publisher."

He took a triumphant swallow of Scotch, the unfair analogy, by his lights, irrefutably proving his point, and went to refill his glass. I could do nothing except stare at him. The display of egomania was so overwhelming that it left me stunned. How could I argue against it? How could I defend my friend? It was a juggernaut.

"Have you discussed this with Arthur?" I asked at last.

"No."

"So as far as he's concerned, he thinks you're pleased with the editing, or at least have no objection to it. You had once told him you'd welcome his suggestions about *Anderson*, so he probably thinks—"

"I don't give a fuck what he thinks. For all he knows, I haven't had a chance to look it over. It only came yesterday. I called you the second I saw what he had done."

"Then are you sure you're not being precipitous?"

He wheeled to face me. "With every passing second, my fury grows."

My stomach convulsed. "What are you going to tell him?"

He grinned without humor. "I'm not."

"Then—"

"You are."

I struggled for breath, but it was a long time coming. My mind was clear, though I knew I had to fight against my rage overwhelming it. "You want me to call him to tell him you're leaving him?"

"Of course. I told you when you came in I wanted him fired."

I allowed myself one angry sentence. "Because you don't have the balls to do it yourself?"

His face darkened. "Because you're my agent."

"An agent, true, but not an executioner."

Now his face contorted with rage. "It's executioner if I want it to be," he screamed. "What did you think your job was? To get close to half a million dollars just for sending packages to Diadem? To be my fucking nursemaid, and not a very good one at that, on a publicity tour?"

I could feel my face flush. Agents have long been called parasites. Without Eric's using the word, he had demeaned my profession and debased me. "I thought I had done a lot for you," I said steadily, marveling at my self-control. "It wasn't too long ago that you were grateful for it."

"Never!" he roared. "One is not grateful to people who are hired to do a job and then do it."

"Servants?"

"It's your word, not mine."

"Then I'll use it. Because that's what you make me feel like. I hope the new house has a tradesman's entrance."

He paused for a moment, mouth and eyes hard and relentless. "If you don't call Arthur tomorrow to tell him I'm leaving, that I'll never have another book published by Diadem Press, then you will cease being my literary agent, now and forever."

I had been expecting it, preparing for it. To hear it said so baldly and so ruthlessly only strengthened my decision. I felt light-headed, joyous. "I'll call him, of course," I said. "I couldn't countenance the prospect of your doing it. I'll tell him you've fired him and I've fired you, and we'll drink to your new publisher and your new agent. I venture to say it will be one of the happiest days in our lives."

I looked at him, registered with exaltation the shock on his face, and headed for the door.

"Call me a taxi, please," I said. "I'll wait outside until it comes."

thirteen

ANNE AND DAVID CAME HOME FROM THEIR TREAT while I was waiting, but I stepped back into a shadow and hoped they would not see me. David was howling, obviously exhausted, and Anne, rather than trying to comfort him, pulled him along toward the house, a calf being led to slaughter. She was too distraught to notice me. Ashamed at having witnessed the scene, I turned my head away.

"Oh my poor darling, what agony for you!"

Judy, as usual, gauged just right. For by the time I got home, the adrenaline produced by my confrontation with Eric had dissipated, and I arrived depressed.

I told her the story as objectively as I could, trying to recall it all in the lateness of the hour (three A.M. French time), if anything downplaying Eric's brutality and my turbulent reaction to it.

Judy listened without comment, pitied me when I had finished, praised me for my bravery, and then asked the question I had been asking myself ever since I had left Eric's house.

180

"What are you going to do?"

"Meet Arthur tomorrow and break the news."

"No, I mean about yourself."

"I really haven't thought it through. *Diamonds* will bring us enough money to keep the agency going as it is for a while. After that, we'll have to see what happens." I had had time on the ride home to begin to think of the material consequences. Contemplating them, I felt a kind of giddy recklessness. I'd just have to work harder, take on more writers, negotiate more acutely. Surely sooner or later I'd find another best-selling author.

"You'll miss him," Judy said softly. "Or at least your vision of him."

"Yes."

"Come to bed. Maybe I can take your mind off it."

But I told her I was too agitated to sleep or to make love, and so she went off to bed alone, while I sat in the living room, thinking. Finally, I picked out a copy of *Success* and started reading it. It had been a long time since I had done so.

The cruelty in Eric was there, the pigheadedness and megalomania. Much of what I had seen that evening was barely disguised in the pages. But there was human longing, too, and pain and love and an ennobling spirit. Had his own life disguised these feelings in the man himself? I could not believe it.

Remember the scene in which Alice asks Ben's forgiveness for the death of the child, and he grants it?

That scene made my heart ache.

❈

Next to the King Cole dining room in the St. Regis Hotel is a quiet bar. Though it has overhead lights and candles on the tables, it is a dark place, made for conversation where one can avoid the eyes of one's companion. I did not think of this when I suggested it to Arthur as our meeting place, but as the first to arrive I was pleased with the choice. It would, I thought, slightly ease my pain, though in no way Arthur's. If I chose not to peer too closely through the gloom, I would not have to study his anguish.

Arthur arrived five minutes after I did, looking somewhat rumpled, unusual for him, and obviously anxious. My phone call asking for a quick meeting without telling him why had, as it inevitably would, unnerved him. It could only be bad news; I suspect he did not imagine how bad the news was going to be.

I had ordered a Perrier—again, unusual; Scotch is my habitual drink after business hours, even if I'm with a publisher or author—and he, noticing it, became visibly perturbed.

"Off the booze?" he asked, a joke without a smile.

"I have a stomach ache," I said truthfully.

"So do I," he admitted. "I don't like sudden phone calls for same-day drinks. Especially from friends."

I signaled for the waiter and ordered a Perrier for Arthur, too. We sat silently until it came, Arthur watching me, I wishing he wouldn't.

"It's Eric, isn't it?" Arthur said when at last the waiter returned with the drink.

"I'm afraid so."

"He'll want new contract terms on the next book," Arthur guessed. "Better paperback terms. A different royalty."

"Worse than that."

He took a sip of his Perrier. "Worse?"

I took a deep breath. "Eric's leaving you. Leaving Diadem. For what it's worth, I've dropped him as a client. He wants his next book published somewhere else."

His face went white. I could feel him stiffen, even though we were not touching. Slowly he rose, a soldier with old leg injuries, and, stiff-kneed, took a step backwards, suddenly illuminated by the overhead light. His breathing was noisy. I had to force myself to look at him.

"It's irrevocable?" he asked.

"I think so."

"Nothing I can say or do will keep him?"

"Nothing."

He turned and moved toward the exit. "Then there's not much point in my staying, is there?" He was holding his stomach. The words had hit him like punches.

"Wait," I said desperately. "Don't you want to know why?"

He turned to look at me. I could guess the bitterness in his eyes. "Not really. I suppose he just decided he didn't like working with a faggot."

"Oh, Arthur!" I said, suddenly close to tears, his words revealing too much of his soul. "It isn't that. Good Christ, it isn't that."

He seemed surprised. "Then—?" He sat down.

I told him everything, beginning with the phone call in France, but concentrating on the meeting. I tried not only to give him the words and their tone, but the nuances. I tried to make him *see* Eric's face, hear the inflections in his voice, feel his unreasonable fury. I tried to make him me, listening to the accusations, the rage, disgust, ego.

The only thing I left out was my own rage. His problem was far more serious than mine.

As I talked, even in the dim light I could see stages in his reactions. The first was despair—a blow such as I had given him could, truly, affect the rest of his professional life. But as I went on I could see him switch from resignation to hope, and then, seeing hope was futile, to anger. And, when I had finished, it was anger that governed his words.

"He's an egomaniacal shit. He didn't understand what I was trying to do; you can help and help and serve and serve, you can offer every possible orifice, and still he'll want more."

"Right," I said, "but—"

"Didn't he *know* I was trying to help? Can't he tell he's writing better now than he did?"

"It was the word 'we' that got to him, I think. At least that's what he said. The idea that you would even imply collaboration—"

His valiant anger mounted. "I'll take my glory unreflected, thank you. I'm not a parasite and my sustenance comes from satisfaction in *my* work, not his. I publish for him, not write for him. I edit for him, not create for him. Holy God, Tony, I can't possibly think the way he does."

"*I* know that," I said consolingly. "Convince him."

"How?"

"Call him." I was suddenly hopeful it might work.

"He won't answer. At least if you've reported accurately."

I had reported accurately. "Write him, then."

"He's the writer," Arthur said, such bitterness in his voice I feared he might cry. "It's hopeless, isn't it?"

Unable to say anything, I simply nodded.

"Well, fuck *you*!" he exploded.

The swing in emphasis stunned me. I had not expected an attack, much as I felt I deserved it. "I tried," I told him, understanding what he meant.

"I'm sure you did," he said coldly.

I found myself pleading. "I did. You have to believe me. I think what he did was despicable. I told you: I've left him."

His look softened. "But you couldn't persuade him. Try as you did, it was no use."

I said nothing. The look intensified. "Right, Tony? Right?"

"Stop it!" I said, and then, my voice lower, "Please."

He must have seen how wounded I was by his attack. "I'm sorry, Tony. I'm sure you tried. Only it seems so unreasonable. It's just awful, not having a say. Not having a chance to defend myself."

"It's impossible to defend yourself against megalomania."

"I know." A thought struck him, and he closed his eyes. "I could lose my job."

I had mentioned this possibility to Eric, who didn't take it seriously or didn't care. It was difficult for me now to tell how real the chances were. So all I said was, "Nonsense."

"No. Sense. I lost Reed, that was bad enough. But Eric—"

"Editors lose authors all the time."

"Yeah, but without those two, Diadem's in trouble. Real trouble. Eric brings in millions himself. The loss will be catastrophic."

I thought of him having to go to work the next day to announce the disaster. Matthew White, his boss, had a reputation for violent rages over something as simple as an expense account. What would he do to Arthur in this instance? I felt a wash of horror.

"How can they possibly fire you?" I asked. "After all the money you brought them?"

He shrugged. "What have I done for them lately?" Whatever spirit had recently animated him had disappeared; he seemed more sunk than ever.

"Even if they do fire you," I went on, "you'll get another job. With your record—"

Bitterness returned. "I'd say my market value's decreased, wouldn't you? Without my bat and ball?"

He was right; I said nothing. We sat looking at each other, neither with anything more to say. He fingered a swizzle stick, seemingly symbiotic with it until it snapped. He stood up. "Let me ask one more time. It's your impression that nothing I can do will make him change his mind?"

I shook my head. "I'm afraid not."

"You won't mind if I try to see him? To hear for myself?"

"Of course not. But I don't think he'll see you."

"Or talk to me?"

"No."

"Well," he said, his voice unnaturally bright, "it doesn't hurt to try."

"No," I said again, wishing he would go away, taking my failure on his behalf with him, and hating myself for thinking it.

"That's it, then." He made no move to go, but stood shifting his weight from one foot to another like a young boy confronting authority.

"Maybe he'll change his mind," I said wanly.

He managed a smile. "Sure." And then, surprisingly, he stuck out his hand. "I can at least thank you. My friend."

I stared at him. "Thank me for what?"

"For fighting. For leaving him. It was a heroic thing to do, and I appreciate it."

His benediction made me squirm. "I left him for my sake, not yours. So I don't want your appreciation." I managed a laugh. "Just your business. My next big project's yours; I promise you." There would, of course, be no project as big as a Meredith novel, at least not for years.

I imagined his eyes filling with tears. "I know that," he told me. "You're a staunch ally and a good friend."

Now I took his hand and shook it. His grip was lifeless, as though all will had left him. "I'm in shock," he said. "I don't feel anything now, but I suspect it'll hurt in the morning."

"There'll be other authors. Other books."

"I know. But nothing like Eric. He's once-in-a-lifetime." He shook his head and, bereaved, made his way blindly to the exit.

I stared after him until I, too, went blind.

In a front-page review in the *New York Times Book Review*, Leslie Morrison called *Flaws in Diamonds* the finest American novel since World War II, the first book to put into perspective the joy and pain of growing up in postwar America. (Fatuous, I thought; Eric made no effort to make meaningful a particular time or place except that his characters lived as his contemporaries. I had the feeling that the Greeks would have acted as his characters did, or the Mongolians.) *Time* and *Newsweek* both devoted their entire book pages to glowing analyses of the novel; *Publishers Weekly* interviewed Eric and found him "fascinating"; *People* magazine sent a photographer and reporter to Eric's house. They were told to come back when he had moved. Obviously there were dissenting voices, but all praised the insights and the book's vitality; the quibbles were no more than pinpricks in the body of praise.

Before the official publication date the book moved to number one on the *Times* best-seller list (publication dates are artificially set by publishers; bookstores can start selling a book as soon as they receive copies, and in the case of a major work, such as Eric's, they do, which is why on publication day a book can already be a best-seller). *Diamonds* was outselling *Success* three copies to two; as a full selection of the Book of the Month Club, there were five hundred thousand copies in print by the end of the month.

I spoke very little to Arthur during this time. In some respect, the good news, which he dutifully reported in his most professional manner, hurt us both, and whether out of guilt or shame, we did not exult over the continued triumphs but merely noted them to each other.

Eventually, of course, and far more slowly than usual, the tumult subsided and the book, while still number one on the lists, was no longer the "hot" novel, its place taken by a loathesome affair about three starlets sharing the same bisexual director. Eric moved to his house in Chatham; Arthur stopped calling with news. I became preoccupied with other clients and settled into a peaceful time.

On the Tuesday after Labor Day, the phone rang. It was Arthur. We had not spoken for six weeks.

"I need your help," he said, his voice miserable.

"Anything."

"It's happened. I've been fired."

"Arthur!" I was sitting when he called, but now I stood, grasping the receiver like a rope. "What happened?"

"Diadem's been sold," he said, his voice barely audible. "We've got nothing much coming for next year, so when MCA made White an offer, he grabbed while the best-seller list had our name on it. But MCA plans to pare costs and that means good-bye to the editor in chief and his 'huge' salary."

"What'll you do?"

"Look for another job."

It wouldn't be easy. Editor in chief jobs are rare enough. In times of economic instability, just starting toward the end of the seventies, they were virtually nonexistent. And for Arthur to take a lesser job, senior editor, say, meant a diminution of his power, his prestige, and his salary. Besides, few would want to hire him for the subordinate position; they'd figure he would be planning to climb and was therefore dangerous.

"How can I help?"

"I want to tell any prospective employer you'll be giving me first look at your next big project."

"You've got it."

"I don't want you to tell anybody about Eric's leaving."

Nobody did know. Eric had not talked about it publicly, and I of course had kept silent. White must have told MCA—Arthur would not have been fired otherwise—but they were being circumspect.

"But once it's public you were fired, wouldn't everybody know?" I asked.

"Sure. But"—he paused—"I have a fantasy about his coming back." His voice, which had grown stronger as it became more matter-of-fact, died again to a whisper. "I've been so fucking unhappy. It's the only thing that's sustained me, the thought that it was Diadem he left, not me."

"I see," I said, lost.

"It's so *unfair*." The whisper became a wail. The sound assaulted me.

"Goddamn right."

"If you hear of anything—"

"I'll ask around."

"Thanks." There was another pause, a longer one. "It smarts," he said at last. "You have no idea how it smarts."

I could guess.

"I'm not going to the office tomorrow," I informed Judy that night. "I'm going to drive to Chatham, to see Eric. I'm going to persuade him to go back to Arthur."

"Oh, Tony!" She hugged me so hard my ribs ached.

fourteen

I NEITHER CALLED HIM FOR A MEETING, SINCE I WAS afraid he would refuse, nor did I proclaim my arrival in any way. I decided to come unannounced, take him by surprise. In that way, at least, I figured, he would react instinctively, with truth.

In any case, filled with resolve, I set off for Chatham, to Eric's new home, without telling him I was coming.

The drive itself was a delightful one. It was cool for September, and the sun sparkled. The leaves on the trees along the Taconic Parkway had not yet started to change color, but instead were their deepest green. I had not decided on a scenario before I left, yet rather than concentrating on what I would say to Eric, I let the rolling landscape lull me into random thoughts, and I decided to let instinct govern events; I would think of what to say when the time came.

I knew that Eric worked in the mornings, then had lunch and a nap, so I left New York around two, wanting to arrive before cocktail hour, but after the day's business had been attended to. It took a little over two hours for the drive, and I pulled into the first gas station I saw after I left the parkway.

"I'm looking for Knight's Road," I told the attendant.

"It's a mile from here," he said, pointing east. "First dirt road on the right." He looked at me suspiciously, as though my mission were rape or murder. "Going to see that writer?"

"Yes."

"Figured."

I looked at him and smiled. "How did you know?"

"Wearing a tie," he said, explaining it all.

I suppose I did look foolish, arriving as I had dressed in city clothes in a rural setting, and his remark made me realize how much bravado, but how little sense, was involved in my journey. After all, what did fairness matter to Eric? What use did he have for morality? What was Arthur or I to him? Servants fired as easily as footmen rude to visiting royalty.

I almost turned back, but then I visualized Judy's disappointment, saw her accusing eyes, and resolved to go through with it. Too, I thought of myself, how I would feel the next morning, and that was enough.

I found Knight's Road easily; though a dirt road, the sign was new and legible. I wondered if Eric had insisted it be spruced up, but then, coming on the first house, I realized it was a moneyed road—any of the owners would make sure the sign was pristine.

The first house, to judge from the mailbox, belonged to the Brighams, the second (around a turn and invisible from house one) to the Vaughans, the third (also secluded) to the Levines, the fourth to the Merediths. And what a house it was!

It, too, was hidden by a bend in the road, so I came upon it suddenly, a two-story Palladian house, as close to an English mansion as one could visualize in the Hudson Valley. Elegant in line, refined in bearing, it had two dozen windows and so, I supposed, numerous rooms. Newly painted white (all the houses on the road were white), with gray trimmings around windows and door, it was set about one hundred feet from the road, perched on a small hill, reachable by a circular gravel driveway lined with flowers. In the distance I could see rolling hills, verdant and tree-topped, like the hills of Vermont, but there was evidently a long flat lawn behind it; the acreage was obviously in back.

The house must have been two hundred years old, but workmen
had done a stunning job refurbishing it. For the first time I realized
in concrete terms just how rich Eric was. The change from mouse-
trap to mansion, from lower-than-Levitt to Palladio, was so aston-
ishing that for several moments I sat motionless in the car, simply
staring at the house, not able to digest its significance.

A Mercedes-Benz was parked in the driveway, Eric's I assumed,
though I had never seen it before. Knight's Road was the kind that
accommodated Mercedes.

I drove up behind the Mercedes, parked, and got out of the car.
The sun was hot on my neck, but there was a cool breeze to go with
it, and birds sang. Under the bright blue sky, the grass seemed
lustrously green.

There was no sign of activity from the house; though the curtains were drawn back in what was probably the living room, and
I could easily see in, I caught no glimpse of Eric or his family—
perhaps they were on the lawn, I thought.

Still, politeness made me walk to the front door and rap on it
with an ornate brass knocker cast in the form of a whale.

No one answered. I rapped again, harder, heard and saw no
movement, and so tried the doorknob. It turned easily; the door
swung open. Forgetting that I could have walked around the house,
not through it, I stepped into the hall.

"Eric," I called.

Silence.

Directly ahead of me was a flight of stairs, its banisters newly
waxed. On my right was the living room, and I glanced at it, getting
a quick impression of a long, flowered-print sofa, antique chairs,
modern abstract painting, a rug thicker than the lawn outside. An
aristocratic room, but not as formal as the dining room, which
loomed, heavy and funereal, on the other side of the hall. Here
was a room more suited to Newport than Chatham. The huge table
that dominated it accommodated twelve Chippendale chairs, while
four others stood in repose along the far wall. The table had been

formally set for three; graceful candelabra stood holding fresh candles; at night, the overhead chandelier would undoubtedly be blazing. The walls were wood paneled and dominated by an immense painting of Susannah and the Elders, the level of art one sees in second-rate Italian palaces. Two windows were cut into the outside wall, but were sheathed by a heavy dark green curtain. The room, it seemed, held perpetual night.

It depressed me, and I did not stay long looking at it. "Eric," I called again, leaving the room and making my way toward the corridor, past the start of the staircase, and on toward the back. "Anybody home?"

Again, silence. There was a door at the end of the corridor, beyond an open pantry which led, I presumed, to the kitchen, and past a clothes closet and downstairs bath, their doors ajar. The door was closed, but since it evidently led to the lawn, I knocked and, hearing no answer, opened it.

Sunlight hit my eyes, so bright it took more than a moment for me to realize I had not come outdoors at all, but rather to an enormous glass-enclosed porch, one of the most charming rooms I've ever seen. Whereas I was certain the interior rooms had been designed by a professional—they had the immaculate, impersonal look of a magazine illustration—the porch had surely been done by Anne herself. The motif was flowers. Three vases of fresh daisies stood in Anne-made ceramic vases on three wicker tables placed throughout the room. There was a long settee, big enough for five, covered in a slipcase decorated with yellow roses; chairs and an ottoman were covered in the same material. Pictures of flowers, from a fine reproduction of Van Gogh's *Sunflowers* to a Haitian original of a field of poppies, adorned the inner walls. The outer, which stretched the entire length of the patio and separated it from the lawn beyond, was entirely of glass.

The view was magnificent. The lawn itself, as dark green as a fairway, stretched out dazzlingly toward the hills in the distance, broken on the right by a huge maple, on the left by a cluster of apple trees bearing fruit. Either Eric or the previous owner had erected a tennis court; its surrounding fence was covered with vines—flowering, I supposed, when the season was right. Farther away on the lawn was a swimming pool, edged with flowers that *were* in bloom.

The boy from Wilkes-Barre had become landed gentry. At any moment I expected a racehorse to stroll by.

I walked to the glass wall and looked out. There was no sign of anybody; the field seemed as deserted as the lawns of Eton when the boys were at chapel. Where could they be? I wondered. Had they bought two cars, or kept the old one? The fact that Eric might not be home had never occurred to me, and now that it seemed true, I did not know what to do. Given the effort it took to get me here in the first place, it would be difficult to leave and come back another day. I was not sure I could muster that energy. On the other hand, to stay without invitation, an interloper, seemed out of the question. I had trespassed as it was. Now I felt uncomfortable, a thief. Uneasiness assaulted me and, suddenly chilled, I turned to leave the room.

"They're there."

The voice came at me before I completed my turn to see who had spoken, and it sent a thrill through me. I wheeled.

David stood before me. Dressed in jeans and a T-shirt, he wore no shoes, which explained how he had crept up without my hearing him. He regarded me placidly, neither surprised nor pleased to see me. "There. Out there." He pointed toward the lawn.

I turned, but could see no one.

"Out there," he repeated.

This time I looked carefully along the direction indicated by his finger. The tree! Of course. Eric and Anne were behind the maple. I couldn't see them from the ground floor; David probably had an unobstructed view from his second-floor window.

"Do you think they'd mind if I went to see them?"

"No."

"Then would you run tell them I'm here?"

"No."

The abruptness of the answer, even from a little troubled boy, disturbed me. "Why?" I asked, rather too sharply.

" 'Fraid."

"Of your mommy and daddy?" I couldn't believe it.

" 'Fraid," he repeated. And then, as though it was I he feared, not his parents, he ran from the porch. Listening for it, I could hear his tread on the stairs; he had evidently gone back to his room, if only to avoid the assignment I had asked him to fulfill. All right, I thought, I'll find them myself.

One end of the glass wall was a sliding door, which opened with a fingertip's pressure. A single step led to the lawn, and I took it gingerly, feeling with my toe as though stepping into a pool of cold water. The grass was soft under the soles of my city shoes, and sunlight soothed my face and hands.

I stood still, reveling in the sensuous peace of the moment, and then started walking slowly across the lawn.

"Eric," I called. "Anne."

There was no response, so I walked closer to the tree, still seeing no movement and hearing no sound. The trunk was easily wide enough to block two people from my sight. I could see roots now; the maple was set on a gentle decline, and the roots were visible, tunneling into the ground behind the trunk.

I thought I saw an animal dart among the roots and concentrated my gaze there. But it must have been a stray shadow, for now all was still.

I was certainly close enough for them to hear me, so I called again, "Eric," "Anne," and received only silence in return.

I began to feel uneasy again. It was possible that they had moved away during the time it had taken David to walk downstairs to talk to me, or both of them could have been sleeping—it was surely the perfect afternoon for an outdoor nap. Too, David might have been lying from the start.

I stopped, uncertain, and stared at the tree, as though trying to X-ray my sight through its trunk. The animal! This time I was sure I saw movement among the roots. I approached a few steps closer and then abruptly stopped again, gooseflesh prickling my arms and neck. It wasn't an animal I saw, but a naked human foot, close to the trunk, a man's foot, its movement involuntary, a series of twitches. From where I stood it appeared severed from a body, but as I crossed to the far side of the maple, I could see it was attached to a leg, a naked leg, and then to a torso.

Eric!

By now I had a full view of the scene previously obscured by the maple. There was not one body, but three, two women and a man, all naked, all asleep (perhaps because of the twitching foot I never supposed they were dead). The bodies were intertwined, with only Eric's foot flung out to its place in the roots; the sight was like an illustration from a Victorian pornographic novel come to life—"How the Rich Spend Their Afternoons," or "Daphne and Phyllis Join Freddie for an Afternoon of Games."

One of the women was Anne. Eric lay partly on top of her, his arm obscuring her face; still, there could be no doubt. The other woman was really a girl, no more than sixteen or seventeen, I judged. She was lying on her back, and both Eric and Anne had fallen asleep with her body for their pillow—she was the cross of the T, the Merediths its stem. Her skin was white, pasty; an occasional pimple showed red against it. Her breasts were full, her pubic hair dark brown, though the hair on her head was hay-colored and fluffy. In sleep she looked innocent.

The only movement was the twitch of Eric's foot and the faintly discernible breathing of the three of them. I watched, riveted, incapable of averting my eyes from the obscenity of the sight, for what must have been at least a minute. I can't remember what my thoughts were—I'm not sure I was able to think at all, and I was surely not able to act. The shock was great, the sight so appalling that I felt my roots were as deeply buried as those of the maple and that I, like it, had become part of the unspeakable tableau.

At last I was able to turn my head a little, only to find my eyes coming upon a glass vial next to the bodies, white powder on the grass beside it. Cocaine? I wondered. No, cocaine kept you awake.

Heroin? Then wouldn't there be a needle?

It was the thought of discovering the needle, though what I would do with it if I found it was impossible to figure out, that allowed me to move. I took a step forward, felt something hard beneath my feet, and looked down. A vodka bottle, discarded. My God, I thought, the combination must have been cataclysmic.

I moved still closer, again with no idea of what I would do if anyone woke, but unable to turn away. Whether it was my actions or some grain of dust in a nostril, I don't know, but Eric stirred, taking his arm away from Anne's face and rubbing his nose with his hand.

Anne's eyes were open, staring blindly at the sky, but I couldn't tell if her lack of expression came from an absence of pleasure or a surfeit. No matter, the sight of her eyes and Eric's movement frightened me, and I realized just how much of an intruder I had become. Obviously, my mission was futile; there would be no talking to Eric this afternoon. I took one last look, fixing the image in my mind (as though it would ever go away!), then turned to walk back to the car.

From where I was standing, the maple blocked out the view of the first floor. But it was not tall enough to shield the attic, and as I looked up my heart froze. For in the center of the attic was a window. It was open; there was no screen or glass. And in that window, as visibly defined as a white silhouette against black paper, was David's face. I saw it so clearly I could make out its calm, grave expression.

Stupidly I waved at him, an involuntary gesture, as embarrassed by his stare as if I had been naked myself. He made no motion nor sign, but merely kept staring. I forced my eyes from him and started back across the lawn toward the house.

How much more had he seen? Was he witness to the drug taking and its sexual aftermath, and if so, how many times?

I reached the house but, incapable of retracing my steps by going back in, slunk furtively around the outside like a prowler. Indeed, a thief is what I was. I had stolen privacy from Eric and Anne. Tears stung my eyes.

It was not until I had got into the car and driven as far as the parkway that I realized they were tears of gratitude.

Part

III

fifteen

IN THE NEXT THREE YEARS, BUSINESS SLUMPED. IT did for all publishers and therefore for all agents, as paperback houses, having overspent for books in the early seventies, reacted to a worsened economy toward the end of the decade by buying few books, and those for prices not nearly as high as they had paid before. As a consequence, hardcover houses became more conservative in their buys. The five thousand and ten thousand dollar books I was able to sell in the past were returned unbought in the present; authors complained that I was doing a bad job—at times, I began to believe them—but they soon found that other authors had failed with other agents, so with a few exceptions they remained my clients, although there was not much I could do for them save sympathize.

"Only blockbusters," was the cry I heard from the publishing houses. "We can sell brand names, but virtually nothing else."

I had no brand names as my clients. Good writers, yes; profitable writers, certainly. But were it not for the continuing moneys coming in for *Flaws in Diamonds*—moneys from royalties on the hardcover sales, payments from the paperback sale, pounds, marks, yen, lire, francs, and pesos from abroad—I could not have kept the offices open nor paid for salaries of my invaluable assistants.

We had one good break. A man had written an account of being kidnapped into a cult just as the Jonestown catastrophe was revealed; I was able to sell it to a paperback house for a quarter of a million dollars. And some of my authors' early hard work paid off. A book by the diligent L. L. Lustig made the lower end of the best-seller list for three weeks, and he finally got a six-figure paperback sale, the first (and only) of his life. Cynthia Baum wrote a charming treatise on sex that sold forty thousand copies in hardcover. And Jody Monroe—dependable, a-manuscript-a-year Jody—outdid himself with a book on the mating habits of domestic pets, and the work is still in print.

But these were hard times, and no day was free from worry. I grew increasingly irritable, and strains showed up in our marriage. Judy's work, too, had slackened, and her tensions chafed against mine like flint. Too often, sparks flew.

I remember one fight with her over whose turn it was to take the car in to be serviced. The task would take no more than an hour, and both of us had the time to spare, but neither wanted to admit it to ourselves or each other. We must have fought for fifteen minutes before recognizing the ridiculousness of the struggle, and we ended in laughter tinged with hysteria—too often, we did that.

I knew, of course, that it was a bad time in the American economy, but when one's own financial life is shaky, the misfortunes of others are not much solace. As the months passed, I grew more and more depressed.

❈

Then, in the spring of 1980, Eric called me early in the morning at home.

"Tony?"

I recognized the voice instantly and had to grip the desk to control my dizziness. The surprise was so stunning that I cannot differentiate my emotions. Delight was paramount, I'm sure, with a vestige of rage and subsidiary pain and terror.

I don't know how long it took me to answer; I had to fight to get control of my voice before I did.

"Eric. It's good to hear from you."

"I need an hour of your time."

The world is mad, I thought. There is no reason in it. "You've got it. When?"

"Wednesday morning? Say eleven?"

I pretended to look at my calendar, for I could not focus my thoughts. I knew it was Monday. "Wednesday's fine," I said; I would cancel anything else if there was a conflict. "Can you tell me what it's about?"

"I'll tell you Wednesday. I need you, Tony. I really do." There was intensity in his voice; he was obviously troubled.

"I'm here for you."

"Good."

He hung up, leaving me baffled and in turmoil. Judy was no wiser. "You'll simply have to wait," she told me. "But oh, God, I wish he weren't back in our lives."

❊

He looked awful. His skin was gray, and his once robust body seemed frail. I would not say he appeared old; rather he seemed to be newly recovered from some serious disease, as though he had to adjust to life at a slower pace.

The only other time he had been in the new office was on the night of the disastrous party, and it felt thus doubly strange to see him across the desk from me. Light from the window behind my chair shone directly into his eyes, forcing him to squint, and that simple response highlighted his fragility and made me feel more comfortable. We were at least equals.

He said nothing, simply looked at me and smiled. There was shyness but no sparkle in that smile, nor in his eyes.

"I'm glad you're here," I said. "I missed you."

"And I you." He was silent again for a while, then he said, "Can I have a drink?"

"At eleven in the morning?"

He sighed. "It seems later. The drive was endless."

"I only have Scotch."

"Scotch'll be fine."

I rose to pour him one, and he reached for it quickly, hands shaking as he brought it to his lips. "Look, I'm sorry about our argument," he said. "I want you to represent my next book. Will you do it?"

I had heard those words in my fantasies, and for a moment thought I was fantasizing still. "What about Arthur?" I asked.

He looked at me with tired eyes. "Please. One at a time. Will you be my agent?"

This was not the moment for more heat. I had already melted. "It will be a privilege."

He did not take the hand I proffered. "The book's still some months off," he said. "It's taken an interminable amount of time. I need you now as a friend."

"I'll do anything I can," I told him fervently.

Again, a monotone. "Anne's left me."

"No!"

He smiled ruefully. "I'm afraid so. Would that it were otherwise."

"When?"

"Monday."

"Where did she go?"

"Here. The city. She's staying at the Manchester, over on Madison. It's a nice hotel," he added gratuitously.

"And David?"

"She took him with her. Hasn't really decided what to do about his school."

"Then you've spoken to her."

"Yes. She called me yesterday. On Monday, all I had was a note saying she had left and asking me not to worry. I found out where they were staying when she called."

I ached for him. "But surely she'll come back."

"Not surely. The implication of the note was that she wouldn't."

"Did she say why she left?"

Again, the rueful smile. "Ad nauseam. There was no one specific thing. Mostly it was coldness, my neglect of her and David—she was particularly upset over my treatment of David—my presumed (and imagined) affairs. Good God, there's not an attractive woman in Columbia County—basically, she just couldn't put up with me any longer."

He took a hefty swallow of Scotch and I could see him relax a little. "I confess I'm not easy to live with," he went on, "especially when I'm having trouble with a book—and this new one's a ballbreaker. But Christ, I've written other books; she knows I'll pull out of this one." He ran a hand through his hair. "I don't understand why now, when I love her more than I've ever loved her in my life—all right, maybe I was a little rough on David."

I thought of the tableau beneath the maple, of the drugs, of David's face, of Eric's cruelty toward Arthur and toward me, and still I wanted to comfort him, reassure him; and so I said, "It sounds like a temporary aberration. She'll come back."

He shrugged, neither agreeing nor disagreeing. "You understand, of course, that this'll slow down the book?"

I said nothing.

"I mean, I haven't been able to work since Monday. Lord knows I've tried, but nothing happens." He shook his head. "I sit at the typewriter, and all I do is think about how much I miss her."

"She'll come back," I repeated lamely.

"Will the words?" he asked suddenly, his troubled eyes finding mine. "Or has she destroyed me?"

He put his head in his hands, and mumbled something.

"What did you say?"

"— get her back."

"Of course you will."

He raised his head. "No. You. Get her back. You and Judy."

The request was so startling I could only stare at him.

"You will, won't you?"

It took me a while even to ask, "How?"

"Talk to her. You and Judy. She trusts Judy."

I couldn't help myself: I shouted. "You must be out of your mind."

"I am," he said. "That's why I need your help. I swear to you, Tony, I can't work when she's away. I can't live. You've got to see her. You and Judy are my only rescue."

"But what'll I say?"

"Say anything you think is right. Or shut up and let Judy talk for you. The only important thing is that I get my Anne and David back."

His hands shook so badly in his distress that he could barely lift his Scotch. It was painful watching him, yet even in the face of his anguish, I mistrusted him. If he was so desperately anxious to win her back, then it seemed pathetic he had to deputize someone to do it for him. Again I thought of the scene under the maple. If she would do that for him, why wouldn't she return when he asked her?

But all I said was, "I wouldn't have the faintest idea of how to go about it. How do I get to visit her, for example?"

The question visibly pleased him. He was sure of winning now. "Call her up. I told you, she's at the Manchester."

"What if she won't see me?"

He thought a moment. "I have a better idea. Have Judy call her. She'll see Judy, no doubt about it. Women turn to their own, and Judy's her best friend."

"*Really?*" The word exploded before I could check it. Judy barely knew her. Did Anne live in such isolation that she was no more intimate with anybody else?

"Yes. Since we moved from Long Island, nobody's called to keep up relationships. It's one of the reasons Anne's unhappy." He produced a smile. "It's tough to live with an author when the only other person you can talk to is a schizoid son."

My hands went cold. He was not using an epithet, but telling the truth. "David's—"

"Let's say sick," he said. "And Anne's in no condition now to take care of him. She's"—he hesitated, looking for the right word —"distraught."

I thought of white powder. He must have encouraged her taking it, and she, in gratitude, his importation of teen-age whores. I tried to keep my face from showing my feelings of sorrow and loathing. "I think you should go to the Manchester yourself," I said. "Give it another try."

He shook his head. "Impossible. She told me that if I set foot inside the lobby she'll call the police."

"She'd never actually do it."

He grimaced. "You don't know her." Putting down the glass, he reached over the desk to grab my hand. In his eyes was a pleading I had never seen before. He was open and vulnerable; there was no dissembling.

He needs my help and I want to help him. "And if I fail?"

His shoulders sagged. "You'll never see another book from me again."

Rage throbbed in my temple. I wanted to hit him. *Be careful,* I told myself. "I won't or the world won't?"

"The world," he said, and then, understanding, "Holy Christ, Tony, do you think I'd *threaten* you over this?"

Past wrongs flooded back. "You did over Arthur."

"To me, that was business. That was your job."

"And this?"

His glance was direct. "Friendship."

I returned the look. "As your friend, I advise you to handle this yourself."

"I've told you: impossible."

"It doesn't seem much like friendship to tell me I've got to go to her if I want another book from you. I wouldn't do it for that."

"I said that would be the outcome. I didn't say it was the *reason* for seeing her."

"Which is?"

"To repeat: friendship."

I caught something in his voice. "Nothing more?"

His stare, if possible, intensified. I could no longer look at him directly. "If you don't see her—if you don't bring her back to me— I'll go mad."

I snorted at the melodrama of it, but he did not seem offended. "I mean it," he said. "I won't survive." He covered his eyes with his hands, but then he looked at me again. The pleading had returned. He might have shown her his need rather than me, I thought, or his love. Still, I was moved.

We sat silently together. At last he said, "Have you decided?"

"What?"

"Whether you'll see her."

"Yes."

"Yes, you'll see her, or yes, you've decided."

"Yes, I've decided. But I should tell you that I can't decide for Judy."

"Sure," he said impatiently, as though my decision were tantamount to hers. "But for God's sake, Tony, don't draw out the suspense."

I hadn't been drawing it out. Until the last minute, I really wasn't sure what to do. Reason told me I was getting into a personal battle of which I had only the sketchiest knowledge. He was an actor, a moral fraud. Yes, he looked haggard sitting across from me; those were genuine tears in his eyes. I can tell the difference between a real tremor of the hand and a false one. But still, my inclination was to say no. By persuading Anne and David to return

—assuming we could—we might be sacrificing their lives for his.
But he had returned to me, a supplicant. It was a huge victory. To agree meant reconciliation.

"I'll see her," I told him.

sixteen

TO JUDY, THERE WAS NO CONFLICT AT ALL. "SHE'S our friend and she's in trouble. We'll see her if she wants us."

"What if she doesn't want to go back to him?"

"Then she doesn't go." She faced me. "The point is, you don't leave your husband, particularly with a troubled child in tow, unless you're in extremis. Our job is to discover what drove her out, and try to help her look at things objectively. Then if she doesn't want to go back, so be it. We'll help her adjust. Obviously we can't force her decision and equally obviously we don't *want* to force her." She paused, then, gravely, said, "Do we?"

I hadn't asked myself the question and so answered without thinking about it. "No, of course not."

"Good. Because I don't trust Eric here. I think he sees his taking you back as a quid pro quo for forcing you to make her return, and if that's the case, if you're acting only for Eric, I'm not going with you, and without me, you'll get nowhere."

I had suspected, too, that Eric was again simply using me, but Judy had not seen his agony, Judy had not heard the desperation in his voice. "We're going to help them both," I acknowledged. "We're not going to force Anne to do anything."

We had been sitting side by side on the living room couch. Now Judy got up and headed for the bedroom. "I'll call her."

"Tonight?"

"What better time? I doubt she's out."

"Don't you want me to call?"

She thought for a moment. "No, I think it's better if I do it. She'll suspect you're on Eric's side, but she knows I'm on hers."

I wasn't sure how Anne knew it—Judy was my wife; wouldn't her sympathies lie with me?—but, relieved, I simply motioned her toward her task.

She returned after half an hour, frowning, and sat down next to me. "Tough?" I asked.

She shrugged. "It wasn't easy."

"But she agreed to let us see her?"

"I think so."

"Think so? In half an hour, you couldn't make sure?"

Her eyes were sad and serious. "Most of the time she was incoherent."

"Crying?"

"Sometimes, but mostly not. No, she just talked and talked, but she never made much sense."

The reason seemed obvious. "Drugs?"

Another shrug. "I couldn't be sure. It's hard to tell over the phone."

"What would you guess?"

"I'd guess no. Natural hysteria."

Agitated, I found it hard to look at her. "What did she talk about?"

"Ninety percent about Eric."

"And the gist?"

She sighed. "Oh, she talked about what a shit he was, how he had ruined her life and David's. Nothing you wouldn't expect."

I caught a note of evasion in her voice. "Nothing?" I asked gently.

She looked at me as though wondering whether to trust me. "She accused him of trying to kill her."

The words hit with the force of a slap. "Jesus! How?"

"That's the funny part of it. I kept asking how, but all she said was, 'With his book.' I couldn't understand what she meant."

"She didn't explain?"

"No. She just kept repeating the phrase. 'He's trying to kill me with his book.'"

I thought back over Eric's three books. When I spoke again, my voice was choked. "But he's been kind to her, adoring. Think of the love Ben has for Alice in *Success*."

She took my hand, a gesture of comfort. "I know. She must mean the new book."

I cupped her hand with my other one, signaling unity. "Impossible," I said. "He'd never let her see—"

The thought occurred to her as it occurred to me. "Unless he wanted to kill her with it," she said.

We looked at each other, realizing the implications, saying nothing. Finally, I stood, shaking my head as though to clear it from being too long under water. "This is silly," I announced. "We're speculating. Besides, if she wants to see us, shouldn't we go?"

Judy held up a restraining hand. "Not tonight."

"Then when?"

"Tomorrow morning. We're due there at noon."

"Out of the question," I told her. "I've got a lunch with—"

Her glance shut me up. "So do I," she said.

I avoided her gaze, deflated. "Of course. I'm sorry."

She stood too, smiling wanly. "We'll probably be there most of the afternoon. I'd better get some work done now."

I watched her turn toward the door. "Wait," I said. "One last question."

She turned back. "Go on."

"Did she talk to all about David?"

Judy's face flushed deep red. Her eyes were dark with sorrow.

"It was only when she did that she cried." Her own tears appeared. "Ah, Tony, Anne's only half right. He's killing them both."

❊

The Manchester is one of the many residential hotels throughout Manhattan. Built in the 1920s, it has undergone a variety of decorating styles. Its lobby combines antique and modern furniture without any underlying plan, so the effect is resolutely impersonal, as if the space had been worked over by a series of second-rate decorators who had each run out of money before he could complete his transformations.

The look was particularly offensive to Judy. She had plenty of time to study it since, when we presented ourselves at the reception desk and the concierge called upstairs, we were asked to wait before Mrs. Meredith could see us. The reason for the delay was never explained, but we sat for over fifteen minutes before she called the front desk and invited us up.

"Keep your fingers crossed," Judy said, making sure that I couldn't by taking my hand and squeezing it, transferring her own nervousness to me.

I'm not sure what I expected. A drug addict in the throes of hysteria; a woman so depressed it took her fifteen minutes merely to tell us to come up; a vengeful woman or a grieving one. I thought back to Anne's benediction at the wedding, her hope that our love would endure. Impulsively I put my arms around Judy and, in the privacy of the self-service elevator, hugged her.

She put her head against my shoulder and returned the hug without speaking. But I could tell she was moved.

The moment of peace lasted only for as long as it took the elevator to reach the fifth floor. Then we got out and, once again anxious, no longer touching, not even holding hands, we walked solemnly down the long, drab corridor until we reached Anne's door. The bell chimed, like the ring at a dentist's office; it took over a minute for Anne to answer it, and for that time I thought she had decided not to see us after all.

But at last I heard an interior door close, and then the hall door opened and there she was. For a moment, I could not bear to look into her face, and so my eyes took in the room behind her—the sofa, the two armchairs, the glass-topped table, the attractive posters, the tiny kitchenette, the curtains drawn against the light outside the window, the closed door hiding the bedroom of what I took to be a two-room suite. Terrible physician that I am, I was afraid of being repelled by her wounds.

Yet when I at last looked, I could discern no dramatic change in her. Partly this was because she wore sunglasses and I could not clearly see her eyes. And partly, I suppose, it was because her natural beauty and her good skin, muscle tone, and youth seemed to have combined in her defense.

She made no gesture of greeting, and the three of us stood immobile for a few moments, until Judy, with an effort, said, "Anne, you look amazingly well," and approached her.

Anne let herself be kissed, turning her cheek to her friend, and making no effort to reciprocate. Indeed, she seemed stunned to see us there, although she had just asked us to come up. I, who had kissed her many times, this time merely took her right hand in both of mine and held it, feeling no response.

I could think of nothing to say, though I had rehearsed my plea in my imagination, so it was with relief that I heard Judy speak, breaking the extraordinarily awkward silence.

"How's David?" she asked.

The question galvanized Anne as the platitudinous greeting had not. At least, she moved away from the doorway, allowing us to enter, and even made a small gesture, indicating the sofa and chairs behind her. I sat on one of the chairs, Judy on the sofa, both of us tentative, as though afraid of David's magic.

"He's with you, isn't he?" Judy said.

"Yes, of course. He's in there." Her voice was timid and soft, unnaturally high. She motioned toward the closed door, and I became aware of the sound of gunshots coming from behind it. "I don't know what to do except let him watch television," she went on. "He won't do his homework, and I really haven't the heart to pressure him." Speaking seemed to relieve her, for her voice grew stronger and she seemed more composed, less fragile. "I've taken him out of school for the week—it would be impossible to commute back and forth—but I wish he'd do a little reading, or at least a little running around. He won't go into the park, even if I promise not to leave his side."

"Does he miss Eric?" Judy asked.

She sighed again. "I really don't know. He's so noncommittal, doesn't even tell me what he's feeling. He seems more depressed than usual, and I wouldn't blame him if he was, but maybe I'm simply projecting."

"Yes," I said. "I think the important question is how you're taking it, not David."

Instead of answering, she simply removed her glasses. I sat back, stunned, and I could hear Judy's gasp from the couch. For I have never seen such eyes. Rimmed with blue-black, as though somebody had punched her, they seemed to be set much further back in her head than I remembered, and their expression was one of an anguish one sees in a Raphael *Pietà*. I tried to discern if the pupils were dilated, but the light hit them wrong, or the dark rings around them acted as natural shades, for it was only her overall expression which was clear—and that was powerful enough to make me sit back in my seat.

"That bad?" Judy asked gently.

Anne nodded and put back her glasses.

"Do you want to tell us what happened?"

"Nooo." Her voice was an eerie wail. The sound made my skin prickle.

"It might help you to talk," Judy said. "It does no good to bottle it up; it'll have to come out anyhow."

Again Anne nodded, and brushed away a tear. "I know. Only it's difficult."

"Of course it is. But please realize that we're your friends, both of us."

Anne looked at me suspiciously.

"It's true," I said. "Sure, Eric's my friend and client, but this goes rather further than that. We want what's best for both of you."

She remained silent, but at last sat down on the far end of the couch, glancing from one to the other of us as though we were participants in some sort of silent debate.

"I don't know where to begin," she said, brushing a strand of hair from her face, her voice tremulous. "Obviously, you know we've had difficulties. We had had them long before we met you. Part of the old difficulties was money; we didn't have enough; Eric kept telling me I spent too much. Then all that changed, and so did the problems, only they got worse." She waved her arm in front of her face, chasing away memory. "But oh, they were insignificant compared to the love. I told you about that, Tony, at your wedding. He was so strange to me. I'm not a writer, not a creative person at all. The pottery doesn't really count. And here he was making up stories about us, stories that explained him to me, explained *me* to me. And still I didn't know *him*, not wholly—all I could see of his soul was in his books, and he had control over them." She paused, reflecting. "At least he did before this one."

Judy caught her up on that, interrupting before she could go on. "What do you mean, 'before this one'?"

Again she waved her arm. "I'll get to that. I have to. But you need the background." She got up from the couch and walked to the door shielding David. Again I became aware of the noise of the television—too loud, but evidently suited to her purposes, for she returned to the couch and sat down again.

"I recognized myself in his books," she continued. "Of course it was me filtered through him, but the filter was love. I mean he loved his women characters so much, and I knew he was speaking to me, telling me he loved me in ways he never said face to face, even when we were making love." A blush started at her neck. "When he spoke harshly to me, or, worse, when he ignored me, or even worse, when he ignored me and David, I would remember the words in the books, the feelings in the books, the *me* in the books, and I would be comforted. He was—is—so wise, sees so much, that I could not believe he didn't know what David or I was feeling. The *real* Eric, I knew, was Eric the writer; writing defined both him and me. I had no other definition." She looked at Judy. "Do you understand?"

She nodded silently, engrossed.

"I was the wife of a writer, mother to a writer's son, and not even up to that task. But he loved me, even though I failed with David and failed with myself. He loved me and he told me so, passionately and eloquently, in his books." She stopped and began to cry, the tears rolling down her cheeks, though she made no sound.

"Keep talking," I said fatuously, feeling simultaneously moved and uncomfortable. "Judy's right. It'll help."

"I'm trying," she answered, asperity in her tone, but when she continued her voice was again soft, hiding much of the emotion that lay beneath it. "And so I forgave him his infidelities, even Kitty and Constance eventually, although I thought it was hateful of him to drag you into it, Tony, didn't you?"

The question came as a surprise; I had not expected it to be put so bluntly, or at that time. But at least she had seen through my lies. I lowered my head.

"Yes," Judy answered for me, but I would have told her so myself.

I thought of the scene on the lawn, of her own participation. She answered as though I had spoken the thought aloud.

"I came to realize that he needed his Kittys and Constances, but that I was superior to them, for hadn't he said over and over again —indeed, I imagine, for as long as the written word will exist— that I was his love?" She smiled wryly, the smile remaining but the eyes, dry now, full of bitterness. "Sometimes, it wasn't so bad. He gave me drugs, cocaine, to make me feel better."

"I knew," I told her.

She looked at me in surprise. "Of course. The Four Seasons. I thought I had hidden it. Ah well, there are worse vices. And this week I stopped. The moment I walked out of the house, I gave it up." She bit at her fingernails. "It's made it mercilessly hard here, but I haven't gone back and I don't intend to."

"Bravo," Judy said, looking at her with compassion, a sister.

She started on a new theme. "The money started coming in, lots of it. It helped me for a while; I had the new house to think of, I could buy the best tools for my pottery, I could find a good school for David. But the money was bad for Eric. It drove him berserk. He acted like he didn't deserve it. So he spent more and more time with his writing, trying, I thought, to *earn* it. But he obviously never felt he did. You've both said you think he's a genius. I know he is. But mostly he thinks he's shit."

"He knows he's a genius too," I answered her pompously. "All writers vacillate."

She sighed. "Whatever. It doesn't make it easier for the person living with him." She reflected for a moment, then added, as though the thought were new, "It probably doesn't make it any easier for him, either. If he knew that other writers felt the way he does, it wouldn't matter to him. It's his feelings, his thoughts that matter, and when he feels like shit, when he thinks his writing's worthless, he takes it out on us, David and me."

"On all of us," I told her.

But she had already dismissed me and now talked only to Judy, facing her directly, her profile to me. "Things got worse when we moved instead of better. God knows, he wanted the house. He needed the space and seclusion—the Bayshore house was awful, it was like living in a trailer. But while we fought there, so badly it almost destroyed our son, in Chatham there was nothing but silence. He made one room into his private study, something he's wanted for as long as we were married; but then, Judy, he disappeared into it." I saw a tear form in her right eye, a small pearl growing larger until she blinked and it dissolved. "I don't mean he actually disappeared—he came out for meals, and sometimes to do the shopping, even to play with David. And of course he slept with me, often spent the evenings with me, reading or watching television, or sometimes even talking. He did jobs around the house, too, to work off the tension. But he disappeared all the same."

She paused, letting Judy say, "I'm not sure what you mean."

"Just this: The man who came out of that study every night might have been Eric's double. He looked like him and his voice was the same and he moved in a familiar way. But it wasn't the Eric I had married. When he shut that door to his study, not only did he shut himself in and shut me out, he made it so that even when he opened the door it was an impenetrable barrier." She shrugged, blinking out another tear. "Does that make it clearer?"

Judy hesitated before answering. "A little."

"The point is," Anne continued rapidly, "all connection broke. He became perfectly pleasant, perfectly polite—good God, *Eric* pleasant and polite! It was as if when he came out of the study he left his soul behind. I couldn't sense it anymore. I had no access to it."

Again I thought of her naked on the lawn, of the girl and Eric between them, and again she seemed to read the thought.

"Sometimes he'd turn wild. Rarely, but it was there. Then he'd want to party or get drunk or take some of my coke. But in those times too I wasn't present. I was just a body or a supplier or a convenience. I liked those times better than the voids; at least he was touching me. But it wasn't really Eric, it wasn't Eric at all. Why, a few times, he made me—" She broke off suddenly, turning toward me. I knew what she was going to say, but Judy, who knew too, held up a hand.

"Don't say it," she whispered. "We understand what it was like."

"Oh, do you?" Anne's voice held the relief one must feel when one has confided his most sinful act to a priest and been absolved from it. Impulsively she took Judy's hand. "You see why I can't go back," she said.

"I see why you left," Judy said. "It's not the same thing."

Anne considered this for a moment. "It's not why I left. Not precisely. He did something awful."

Involuntarily, I shivered. "What?" Judy asked, unable to hide her own anxiety.

"It happened last Sunday afternoon," Anne said. "As you remember, it was a beautiful day, hot and dry. Eric was working in his study, David was in his room playing, and I was sitting outside on the lawn by a large maple tree, our favorite tree. I had taken down a copy of *Art News*. I was going to read a story on ceramics, but the article was badly written, so I stopped reading and simply lay on the grass, thinking a lot of unrelated thoughts, dreamy and comfortable, enjoying myself as much as I could. In fact, I remember thinking I was really glad we had moved to Chatham. I felt optimistic, and thought how nice the house and grounds looked.

"Eric came downstairs and out on the lawn. He told me he had finished work for the day and was going to drive into town to buy some mixer—evidently I had committed the unpardonable sin of allowing the tonic to run out. Since he rarely drinks when he's working, this didn't seem so hideous to me, and he even teased me about it. I felt a kind of gratitude for that; teasing is, after all, a connection.

"So off he drove, and I lay back on the grass, looking at the house. Even though there are screens, in the late afternoon the light hits the house in such a way that you can see into the rooms when the windows are open, and naturally they were last Sunday since the weather was so warm."

(I wonder if there are screens in the attic now, I thought irreverently, remembering.)

"I could see David in his room, sitting near the window, either reading or playing a game, for his head was bowed. But in a little while he stood up and moved away from the window. I presumed he was going to get a new book or game, or even just go to the bathroom.

"I must have turned my head away for a minute. When I looked up I could see David in Eric's study. I couldn't figure out how he got there—Eric always keeps the door locked—so the sight was disorienting, and I felt a little panicked. Something was out of kilter."

She stopped for a moment, swallowing. Her voice had become agitated, high-pitched and strained, and I could see tension lines around her eyes. I looked at Judy to see if she had noticed the change in Anne, but she was staring directly at her without altering her expression of compassionate interest.

"Things happened so fast," Anne went out. "I saw a match flare in the study, then a lick of flame, and I stood up, not believing. The flame went out, but the whole thing was repeated—the match, the flame, then everything normal, except that it was David in the study, not Eric. I started to run toward the house, but before I reached it I saw the flame for the third time, and then I was indoors and climbing the steps, realizing what David was doing.

"The door to the study was open, and I could smell the smoke and see the ash. David had brought in his metal wastebasket and, page by page, was systematically burning Eric's manuscript. He looked at me calmly when I burst in, and in a quiet voice told me he had picked the lock with a clothes hanger. He was about to light another page, but I grabbed his arms and tore the matches from his hands. He started to cry, and I was crying with him, but he would not let me lead him from the room. When I asked him why he was burning Eric's book he refused to answer but only increased his screaming. His face was black from the tears and the ash.

"Finally we both cooled down a little, and I was able to hold him against me. After a while I could feel his body relax. He was my David again. I knelt down to embrace him more fully, so that I could kiss his face instead of the top of his head, and he responded by kissing me back and then burying his face in my neck. My God,

Judy, I think it was the first time in months that we were that close!"

She inched herself along the couch nearer to Judy, as though needing the contact for her own comfort. "Anyway, there we were, the two of us, David and me, hugging in Eric's study, oblivious to anything but our own sadness—when Eric came home."

She paused and a look of fear came into her face. "He was savage, Judy, relentless. It took him no more than a second to figure out what had happened, and then he attacked David—his own son—with his fists." She shuddered. "I can still see it. I still *hear* it. My God, the sounds Eric made. Wild sounds.

"I tried desperately to stop him, to somehow get between him and David. But if I had been ten times as strong, it wouldn't have helped. Eric simply shoved me away, pushed me so hard I fell against the desk—I still have the bruise from it. And all the while he was hitting David and screaming at him and—oh God—roaring. Finally I grabbed him by the arms, and this time he let me stop him. Maybe he was exhausted, maybe some part of his sanity returned. Whatever, he let David fall to the floor and stood over him, panting like a dog, saliva at the corner of his mouth—like a dog.

"It was quiet. I could hear his breathing, hear David whimper, but compared to the noise before it was like dead silence. Then, miraculously, Eric started to cry, also silently, huge tears just running down his face. He tried to come to me, to put his arms around me, but I screamed at him, called him a child beater, a killer—for he was killing David, killing me, no doubt about it—told him I was only sorry David hadn't burned the whole book, because the book was killing us both.

"He didn't try to argue, just stood there crying. Mr."—she spat the word, eyes blazing—"Macho, the genius, just stood there crying, sorry for himself."

She started to shake so violently that Judy had to put her arms around her to soothe her. "You don't have to go on," she said. "You don't have to say another word."

Anne shook her head. "There's not much more to tell." She took a breath, holding it till her face got red, then exhaled slowly. "I leaned down to look at David. He was motionless on the floor. I couldn't tell if he was conscious or not. I had trouble picking him up"—she smiled wanly—"my big, heavy boy. Eric had enough sense not to try to help me. I'd have killed him, I swear it, if he had taken a step toward us. But he just stood where he was.

"I carried David to our bedroom and laid him down—he still didn't move. Then I packed some things for me, went to David's room to pack for him, and carried the bags to the car. Eric made no effort to help me or stop me. I went back to get David. He was conscious. His eyes were open and he tried to mumble something, only I couldn't hear what it was. His face was swollen and cut. There was blood all over him."

She sighed so deeply the sound was guttural. Once more her own tears started. "I took him to the hospital in Hudson, to the emergency room. I could tell how badly he was hurt by how fast the doctors grabbed him from me. They rushed him away, and I was left alone in that terrible room, waiting for word. About an hour later—an interminable hour!—a doctor came out and told me David would be all right, that nothing was broken, but that the swelling and discoloration would last for weeks and would get worse before they got better. Still, it was a tremendous relief that nothing was badly damaged.

"The doctor doped him up with painkiller, so when I finally was allowed into his room to see him, he was out cold on the bed, and I didn't dare shake him to rouse him, much as I wanted to comfort him. Seeing him so—*fragile* twisted me up inside in a way I had never felt before. And in the quiet of that room—not until then—I decided to leave Eric forever, that my obligation was to save David and myself."

So there it was, I thought. Her decision. What words of mine could possibly bring her back to him?

"I didn't hate him at that moment," Anne said. "Or if I did it was not because of what he had done, but because of what he *was*.

I knew I couldn't change him, I didn't even want to change him, not anymore. I couldn't understand how this man, who knew so much, who understood me so well, and whom I once loved equally in return—I couldn't understand how he could savage his own child. And I knew that because I didn't understand it, and because I didn't want to go on trying to change him, and most of all because I no longer wanted to be loved by that *thing*, I had to leave him forever."

The tears had stopped and she spoke quietly, reflectively, in the determined manner of someone who has thought it all through and made up her mind. "I don't know how long I stayed with David, thinking all this, but eventually the same doctor came in and asked if I needed anything. I told him no, but he looked at me closely and said that at least he would give me a tranquilizer to take when I got home. I announced that I wasn't going home, and he said that of course I could stay overnight in the hospital, that they would set up a cot in David's room, and I could sleep on that.

"Only after I had accepted and the cot had been brought did he take me to his office. It was, he said, an obvious case of child abuse. Nothing else could have accounted for the injuries. Could I tell him what happened."

Her agitation returned, though not with its earlier intensity. I could see the tremors, though; her energy was running low, her emotion had exhausted her. "I—I didn't know what to say. Oh, it had occurred to me to report Eric to the police, to punish him in every conceivable way I knew how, but sitting in that antiseptic office, I couldn't do it. I *couldn't*. So I merely explained that David had set fire to Eric's manuscript and Eric had hit him because of it.

"It must have been the first time he realized just which Meredith child he was treating, for I watched his mouth fall open, and though he tried to keep his composure, it was obvious he was struck with the magnitude of his responsibility.

"I was so exhausted I didn't care about his surprise. In fact, I thought it grotesquely amusing. Still, I told him I wouldn't be pressing charges and that I preferred that none of the details be made public." She smiled. "He really was a nice man. He told me that legally he was obliged to report it, but that in our case he would bend the rules and that the secret was safe with him, and in fact he's been as good as his word, for I've seen nothing in the papers."

She shook her head. "It's silly, isn't it. Five years ago the same horror would have meant nothing to anybody except us. Now it's a scandal. Anyway, we talked a little more. He told me he would let me stay with David for as long as I wanted, and that there would be no charge for my being there." She smiled again. "The rich get richer. Then he left to attend to his other patients, and I took a piece of paper and wrote Eric the note which must have made him call you, since I wouldn't see him myself."

She was in control now; I could feel her strength in the room. "I asked one of the aides to deliver the letter to Eric. I was god-damned if I'd ever set foot in that house again.

"Anyway, the next morning I made some phone calls, reserved this suite at the Manchester, got David released, and the two of us drove to New York. Except for your phone call, Judy, and Eric's, we haven't spoken to anybody since we've been here. And I've gone out only to buy some necessities—I hadn't packed enough underwear for David, and I needed a few cosmetic things for my-self. David hasn't gone out at all. I'm afraid he'll go blind from all that television."

She had finished, stronger, I suppose, than when she had started, relieved to have gotten it out. My own feelings seemed to slam against each other. Terrible as her story was, perhaps it was only one side of it. I knew little of Eric's troubles with David, troubles that could not have stemmed from Eric alone—Anne must have had some part in them. And I realized how little I knew about the dynamics of the marriage. Because of Eric's novels, I felt I knew their relationship intimately. But of course it was a *fictional* rela-tionship I knew—based on facts, apparently, but transformed into art by one of the protagonists.

"What are your plans?" Judy asked.

Her voice was low. "I have none."

"You can't stay here forever."

"I know that. But I've been too depressed to think. Maybe your coming will start me off."

"What about David?" Judy persisted, businesslike. "He's in school in Chatham?"

"Yes, there's a school for special children half an hour from the house."

"There's a good one here in the city," Judy said.

Anne bristled. "I know. I'll have to get him in there, or somewhere. But I can't do it right now." Her voice caught. "I really can't."

Judy's tone was comforting. "Of course not. First you've got to get your own life started."

Anne smiled as though this were a revelation. "Precisely."

"You've decided to stay in New York?"

"Yes. I couldn't go back to Long Island, and I don't want to go to some place strange."

"So. New York. But you can't stay at the Manchester."

"I *could*. It's fantastically expensive, and at least that would serve Eric right—he'd have to pick up the American Express bills."

"But there's not enough room."

Again she smiled. "Exactly. I'll have to find a place even more expensive."

"I'll look for an apartment for you," Judy said. "I've lots of contacts."

"It would need work space," Anne said. "I'll go on with my pottery. I've started to sell some more recently, although it might have been more because of Eric's fame than my talent."

"Your talent," Judy said firmly. "Remember, I've seen your work, and I'm the one with taste."

It was precisely the right thing to say. "It'll keep me going," Anne said, her voice more animated. "Eric'll have to give me some money, and I'll make some myself. We'll get along fine."

"Then you're divorcing him?" I asked.

Anne looked at me in surprise. I think she had forgotten about me altogether. "I really haven't thought that far ahead. For now, all I want is to be away from him."

Was there then a chance she would go back? I dared not consider it.

"I wouldn't make any decisions now," Judy counseled. "Wait till the shock wears off."

"I suppose I'll have to divorce him," Anne said, as though thinking of it for the first time. Again, she started to cry. "Oh God, that means lawyers and mess—and hurting poor David even more." The tears increased. "And I'll have to see him again, won't I?"

Judy nodded. "But not alone, if you don't want to. You'll have a lawyer with you."

She wailed. "I don't *know* any lawyers."

"I'll help you find one."

"Or maybe," I said, "you'll change your mind."

There was silence. Anne looked at me with a terrible coldness. "You'd like that, wouldn't you?" she asked at last. It was an accusation.

Merited. I grew warm with shame. "Indeed I would. I want you to be happy—and Eric to be happy."

"And we can only be happy together?"

I tried to keep my tone light. It was a disaster. "Of course not. Only I'm a romantic. I like reconciliations. I'm your friend—"

"Not ours. His. *He* sent you here."

"Yes, but—"

"Well, tell him I'm not going back." Her voice rose. "I hate him!" she screamed. She turned to face me, her eyes lunatic. "Do you want to know why I won't go back? Do you want to *see* why?"

I sat still, breathing rapidly, waiting. She got up deliberately and with slow steps walked to the door of the bedroom. "David," she called. "Come say hello to Judy and Tony."

He answered, but the words were indistinct. Anne must have understood, however, for she said, "Yes, you really have to," and

I heard the television set being shut off. It seemed to take minutes before he appeared, but at last the door to the bedroom opened, and there he was.

"Oh my God!" It was Judy who spoke, unable to control herself. I had to bite my lip to keep from crying out in astonishment.

David was unrecognizable. His face was puffed up like a macabre beach ball, only there were ridges and welts on it, and two knobs over the forehead which, by swelling, had narrowed the eyes to slits. There was a jagged tear at the side of his mouth where black sutures had been taken, giving his face the look of a Frankenstein monster, as though he had been pieced together from other faces into this horrible one. His face was red, blue, black, green— anything but flesh-colored. One of the blows seemed to have caught him in the throat, for his hello was hoarse, strangled.

He walked stiffly, as though in pain; but he made it to both of us and gravely shook our hands. Anne walked with him. He kept his left hand on her skirt while he touched ours with his right. His grip was limp, without tone or muscle. He was just alive enough to know he had a duty to perform, and too weak to refuse to do it.

"Do you want to stay with us for a little while?" his mother asked.

He shook his head.

"Okay, then, you can go back. Is the program good?"

He did not answer, but merely retreated to his room and shut the door. In a moment, we could again hear the sound of the television.

"The discoloration should lessen in a week or two," Anne told us matter-of-factly. "As I've said, nothing's been broken. By the end of the month, the doctor said, he'll be physically normal."

Then the reserve, her control, broke, and she started to weep, great sobs wracking her as though she were asthmatic. "But oh his head," she cried. "His poor mind. What's he done to *that*?"

She turned to us, panting as though she had run a marathon, her back pressed against the closed bedroom door; she would have fallen if it had not been there. Sweat stood out on her forehead.

The sight of David must have made her relive the scene in Eric's study. She glared at us, defiance and something close to exaltation in her eyes.

"You see now," she said, "why I can't go back. Could never go back." She paused, chest heaving, holding onto the doorknob for support. "I'd have to kill him," she explained, her voice unnaturally calm, her breath coming hard. "You can understand that, can't you?"

"Yes," Judy said.

"Yes," I added fervently.

seventeen

I CALLED ERIC THAT NIGHT TO REPORT.

"We've failed," I told him.

"Failed?"

"She won't come back."

There was a pause. I could hear him breathing. "Details," he said.

"She's in a suite at the Manchester," I began.

"Christ, Tony, I know that." His tone was exasperated.

"I wasn't sure you knew it was a suite," I said. "Besides, I've got to start somewhere."

"Sorry," he said, without a hint of remorse. "I'm a bit tense, as you can imagine."

"It'd be easier for me if you asked questions," I said. "I'm having trouble getting my thoughts in order."

It seemed an acceptable plan, for he started right up. "How does she look?"

"As beautiful as ever." I said it sincerely.

"Tired?"

"Probably, but she didn't complain."

"Upset?"

I thought of her tears. "You might say that."

"Don't play games," he said.

"Okay. Yes, terribly upset."

"Did—did she seem to you to be taking anything? Pills, I mean. Tranquilizers, something like that?"

It wasn't what he meant, I knew. "No pills," I reported. "Nothing of any kind, so far as I could see." I decided on frankness. There was no sense in being coy. "She told us she had given up cocaine."

There was a brief silence. I couldn't tell whether he was relieved by the news or not. Finally he asked, "What else did she tell you?"

"That she had definitely decided not to come back."

"No. I mean about what happened, what drove her out."

I was prepared for the question, but still I proceeded carefully. "She told me what happened in your study."

He groaned. "I went crazy, Tony. Blind crazy." There was nothing but gentleness and regret in his voice. "When he set fire to those pages it was as if he were setting fire to *me*. So I fought back, lashed at him. Struck my own little boy." He was quiet, and I wondered if he was crying. "Obviously he was getting back at me. I should have recognized that. But he hit me where it's most painful: in my soul."

"Don't you have a copy of the manuscript?" I asked.

"Sure. That's not the point. If he had burned the book after it had been published, when there were hundreds of thousands of copies available, it would have produced the same pain."

"Maybe he didn't realize what he was doing."

"Maybe not," he said testily. "I *know* I didn't, Tony. Did you tell her that?"

I hadn't, of course. Now I wondered why. "It wouldn't have done any good."

"Why?"

"She was too hurt and too angry."

"Did you tell her that I love her?"

A dust of anger formed at the pit of my stomach. Whatever fear I had felt at the beginning of the conversation had dissipated. "She wouldn't have believed me."

"But she *would*. She *knows* I love her."

"Does she?"

"My God, yes."

"I don't think she'd tell you that if you asked her."

"But *you* didn't?"

The dust swirled. "Don't you think it's a question you should ask directly yourself?"

"I told you why I wanted you to go." His tone was cold. "And you failed."

I snorted with laughter. The accusation was absurd.

"You admitted it yourself," he went on.

"Then why don't you?" I said. "*You* failed, not me."

His voice grew higher. "I didn't!"

"My God!" I shouted. "Did you see his face? *Did you see what you did to his face?*"

There was a long silence. "The memory will haunt me for as long as I live," he said at last, his voice low and soft.

Exasperation mounted. "Then how do you think she can believe you love her?"

"Because she'll understand eventually. She'll know why I did it —she knows now."

I was unimpressed. "And David?"

"Someday he'll understand, too."

"You really believe that?"

There was no hesitation. "Yes." As though to deflect the staggering arrogance of the answer, he hurried on. "Did she say what her plans are?"

"She hasn't made any."

"And David's school?"

"Undecided."

"So for the moment she stays at the Manchester, tending to his wounds and hers, and resenting me?"

"I don't know if 'resent' is the right word."

"Hating me?"

"She may be too numb to hate. But it's closer."

"So let me review," he said. "You didn't tell her that I love her?"

"No."

"Or wanted her or needed her or could not go on without her?"

"No."

"In fact, you merely took her word, then called me to report you had failed."

"Judy was with me," I said hotly. "Ask her. There wasn't anything we could do."

"Want to bet?"

"Yes!" I shouted the word.

He sighed. "There's one person who can do it."

"Who?"

"Me," he said. "I'll get her back myself."

✠

Later, when I reported the conversation to Judy, she grew somber. "This time he'll get you," she said, "for revenge."

"Revenge for what?"

"You've seen him at his weakest. You know too much about his life. His real life. With you, he can no longer hide behind his books."

"I'll be careful," I promised.

"He'll resent you. He'll try to destroy you."

"What about you? You know what I know."

"He'll get at me through you. He knows how much I love you. Give him up forever. Please, Tony, I beg of you." Her voice was high, her passion powerful.

"He's already fired me once," I said. "What worse can he do than fire me again?"

She shuddered. "Let's not find out."

I considered. Whatever sense of reconciliation I had felt was gone. The scene at the Manchester was ineradicable. But the agency was now in severe financial trouble. Only a new book by Meredith could save it. "I'll give him up after the next book."

"That could take years. He said he couldn't write without Anne."

"I don't believe that," I told her. "He told me he'd been working, and my guess is he's been working for a while. It's been a long time, after all, since *Diamonds*. No, I'll represent the new one. He owes it to me, anyway; it'll be payment for past sins."

She winced at my jocularity. "Please give him up now."

I put my arm around her. She was actually trembling. "After the next book," I assured her.

❊

Six weeks later, an event occurred that changed any inclination I might have had to drop Eric as a client.

On the evening of July 28, 1980, just after we had eaten dinner, a radiant Judy Silver—my one love, my wife—announced that she was pregnant.

❊

In the weeks between my conversation with Eric and Judy's glorious news, we had only brief contact with Anne. Judy called her, and once actually saw her—to go with her to look at an apartment that Judy liked but Anne did not. She reported that it was an uneventful outing. Eric had tried to reach Anne on several occasions; each time, she had refused to speak to him. He had written a long and passionate letter, full of apology and self-abuse; she had not answered it. David's school was not yet set, but Anne was looking into several possibilities and had no doubt that the matter would be settled by the time the new term started. The boy's face was healing nicely, and the time alone with his mother seemed to have calmed him. He was more cheerful, more open, than he had been in years. He had begun daily therapy in the city, and that too was helping. So Anne, while still angry and still hurt, was faring well.

Then one day when Judy called the Manchester, she was told that Mrs. Meredith had checked out, leaving no forwarding address. After some discussion—could she have gone back to Eric? No. Could she have been hurt? No. Was she avoiding us and everybody? Yes—we decided she had found an apartment without Judy's help and had moved in. When she wanted us or needed us she would call. It occurred to me to call Eric to ask her whereabouts, but Judy vetoed the idea. Anne had refused to talk to him. Our calling him could bring only distress without a chance of eliciting information.

So gradually over the weeks, Eric's pain and Anne and David receded from our lives. There were clients for me, new assignments for Judy. And three huge checks arrived from abroad covering royalties on Eric's books. He was becoming as popular overseas as he was here.

It was not that we forgot the Merediths. They would remain part of us forever. But we did go on to other concerns, and the summer imperceptibly disappeared. By Labor Day we had not heard from either of them for over a month. Judy was now beginning to show, and I too had grown stouter, sleek the way a prosperous New York agent should be. Yet with all the pleasure of those weeks, I remember feeling that something serious was unresolved. With the fate of all three Merediths uncertain, real contentment, for me if not Judy, was impossible.

❈

In the third week of September, Eric came to my office unannounced. It was a little after ten in the morning. I was opening the mail when he poked his head around the door and said, grinning, "Mind if I come in?"

I leaped to me feet, as startled as if he had been Jimmy Carter. "Eric! My God!"

He looked relaxed, confident. His skin was tanned and the worry lines around his eyes, so noticeable when we had last met in my office, had disappeared. I wondered briefly if he had been on vacation, but, knowing how much Eric preferred his home to any-place else, dismissed the idea as preposterous and wondered instead where the ease, the health, the *life* had come from. There was no sign of trauma or despair; except that he wore slacks and an open-neck shirt, he could have passed for a young executive just given a raise for a job well done. He shone with self-satisfaction. I was dumbfounded.

He was carrying a manuscript box, so, rather than take my hand in greeting, he simply filled it with the package.

"What's this?" I asked.

"My new novel."

I glowed. "The *new* one."

"Indeed. The others are already published. If I had wanted to give you one of those, I'd have brought the bound book."

There was no malice in the remark. He was teasing me, enjoy-ing it.

"But you were having such trouble!"

"I was inspired," he said, his grin enormous.

"By whom?"

"By Anne."

"Anne!"

"Yes. When she came back—" He noticed my look of astonish-ment. "But you didn't expect her to come back or know she had. You didn't believe me when I told you I'd do it. Anyway, she came back and David came back, so the circle is complete, and I can work again. Not having her back for a time—a black time, let me tell you—sent me under. When she came back, creativity flowed."

"But how did you persuade her?" I made no effort to hide my amazement. "She was so adamant."

"I called her every day," he said, his voice grave, "but she never would talk to me. So I wrote her, over and over again, asking only that she see me, let me talk to her. I knew she must be going through hell, cooped up with David, no one to talk to except Judy, particularly if she wasn't taking drugs, and I doubted that she was. I actually counted on her abstinence; it would weaken her, I figured, depress her. For I knew that once she let me see her, once I got inside that suite, she would agree to come back to me."

"Eventually you broke her down," I said.

"*She* called *me*. She was crying, didn't know what to do, was going out of her mind. Well, I drove down there in two hours, and five hours later, we were all three of us back here in Chatham."

"What did you say to her?"

"You've got to remember that deep down she longed to come back. *Had* to. I promised her I'd reform. No more tantrums. No more outbursts. I told her I was hers in every way—and God bless me, Tony, if I'm not. You're looking at a model husband, monogamous lover, patient father."

"What *about* David?" I asked.

"Set up in his old school, happier than he's been in years." He preened. "Oh, it took a while. He was scared of me at first—it was particularly bad in the hotel. But about a week after we got home, we had a long talk, the best talk I've ever had with anybody. I explained that people go crazy sometimes, even people who can love, even fathers against their sons." He looked at me hard. "And he understood, Tony. I swear he did."

I did not believe him; it was inconceivable that a preadolescent boy could "understand" so savage a beating. But I pressed him no further. Something had brought the family back together, and I held the result of that reunion in my hand. "You're pleased with the book?" I asked.

He grew fatuous. "I'm never really 'pleased.' Every time I finish a book I panic that it's not ready. When I gave it to you, I thought of two things I could improve."

"But you did hand it over," I said, smiling, "and I'm goddamned if I'll give it back. You can mail me the changes."

"I hope you like it," he said, and when I tried to assure him I would, he held up his hand. "It's different from anything I've tried. More experimental. I think it's powerful, but that's for you to judge."

"Then you *are* pleased."

His eyes bored into mine. They were troubled eyes. The ebullience of moments before had vanished. "It was agony writing it," he said. "More pain than I've ever known in my life."

"All writers—" I began, but again he stopped me.

"Suffer. But I don't give a shit about all writers. I only know my own pain."

It sounded whiny to me, and I was sick of it. "Still—" I said.

"Yes," he replied. "The book is a fucking miracle."

eighteen

ERIC CALLED HIS BOOK *TWILIGHT*, BUT IT SEEMED TO me written in the darkest part of his psyche. For while once again staying in the small framework of a man, his wife, and their child, Eric opened up the door of pain, and in their personal agonies depicted the cruelty and psychological depravity that lurk in all of us.

Yes, the book is autobiographical, both in the sense that all great works of art are, and in the facets of the story that closely paralleled Eric's, Anne's, and David's (in the book, as you remember, Martin is shown as schizophrenic, a child who is also a killer, able to relate only to the jungle animals he sees at the zoo).

Eris is merciless to all three of them, but particularly to Beatrice, the innocent Michigan girl who, in marrying Geoffrey, marries the drugs and sexual excesses that eventually destroy her. In light of my earlier conversations with Eric, there was one passage that seemed to me particularly revealing. Husband and wife have just made love; husband has climaxed. He lies spent on her body for a moment, then raises himself up on his elbows to look down at her.

He studied her intently, as though perusing an ancient document whose writing had grown indistinct. Her hair held strands of gray. Her eyes were closed, but leading from the greenish lids were small pathways of age, radiating out like ribs of a fan toward ears grown pink at the edges from her recent athleticism and down toward a nose now spattered with ruptured capillaries. There were lines around the mouth as well, and although the skin of her face was still smooth and young, he sensed decay beneath the surface, death endeavoring to push out from the inside.

Her full breasts, moments ago familiarly soft and exciting, sprawled loosely across her chest, the once pink nipples brown, the once translucent skin wrinkled. I know why men have affairs with younger women, he thought suddenly. Because in night after night of sleeping with their wives, each act of sex is not "a little death," but a step toward death, a portrait of the inevitable future.

I hated the book. Its power frightened me, its morbidity depressed me, its cruelty was to me oppressive. I read it compulsively, drawn to it with the fascination one feels on seeing a terrible accident— I had to investigate it and could not turn away. For once, I did not think about its commercial possibilities or its literary skill—both those would be pondered the next day, after a healing sleep. I simply let myself wander through his terrifying world, almost completely severing my ties to mine. I let his vision, his pessimism, his brutality invade my gentle soul.

It was an awful experience and it left me shaken. I snapped at Judy when she got back from work with a harshness that provoked a flare-up in return. In apology I handed her the manuscript, and told her that Anne had gone back to Eric. She read the book that night and greeted me bleary-eyed in the morning, her face pale with fatigue.

"Poor Anne," was the first thing she said.

I smiled, remembering the phrase from before. It seemed to me the torment was Eric's, not his wife's. "Again, not 'poor Eric.' "

"No. He's expunged his furies. She has to live with them."

"It was her choice to go back," I reminded her.

"Do you think she had a choice?"

The words startled me. "Sure. We both heard her in the Manchester. She was positively not going back."

Her eyes grew moist. "That's why it's 'poor Anne.' That's why it's poor us!"

The next morning I had another unexpected visitor: Arthur. Briefly I thought he looked his old self, his gray trousers and beige jacket unwrinkled despite a muggy day. But I saw his face was drawn with deep lines, and the skin around his eyes was dark.

Just after he had been fired we saw each other a few times—I took him to lunch as often as he would allow me to. But soon he stopped calling or accepting my invitations, and I was only dimly aware that he was supporting himself with free-lance work; nobody, it seemed, wanted to hire an ex-editor in chief who had lost his two most successful authors. Every time I heard of a good opening, I called to recommend him. But though they eased my guilt, the calls did him no good. Others got the jobs.

So we lost contact, he, I suppose, out of shame, I out of helplessness. And now his reappearance delighted me. I had always known he was a fine editor, but more, I thought he had in him Wordsworth's "still, sad music of humanity." He cared.

We spent the first half hour reviewing our lives, keeping the important details back, as former close friends will during reunions. But eventually he came to the point.

"I need a full-time job."

I looked at him inquisitively. Because of his expensive clothes, I never associated Arthur with financial difficulties. "Money troubles?" I asked.

"My mother's in a nursing home. The one on Lexington and Seventy-ninth. Do you know it?"

I did not, and said so, surprised that his mother was alive. This was the first time he had ever mentioned her.

"She's been in the home for over a year," he told me. "Those places drain you, though. We ran through whatever she had left in the first six months, and then we started on my savings. They're almost gone and when they've disappeared, I'll have to move her. To say nothing of me. And I don't want to, Tony. She's best off there, and I like where I am. So you can see the urgency. You can see why I literally can't afford to wait."

I saw. "Where have you tried?"

He shrugged. "Everywhere. They've *got* editors in chief."

"But you'd take a job as a senior editor?"

"Naturally. But they say I would make the present editor in chief nervous. And besides, I don't have any big money authors I can bring with me. With things as financially rotten as they are, nobody's hiring unless you can promise an instant money-maker."

He looked at me so pleadingly I had to turn my head away. "Arthur, I'll try," I said. "I'll call anyone, promise you my next big author—anything I can do. But I don't see—"

He cut me off. "Neither do I. Besides, you told me all that when I was fired. I used it, but it didn't do any good." He was breathing quickly. "Diadem will take me back."

I sat up straight. "I don't believe it!"

He grinned ruefully. "Yup. Seems they haven't been able to get anybody as good to take my place."

"But that's marvelous. Swallow your pride and take the job."

Again, the smile. "Swallowing's easy. But there's a condition."

With a heart that dropped like a steel sinker in my chest, I knew what it was. "That you bring in Eric Meredith's new novel."

It was his turn to avert his eyes. "You got it." Now he looked at me squarely, the motion an effort. "Meredith's back with you, right?"

The question made me feel suddenly guilty. "Yes. It's a long story—"

He waved his arm. "You've told me some of it. I can guess more. And God knows, Tony, I'm not accusing you of being disloyal. Here I am, begging for another chance to work with him. The point is, you *are* his agent, and you can intercede for me."

In an instant, I realized what the request must have cost him. This proud and troubled man was begging.

"Oh shit, Arthur, he'll never agree." And yet, I thought even as I said it, that when I brought it up, Eric had not actually *refused.*

"Please," he said, his voice gentle.

"It won't do any good," I told him.

He heard the acquiescence in my voice and embraced it. "It just might. It really might, Tony! You know how mercurial he is. If he got rid of me for no reason, he may come back for a good one. He's a human being, goddamn it. Read his books. There's compassion in him. Now's his chance to show it. Any man who can write that way can't be as cruel as he's been to me."

I thought of *Twilight*, which of course Arthur had not read, and did not have the stomach—though I had the proof—to refute him. Still, *Twilight* as yet belonged to no publisher. This would be the right time to ask.

"Give it a try," Arthur said, his voice husky with urgency.

"I need twenty-four hours to think about it," I said, knowing already what my answer would be.

He hesitated. But finally he said, "Sure," and then clamped his mouth shut, as though willing it to say no more.

"I'll call you tomorrow morning," I promised. "Will you be home?"

"It's my office," he reminded me.

"Tomorrow, then."

"Thanks." He turned to go, then took my extended hand in both of his. "Remember," he said, "it's my *life*."

"I've got to try," I told Judy that night. "No matter what happens. If he fires me again, poverty is good for babies. It toughens them."

The light in her eyes, the joy in her voice, was wholly for me. "I love you," she said. For once, I could understand why.

❈

"It's Tony Silver."

There was no hello in response. He merely asked, "What did you think of it?"

"Think of what?"

"*Twilight*," he said, exasperated.

I had not forgotten I had yet to report. But Arthur's troubles had taken precedence over it in my mind. "I thought it was magnificent," I said.

He must have caught something in my tone. "But——?" he asked.

"It's troubling, Eric. The book depressed the hell out of me."

He chuckled. "It was meant to."

"It's a downer," I said. "You can't expect the kind of sales you had with *Diamonds*."

"You know I've never cared about that." He paused. "But it'll sell *some*, won't it?"

"Sure. If for no other reason than you're a brand name."

There was asperity in his next question. "There are other reasons, though, aren't there?"

"The book's heartbreaking. Beautiful. It's a masterpiece."

Fist in hand. I could *feel* it over the phone. "I'd like to come see you," I said.

"Why?"

I did not want to mention Arthur over the phone. "Things from the past and a review of what we're going to do with *Twilight*. There's strategy to discuss."

"I don't know," he said. "I need a little solitude now that I'm finished."

"It won't take more than a couple of hours," I assured him. "I could come up this afternoon and you'll be free from then on."

He sighed. "Okay, let's get it over with."

Impatient as I was, it nevertheless took me half an hour to bring myself to make a move toward my car.

✣

And so, on an equally beautiful and therefore equally ominous day, I found myself for the second time heading north toward Chatham, determined this time to go through with my advocacy, no matter what. Past Poughkeepsie, the leaves had already started to turn and their reds and golds against a dazzling sky made me realize, not for the first time, how happy I was to be living in the northeast. There were only a few other cars on the road, but I drove slowly, less from enjoyment of the scenery than reluctance to arrive at my destination. Though I tried to puzzle out various scenarios for how the conversation might go, I found myself unable to concentrate, and let my thoughts drift with the miles, a contentment only half-willed coming over me.

The contentment vanished the moment I turned off the highway. The familiar turn and then the dirt road brought back sharp memories of my previous visit, of the debauchery I had witnessed and the young boy who had watched with me. I wondered with a shock what new scenes awaited me. The fear of it was so great that I did not worry over Eric's reaction to my mission—I had determined to fight for Arthur, and even if Eric exploded, my own conscience would be clear. I was doing what I knew to be right.

Again the house seemed deserted when I approached, but this time there were two cars in the driveway, twin Mercedes, and I reflected that the entire family was probably indoors. The time was around noon, and the house, casting no shadow, seemed newly painted and surreal; it was a supernaturally bright world I was entering.

I parked, walked up the driveway to the door, and rang the bell, feeling an accelerated heartbeat in my chest. Within moments, the door opened. Anne stood in front of me, smiling wanly. She looked older, and her eyes were lusterless. The black rings that had sur-

rounded them had not altogether disappeared, and she seemed
thinner, more fragile, a patient not yet recovered from major
surgery.

"You look—terrific."

"It's the clean life," she said, glancing at me significantly. "Eric
and I have both reformed."

"I couldn't be more pleased," I said, meaning it. If they were
truly at peace with one another, then at the least my mission might
succeed. I felt a burst of hope for all of us. "How's Eric?"

"Relaxed at last."

"The book's finished."

"That's part of it. And, after all, he persuaded me to come back."
A thought struck me. "Have you read it?"

"The book? No. He's asked me not to. Says he only wants to
show it to me when it's perfect."

"But he's given it to me."

She seemed surprised. Worry appeared in her eyes. "Really?
Maybe he wanted your advice."

"I've none to give. The book's magnificent."

She brushed back a strand of hair. "You liked it, then. I'm so
glad."

" 'Like' isn't the right word. I was moved by it, overwhelmed
by it. Troubled by it."

"Then he's rid himself of his pain." She sighed, looking steadily
into my eyes.

All this while we were standing in the hall. Now she took my
hand and led me through the house to the back porch. They had
added flowered pillows to the couch. The room smiled with light.

"Tony!" Eric entered, hand extended, beaming. When I took
the hand to shake it, he put his left hand over mine and squeezed it.

Anne asked me if I wanted lunch. I refused, but accepted the
offer of coffee and she went to make it. Eric and I sat at either end
of the couch; there was an ease to his manner I found remarkable.
It seemed as if Anne was right: he had expunged the pain and was
at peace.

"Tell me!" he said. "Don't keep me in suspense. What do you think of it?"

He leaned toward me with the air of a man politely interested in my opinion, but not about to be swayed by it.

"The book's perfect. I couldn't think of a word that should be changed."

He smiled and settled back on the couch, looking at me expectantly. I kept quiet. "That's all?"

"I told you on the phone: the book is so painful it might not sell as well as the others."

"And I answered that I didn't care." He leaned forward again. "Surely you didn't drive up here to repeat something you'd already said."

"No, I came to talk strategy."

He crossed his legs and put his arm over the back of the couch, the lord of the manor. "Right. What are your thoughts?"

"Diadem has an option on the new novel—they have the right to see it first." He started to speak but I hurried on. "I don't think that's much of a problem, though. We can reject any offer they make, and simply send the book out for open auction."

At last I had him interested. "Fine. But only include the good houses in the auction. Random House, Simon and Schuster. Knopf. Dutton. The big names with the most prestige."

"I could draw up a list and show it to you."

"Good." His eyes narrowed. "But wouldn't Diadem have to be included? What if they outbid everybody else?"

"The chances are slim. Money doesn't have to be the only consideration. There are advertising guarantees, royalties, division of the paperback money. Even though it's been sold, Diadem's still a small house. I can't believe it could compete with the Goliaths."

He glowed with satisfaction. "It could be an exciting auction."

"Could or couldn't."

The satisfaction disappeared. "What does that mean?"

"That *Twilight* might not be as successfully auctioned as all that. I told you, it's depressing. Gorgeous. Magnificent. But it doesn't have the verve of your earlier books, the sex appeal, if you want to call it that."

"If we don't auction, what's the alternative?"

"For this book, and this book only, stick with Diadem."

"*What?*" The word exploded.

I spoke rapidly, warding off his attack. "Diadem will pay enough. I told you before: lose you and they're lost. And this time there *is* an argument to stay with their sales force. They'd only have to say it was the new Meredith, no explanations of why you switched houses—no explanations of the *book*—needed." I swallowed. "It's best for the novel, Eric. It's what I think you should do."

I watched his face darken, a severe storm. Yet he said nothing, simply sat and stared at me, his pose casual, though I could detect a tremor in his cheek, and there were wrinkles in the cloth of the couch where his hand clutched it.

"I understand Arthur Collins was fired from Diadem years ago," he said, his voice saccharine.

"He was."

His stare hardened but his tone was still sweet. "My remaining with the house wouldn't mean his return, would it?"

"What difference," I asked, my face growing hot. "You wouldn't have to—"

I could see him control himself—the effort was palpable. "It's a dead subject. The man betrayed me. *Keep him away from me!*"

"His mother's sick."

He looked at me in horror. "Collusion," he said. "You're working for him, not for me. The two of you have cooked this up together."

"She's *sick*," I went on idiotically, determined to finish, dimly realizing that in some sense he was right: I was not representing his interests. "Arthur's had to put her in a nursing home. They've run out of money. Arthur'll have to move her to one of those horror places."

He had risen, and now walked stiff-legged toward me. I flinched when I saw his glazed eyes, but he walked past me to the inside door, then left the room.

"Where are you going?" I called after him. He did not answer. I waited for him, not knowing what to expect. He returned in less than a minute, carrying a check, and stood looming over me, giving me a glimpse of what David saw routinely. He dropped the check in my lap and walked toward the door. There he stopped. "Get out."

I looked at the check. It was for a hundred dollars, made out to Arthur. His disdain filled the room like an odor. Appalled, I stood, revulsion washing through me. I ripped up the check. "You are the cruelest, most evil—"

"I said get out!" He was screaming.

"I don't give a fuck if you're fifty kinds of genius. You're the most disgusting, insensitive, depraved human being I've ever met!"

He ran toward me and grabbed my arm, pulling me toward the door. "I'm going," I yelled. "I can't wait to get out." But he held me in a remorseless grip. "If you ever show up here again," he whispered, "I'll kill you."

He was palsied with fury, and his face was awful. I pulled away from him. "Keep your fucking hands off me," I shouted, "and stick to killing your own family. You seem to be doing a good job at that."

I ran toward the front door, half expecting a punch behind the ear, but suddenly I felt so sick I had to stop, fighting down the bile in my chest, and despite myself turned to see what he was doing.

He hadn't moved, but stood in the doorway, back toward me, erect and unmoving like a palace sentry. The sight made me sicker, and I thought I could not leave without vomiting. There was a bathroom, I remembered, and I made a dash for it.

Anne was bent over the sink, tears running down her face, sobbing. She wheeled as she saw me, and let out a little moan. "I heard it all," she said. "Save yourself."

I felt sick no longer. The sight of her was in a mysterious way healing. "What do you mean?"

"I had to go back," she said. "Without him, there is no me. His hold is too strong." The speech came out in bursts; she was breathing as though she had just finished a marathon. "But you. Run. You're free!"

I looked at her, my heart melting with pity, but I merely said, "Good-bye, Anne," and wondered crazily whether I should kiss her.

Then I fled, closing the door behind me, shutting out her pain and her addiction, and by so doing shutting out mine. Willing myself not to run, I walked cautiously down the hallway, and hesitantly opened the front door, expecting to witness some new catastrophe.

There was only sunshine; it made my ordinary car a chariot. My lungs were suffused with freedom. I walked to the door on the driver's side and opened it, trying not to glance back. But my curiosity was too strong, and I unwillingly turned one last time, already sensing what I would discover.

Sure enough, David appeared in an upstairs window—I had the momentary mad feeling that a David would be visible in any window of that house. And even as I turned away, frantic to be with Judy, my salvation and my sanity, I saw him wave farewell.

nineteen

MY OFFICES, OPENED WITH SUCH FANFARE AND drama, were sublet to a jewelry designer. Paul Kieling and Erika Eliasof, my able and ardent assistants, were with deep regret dismissed, taking with them guiltily gaudy letters of recommendation and severance pay of $500 each, all that the once-affluent man-about-the-south-of-France could afford.

I calculated that by not representing *Twilight*, I would lose in excess of $200,000 in the year of its publication—a setback all my other authors, and the income from Eric's past books, could not overcome.

For a week or so after my confrontation with Eric, the pain and realization of loss did not penetrate to any sensitive spot. I was perfectly placid as I negotiated the transfer of the offices, upset but not devastated when I fired Paul and Erika, and so good-natured at home that Judy praised me as a saint to all her friends and treated me with a gratitude that manifested itself in small cheer-up presents and uncanny ardor in our lovemaking.

But ten days after our fight an ominous letter arrived that broke through my defenses and brought on a depression so severe that even simple tasks became chores and the more difficult ones the letter presaged seemed insurmountable.

251

The letter was from the law firm of Samet, Goldman, and Salcedo, and it informed me that I was being sued by Eric Meredith, an author and former client of mine residing in Columbia County, New York State. The charge: willful collusion between Arthur Collins, then an editor of Diadem Press, Matthew White, former owner of Diadem Press, and me to defraud Meredith of his rightful moneys by paying the advance of $500,000 for his third novel, *Flaws in Diamonds*, in such small increments that Meredith was denied substantial interest accruing on the money, interest that was rightfully his. I had further compounded my malfeasances, the letter asserted, by using my professional position to make sure that Meredith remained with Diadem, despite his express wishes that his future books be published elsewhere. The actual monetary loss to Mr. Meredith was easily calculated. The loss due to mental anguish was more difficult to assess. But $2,000,000 would cover it, Mr. Samet and Mr. Meredith were sure. A date was set by which we had to reply. They were looking forward to hearing from us.

The letter hit me hard. It was the most vicious kind of reprisal. In a panic, I hand-carried it to my own lawyer, Bob Frankel. "It's the only thing his lawyer could invent to hurt me with," I told him. "There was nothing else out of the ordinary. And even this is rubbish."

"Did Diadem pay out that slowly?" he asked.

"Sure. They were having cash flow problems. But Eric *welcomed* the slow payout."

"Do you have that in writing?"

"No. He told me on the phone. He said he would use the money for mortgage payments, told me he didn't want large sums of money coming in all at once because of Anne's cocaine habit."

Frankel's eyebrows rose. "He actually said she had a habit?"

"Not then. He called it 'her frivolities.' But it was obvious what he meant." I stared at him. "Does he have a chance of winning?"

Frankel sighed. "Not much, but some. You'll have to fight it. At the least, he can make life hot for you."

✻

"Hot in what way?" Judy asked that night, when I told her what had happened.

"The publicity would kill me. All he'd have to do is leak the story to *Publishers Weekly*, and I wouldn't see another client for years."

She began to cry. "That shit!" she said. "That monster. Oh God, Tony, he *can* destroy you. He wants to. How far will he go?"

I held her, and tried to will away her tears. "I'm scared," I said.

✻

I reached my low point at the farewell party for Paul and Erika, held in our offices—the last day they would be in my name—and attended only by the two honored guests, and by Judy and me. When Paul and Erika departed, arm in arm and champagne-gay, Judy and I were left alone among the detritus, all my valuable papers having been picked up that afternoon and moved to our home. Just where we would put the baby (it was typical of us that Judy wanted to know its sex before birth, but I forbade it on the ground that I *liked* suspense) was a question we had not settled. For the first month, at least, we would place the crib in our bedroom and use the living room as my office.

The sight of the Silver & Associates offices was particularly depressing. Torn cardboard boxes containing unneeded books, rejection letters from years back, old newspaper reviews, and papers scribbled on by my hand, but meaningless now, littered the floor. Blotters removed, the desks looked naked and forlorn, their impersonality a bleak comment on the enthusiasm with which we had covered them in manuscripts and personal artifacts.

I wandered into my own office and stared out the window into a New York twilight. The buildings around me were lit and still bustling, and I envied even the secretaries—they had their professional domiciles, while I was homeless. Not only homeless, I reflected miserably. There was a good chance I would have to find a new profession.

Judy came up behind me, put her arms around my stomach, and nestled her head against my back. "It was nice while it lasted," she said.

"It *hurts*," I said.

❊

Six weeks later, I got an amazing letter from Eric:

Dear Tony:

First off, let me tell you I'm dropping the lawsuit. It was an act of anger, not reason.

Yes, yes I was wrong. You had every right in the world to intercede for Arthur, and it was despicable of me to have so cavalierly dismissed your plea—to say nothing of yourself! And then to have attacked you as I did, in your work, was indefensible.

For weeks after I've finished a book, I'm in a terrible condition—you above all should know that—and my only excuse for my behavior is that I was so self-involved, so selfish and introverted, that I did not then realize you came in friendship on an act of friendship, and that a friendly response was mandatory.

My response, I must tell you now, was "no" then and it is "no" today. I simply cannot work again with Arthur—irrational as my attitude toward him might have been, our relationship would inevitably have overtones to it that transcend the clearest consideration of my writing. I need a neuter for an editor, a professional sounding board, and nothing more. In fact, I have promised myself I shall not meet the new editor who will be handling my books, for fear I will become friendly with him. So forgive me: I cannot work with Arthur again. But this does not gainsay the fact that you were right to ask on his behalf, and I had every right to say no.

Yet while I cannot have an editor for a friend, I *can* have a friend as an agent—

Felicitous phrase, that!

and so please try to forget the events of two months ago and agree to represent me once more. You have done a good job for me, Tony. You have made me rich and world-famous (although I am not so modest that I do not think my books had something to do with it). Besides, we are a team—hail, hail, Los Angeles— and my good daddy told me it is a mistake to break up a team when it's on a roll.

To sum up, this letter is to ask you (a) to return as my agent and (b) to forgive me for my perhaps excusable (but only because I am a "creative artist") but surely unwarranted behavior. I have not shown *Twilight* to anybody else in publishing—indeed, I have not even shown it to Anne. You would be handling a virgin.

I look forward to hearing from you. Please respond as soon as this reaches you.

Best
Eric

P.S.: Anne has been ill and lies abed. Nothing serious, but debilitating all the same. If she were by my side, I know she would send love to you and Judy.

The letter hit me so hard I had to sit down to read it again. I felt no elation from it, no sense of vindication, no excitement, no joy. Rather, it filled me with gloom.

It was neither Eric's voice nor his manner. So convinced was I that the letter was spurious that I double-checked the postmark— Chatham it was—and even the signature against an earlier letter of Eric's; as far as I could tell, the writing was genuine.

Still, there was something wrong. The sentiments in the letter were lies, the apologies reeked of insincerity. Reading it a third time, I was afraid.

That night, I showed the letter to Judy.

"Oh Tony," she said, with a breathlessness uncharacteristic of her, "how wonderful."

I looked at her quickly. "You're not disappointed? Upset?"

She avoided my eyes. "Why should I be?"

"Because it brings him back into our lives."

"It means you can go on working at what you love," she answered. "It means success for you. It means getting rid of that awful lawsuit."

"But you hate him. Hate what he does to me."

"I think you know what he is now. I think you can divorce the books from the man. Besides, didn't you tell me once he was—let me get the words right, it's important—'the writer you could never be'?" She paused; I could sense her tension. "Isn't that right?"

I considered it. "Please tell me," she went on. "I really have to know."

Her intensity surprised me. "It's right," I said, smiling at her abashedly. "You've helped me grow up. I don't need *Eric* anymore. But his work still thrills me, and I think I can represent it as well now as I ever could. He's the better writer. I'm the better man."

She relaxed. "Ah."

I took the letter back from her. "Why do you think he changed his mind?" I asked.

"He came to his senses. You read the letter."

"But it's so unlike him. He was just as intractable about Arthur, and he didn't change his mind, even though he was as unreasonable then, too."

"You're closer to him than Arthur."

"I don't think that makes a bit of difference," I said. "If he'd betray Anne, dropping me wouldn't bother him for an instant. He's told me so many times." She fidgeted, obviously uncomfortable, and did not answer. "There's something wrong with the tone," I went on. "A conciliatory Eric is a dangerous Eric. Wouldn't you agree?"

"I wonder what's happened to Anne," she said. "Whether she's really sick, I mean, or just temporarily."

"I don't know," I answered, suddenly uncomfortable. "I'll ask him when I speak to him."

She smiled, and I could hear her breathe more normally. "Then you *will* speak to him? You've decided to take him back?"

"I'd be a fool not to," I said. "Why haven't you answered my question?"

Evasion lurked in her eyes. "What question?"

"Whether you believe what's in the letter?"

"Sure I believe it. Why would he have written it otherwise?" I could not decipher her tone. She sounded forced, unnatural, the way she talked when speaking to a client she did not really like.

"I don't think it's from his heart," I said.

Now she looked at me, lines of worry around her eyes. "Then why would he write it?" She picked at an imaginary piece of lint on her sweater, a habit she had when she was nervous.

"Something made him write it," I said.

"What?"

"More accurately, somebody."

The plucking intensified. "Who? Anne?"

"I don't think so. She hasn't that kind of power over him."

"Then who?"

"I haven't the faintest idea."

She stood up, taking a deep breath, staring at me defiantly. "I did," she said.

❈

Years later, as I write this, I cannot swear I had no suspicion; I think I did. And thinking of it makes me realize how brave she was to tell me, and how loving and loyal her act. But then, after her confession, I felt weak and unbearably ashamed. Had I been standing, I would have fallen.

She came toward me, head bowed, a penitent. She took my head in her hands and drew it toward her body, cradling me as though I were a child. "You wanted it so badly," she whispered.

My weakness passed. "Tell me how," I said, fighting for calm.

She shook her head. "There's nothing to tell."

"Everything costs. Eric comes expensive."

She kept her gaze toward the floor. "Not this time."

I took her hand and pulled her down beside me on the couch. She sat unwillingly, resisting, but I forced her and, once she was seated, took her chin in my hand and made her look at me. "I don't believe you," I said.

Anger flared in her tear-filled eyes. "I didn't sleep with him if that's what you're afraid of."

It was exactly what I was afraid of. "Then what?" I asked gently. "You didn't simply call him and ask him to change his mind. He may respect you, Judy, but he doesn't change his mind out of respect. It takes an earthquake."

"No," she admitted. "I didn't just call him."

Now it was I who turned my gaze away. "You'd better tell me."

"I'd rather not. Can't you just be happy he's asked you back?"

"It'll poison things if you don't," I warned. "Every time I see him—or you—or read his books, I'll wonder what happened."

She seemed to agree, for she shrugged and withdrew her hand. "Don't look at me," she said, standing. "Just let me talk to you. Don't interrupt."

"No questions?"

"After I'm finished."

"Agreed."

She paced the room, occasionally brushing her hair from her eyes or plucking at her sweater, but mostly keeping her hands still. Throughout most of her narration she looked at the wall, as though she were reading from a prompter. She kept her voice steady, almost inflectionless, but occasionally despite her efforts it would break like an adolescent boy's.

She started slowly, choosing her words carefully. "I knew how upset you were about Eric. Knew it not only because of what he did to you that day, but because representing him made you happy. It wasn't only because of the money—though God knows I have nothing against the Beaumanière—but because his books fulfilled something in you—"

She shook her head to stop me from speaking. "When I'm finished," she said, and continued.

"He did fulfill something, Tony. Something I couldn't give you and that you haven't found anyplace else. I can't precisely define what it is. Oversimplified, let's call it your artistic soul. You're not a genius, and neither am I, but both of us have ideas and feelings just the way geniuses do, only when we try to express them we're mundane. Eric raised those feelings to art, illuminated them.

"Anyway, in some sense Eric became your spokesman, your personification, if you will, and by representing him you were representing a part of yourself. I don't say you'd *want* to be a genius. Neither would I—good Lord, look what it's done to Eric! But like everybody else, you have yearnings."

Again she silenced me before I could speak. She had thought hard about what she was going to say—had prepared herself for the eventuality of the letter and my questions about it—and was not about to let me detour her. She was deep in her own thoughts and memory, fighting to control the emotion that underlay them.

"Right or wrong, I sensed you wanted him back, but I know you well enough, my darling, to be positive you wouldn't deign to beg, even if you thought it would work." Her breathing grew coarse. "So I decided to approach him myself."

She paused a moment, at the end of a chapter, then hurried on. "It wasn't an easy decision. For one thing, I didn't really know what Eric thought of me. His relationship was with you, mine was with Anne, and I was afraid he'd laugh at my intercession. And I didn't want that, Tony. I'm not a person to dismiss.

"Also, I was afraid that by talking to him I would be hurting your cause rather than helping it. That in time he'd simply have realized how pigheaded he was being and, guilty, come back to you of his own accord without my saying anything. He *is* pig-headed, and I was worried he'd grow more obstinate rather than less, stubborn to the point where all sense would vanish forever."

At last she looked me in the eye, if ever so briefly. "Finally, I couldn't be sure of your reaction. Would you be furious? Embarrassed? Resentful? Grateful? I asked myself what I would have thought if the positions were reversed, and I decided that no matter how momentarily angry I became, in the long run I would realize you did it out of love and out of a desire to do what's best for me—and I hope you know those were my motives, those and no other." She smiled. "When I've finished, you can tell me whether I was right."

She was pacing rapidly now, and her voice was more animated than it had been so far. I sensed an excitement in her I had only felt at times of enormous emotional stress—in our serious premarital fights, for example, or when she was particularly anxious about her parents. It was a contagious excitement. My skin prickled and my own breathing came fast. I felt a mixture of anticipation and terror. I desired her.

She went on, not allowing me to think further. "Having made up my mind, it still took me three days to get up the nerve to call him. He's a pretty terrifying creature, you know. Granted, he's never done anything frightening to *me*, but your stories are convincing enough. Besides, I've read his books."

She stopped briefly, swallowing as though her throat were dry. "I made the call early in the morning, on the principle that you've always told me: the difficult calls don't go away. They hang over you if you put them off. He was astonished to hear from me. Much to my annoyance he picked up the phone himself; I'd have loved to get Anne as a buffer. He assumed I was calling for Anne, but he was perfectly cordial when I told him I wanted to talk to him.

"I had prepared my speech for the phone—I was too scared to meet him face to face—but the friendliness of his voice, the impersonality of his cheerfulness, as though he were talking to a saleslady, made me reconsider. He didn't mention the lawsuit, didn't even ask how you were. I knew that, like it or not, I would have to go see him. If I were to be your true champion, it would have to be in the field."

I knew Eric well enough to have my apprehension increase as she went on. And I knew my Judy, too: fiercely combative when it came to a cause other than her own.

"He didn't ask me what I wanted to talk to him about—it could only have been you. But he did agree to let me come see him (I had no thought of asking him to meet me in New York), and we made a date for the next day.

"I didn't want you to know anything about it, so to be safe I took some money out of my own account and rented a car. It's hard to describe my mood that day. I was scared, but once I started some of the fear wore off, and I took a more philosophical attitude: Eric was a genius, therefore unpredictable. But I, a mere mortal, was simply asking for his help, for help for the person I love most, and this did not seem to me an outrageous thing to do. If he said no, so be it. I would have lost nothing except the cost of humiliation, and I've been humiliated before and survived it. And if he said yes"—here she gave a little laugh—"if he said yes, then I would be repaying the man I love for all the things he's done for me, and all the things that made me love him."

I wanted to rush to embrace her, to say that whatever she did, or whatever happened with Eric, I would love her forever, but she had fallen once more into her narrative.

"So I was quite calm when I reached their house—it's tough to find; did you have trouble the first time?—and I must say I was impressed. You had told me what it looked like, and very accurately too, but even so I was unprepared for how grand it is.

"Our appointment was for eleven, and I was there right on the button, even with the struggle to find the house. I knew David wasn't home, he was in school, but I assumed Anne would be. So I was surprised when the first thing Eric said when he opened the door was, 'Anne isn't home. She had an unbreakable meeting, but she wanted me to give you her love.'

"He was dressed casually, the image of a country squire, tweed jacket and gray flannel slacks, blue shirt open at the collar. I had never before really thought he was handsome, but that day he was —well, at least dashing.

"He led me to the sun porch. What a beautiful room! A decorator's dream. They haven't done much with it, at least I think the flowers are a cliché, but the possibilities are limitless. I remember thinking how sorry I was that no matter how the meeting came out, I would never get to redecorate it. One can't have one's decorator and one's agent in the same family."

"Go on," I broke in impatiently. She was avoiding her story, not telling it. And it worried me that he had taken so much care with his clothes.

"Sorry." She gave me a wan smile, recognizing what she was doing. "He had coffee perking already on the stove, for when I accepted his offer of a cup, he went to get it and returned almost immediately. We sat side by side on the couch, he at one end and I on the other, all very prim. I might have been an interviewer for the Gallup Poll.

" 'I want you to reconsider what you've done to Tony,' I told him right off. Despite his cordialty, I was suddenly uncomfortable and wanted to get the meeting over with as quickly as possible. 'You're punishing him for an act of friendship.'

"I thought it was a pretty good line—it had popped into my head when he was leading me through the house—but it didn't do much for him. He simply shook his head and said, without rancor, 'But it wasn't friendship toward me. Quite the opposite.'

" 'I think he misinterpreted the seriousness of your feelings about Arthur,' I said. 'And just because he's Arthur's friend doesn't mean he isn't yours, too.'

"He smiled. Condescension oozed from every pore. I wanted to slap him. 'But my dear,' he said, 'I don't want a friend for a literary agent, I want an agent. Someone who will look after my needs, take my side exclusively. And Tony didn't do that, did he? Indeed, he and Arthur ganged up against me.'

"I did what I swore I wouldn't do: I got mad. 'Tony's done an incredible amount for you,' I said.

" 'He did,' Eric acknowledged, with emphasis on the past tense. 'In the beginning he put me with the right house, got me a good deal of money.'

" 'He did more than that,' I reminded him. 'He stuck by you in California, he lied to Anne for you, he went along with your betrayal of Arthur, though it nearly destroyed him to do it, he—'

" 'More coffee?' he interrupted.

"I got madder. 'Answer me!' I shouted.

"He moved closer to me and took my hand. 'You love him very much,' he said. 'I admire that. You've got spunk, Judy.'

"I yanked my hand away. 'We're talking about Tony.'

"He stayed calm. Indeed, the angrier I got the calmer he became. But his words were poison. 'But you see,' he said, 'I don't need him anymore. I need an accountant to help me, not my "friends" Arthur and Tony. They're in league against me. Tony's representing Arthur. What kind of an agent is that?'

"My God, I hated him. 'You know he's acted honorably,' I said. 'Always has and always will. All he did was fight for his friend.'

" 'Even if that's true,' he said, 'and I don't for a second believe you, then at best Tony's outlived his usefulness.'

" 'Is that the way you are?' I asked. 'When a friend's no longer useful, that's the end of him?'

" 'If he's interfering with my writing, yes,' he answered. 'And Tony was, with his reproaches and his constant demands on Arthur's behalf.'

"I let that idiocy pass. 'What about Anne?' I said. 'What about someone you love?'

" 'I'm thinking of making Anne my new agent,' he told me.

"I was shocked into silence. Then the ridiculousness of it hit me and I laughed, despite the tension and the anxiety, despite his being so horrible. 'What can she possibly know about being an agent?' I asked.

" 'She'll have to learn,' he said. 'It'll give her something positive to do.' I thought of her passion for ceramics, her skill at it, and I wondered why that wasn't 'doing' something. But of course it was something of hers, and for him that meant nothing.

" 'I'll direct her at first,' he went on. 'Teach her the ropes.' He chuckled, a nauseating sound. 'I guess I owe my expertise to Tony. But she's smart and she'll be able to branch out on her own. It'll mean trips to Europe for her, trips to Hollywood.' He actually winked at me, a traveling salesman sharing a good one. 'Besides, it'll keep the ten percent in the family.' "

She did a remarkable imitation. I could see them on the sun porch, hear Eric's voice, feel his arrogance.

"I stood up, appalled, unable to listen any longer. He asked me where I was going and I told him, 'Home.' He offered more coffee, I refused. And so he got up too, to show me out, I assumed, but we both stood without moving, as though there were something more to say. I don't know what it was, Tony, but I *couldn't* leave; there was a force in the room, and we both felt it.

" 'I haven't told Anne yet,' he said.

"I asked him what if she refused.

" 'She won't.' There was no question in his mind or in mine.

" 'So you'll pick the time and place to tell her?' I said, feeling my anger break the tension. 'Here on the patio? An intimate bistro? In bed? When she has a headache?'

"He looked at me with great curiosity, as though unable to explain my anger or my sarcasm. 'I'll tell her when the right time comes,' he said gently, but the tone of his voice did nothing to make me less angry.

"I turned toward the door. 'Then there's nothing I can do that will make you change your mind?'

"I expected a flat 'No,' but to my amazement he hesitated, started to speak, then said nothing but instead came to stand beside me at the door. He stood as close to me as a person could without touching. I felt suddenly ungainly, as though I were three times more pregnant than I am. Nevertheless, I could sense the electricity in his body.

" 'There's one thing,' he said at last.

" 'Tell me!' I cried, at that instant knowing what it was, but too committed now to stop him.

"He took my hand and moved a step back in an almost graceful motion, as though he were dancing. Now I could see his eyes. They glittered. I've never felt so frightened in my life.

"His voice was harsh with lust. 'Fuck me,' he commanded. 'We have time before Anne gets back!' "

❧

Sometimes great shocks numb the system, but in this case it did not happen to me. There was a buzzing in my brain I could actually hear. I felt splintered, like an autistic child I had once seen in a film whose various parts seemed to pull his body simultaneously in different directions. I had read Eric's letter. Despite Judy's denials, he would not have written it if she had not done what he wanted.

"Go on," I said, even those words difficult to utter.

My demand was superfluous. She would have finished if there had been nobody else in the room.

"He must have seen my horror, my shock at the brutality of his request, for he immediately began to woo me. He told me he had always found me attractive, not just physically, but in brain and spirit. Just my being there was proof—how many women would have had the courage to face him? How many would fight so for their husbands?

"The words meant nothing. I remembered Kitty and Constance, and your story of the scene on the lawn, and Anne's grief in the hotel—but oh, Tony, I didn't leave. *I could not leave!*"

At last she started to cry. I went to her and put my arms around her. As though one, we moved to the couch and sat together on it.

She nestled her head in my shoulder; I could feel her wet tears through my shirt.

"Tell me the rest," I said softly.

She went on unhesitatingly. " 'Look at me,' I said to Eric. 'I'm pregnant.'

"He gave his beastly chuckle and made a joke so offensive I could have torn out his eyes. 'Good,' he said. 'At least you'll know whose child it is.' "

She shuddered and I held her tightly, kissing her hair and her forehead, but when I tried to turn her face toward mine, she resisted.

"He must have realized how awful he had been, for again he started soothing me with words. Now he talked of how beautiful I was, how pregnancy had made me more beautiful still. Then he began to talk about Anne—how inadequate she now seemed to him, how much he respected her as a woman, but how little as a lover—bullshit, Tony, I assure you, the commonest kind of line."

"Why didn't you just tell him to go screw himself?" I asked.

"Because I was there for a reason. I found myself thinking that if I did go to bed with him, it would be no worse than a gynecological examination, a probing, and that in effect he was right: it was your child, and nothing could change that. I *knew* that nothing he could do would hurt the child. One moment's violence, and I'd have killed him.

"So you slept with him?"

"No"—my heart rejoiced!—"not quite. I didn't lie to you before." She touched me briefly with a trembling hand, then stood and resumed her walking. "I told him firmly that if I did agree, if I let him make love to me—for no power on earth would allow me to make love to him—that it was not because I felt anything for him, but because I loved you, was doing it only for you, and that he would have to guarantee he would take you back. I told him too that if I thought he was hurting the baby, I would make him stop. He told me it was a lovely speech, that he expected no less from me, and that if those were the rules he would abide by them. I couldn't tell if he believed me, or thought he could change my mind, or if his ego could *let* him believe, but he did agree, and at that time—as now—I believed him. So the unwritten contract was drawn, a nineteen eighties contract, not one out of *Measure for Measure*. And all I had to do to bring it into effect, to bring you and yes, me, too, those things we love so dearly, was to give him a few minutes of my time and to lend him ever so briefly a body already owned by you, which could belong to no other man for as long as I lived."

I have never loved her so much, yet I was frozen, could not move to comfort her.

"He took my hand and led me upstairs. We walked past a closed door—his study, from your description—and into the bedroom which was neat and blue-and-white. I was far too rattled to notice much more. He was kissing my neck and groping at my buttons."

"I don't want the details," I told her, both wanting them and not.

She smiled. "There are no more details. And there's a surprise coming, a happy surprise.

"I pushed him away, repeating to myself over and over that this was a medical act, not a sexual one. I told him it would be easier if I took care of the buttons myself, and he agreed, for he began working on his own shirt, not mine. I sat on the side of the bed, my back to him, and took off my blouse. I noticed how round my belly was, and thought I was doing this for the baby, too, for both of my darlings, and it didn't seem so bad. I remember being amazed at my lack of embarrassment. I had just reached back to unsnap my bra, so lowering my head still further, when I caught a movement out of the side of my eye—someone was at the door!"

Her body gave a little jerk as she said it; she was reliving the shock. "It was Anne! Staring at us. I screamed and tried desperately to cover myself with the blouse—and then and only then, so help me, Tony, did I feel ashamed.

"I tried to speak. No words came out. Then I looked at Eric, wanting even his help. He was smiling—grinning, really—and he looked hard at Anne without anything like embarrassment, and said, 'Ah, you're home. Come join us.' "

She stood still, facing me, her expression a mixture of shame and anger. I thought I detected, too, a hint of amusement, as though she were mocking herself, a participant in a farce.

"I couldn't tell if Anne was drugged or defeated. Surely she had no will left of her own. She was looking at Eric like a sleepwalker, her face registering nothing. 'Come on,' Eric cried. Anne took a step forward and put a hand on her throat, as though she, too, would unbutton her shirt.

"Well, that tore it. I gave another scream, and I fled from the room. I don't believe either of them tried to stop me, but I didn't look back to find out. How I got down the steps without killing myself I don't know—I was operating on shame, fury, self-loathing, disgust. They were enough to numb my brain until I was in the car and halfway down the Taconic to New York."

Laughter took over. She must have been relieved that she'd told me—there, she had admitted all, and nothing had happened! That, combined with her own knowledge that nothing *had* happened, made her begin to giggle. She sat down next to me, tension erased from the corners of her eyes.

"You know the gas station just before the Taconic narrows at the Danbury turnoff?" she asked. I nodded. "Well, I pulled in there, drove to the end of the station, and quietly but surely had hysterics. If somebody had seen me, he'd have had me committed.

"I must have laughed for five minutes, picturing it all again and again, then suddenly I stopped and I felt perfectly at peace. I thought to myself, 'Well, I tried; you can't say I haven't given it my best shot,' and utterly composed I drove home. I didn't even have to put on much of an act that night. You never knew that anything extraordinary had happened. I made you make love with me—you weren't really in the mood—but I've done that before, and obviously you didn't think I was acting strangely."

Relaxed, herself again, though obviously still affected by her own story, she sat serenely by me on the couch. "There's nothing more to tell you," she said. "The transgression of an American housewife. You can despise me for it—frankly, I don't know how I'd feel if you interfered with my life so profoundly without telling me about it. Or you can just laugh at me for being an idiot." She paused to hug me. "All I ask," she went on, "is that you remember one thing. What I did I did out of love, for no other reason than love."

She loosened her hold, but I pressed her against me. My throat too constricted to speak, I returned her love, as passionately as she had given it, through the strength of my embrace. I *willed* her to know. I think she did.

❖

We've talked little about the episode since. But late that night, after I had spent the day thinking about myself as child, agent, lover, husband, man; and after I had decided what to do about Eric, I briefly brought the matter up.

"I know why he wrote the letter," I told Judy.

She nodded. "I think I do, too."

"Because he didn't have you," I said, "and wants you still."

She did not disagree.

twenty

November 19

Dear Eric:

It has taken me over a week to answer your letter because the day I received it I showed it to Judy, and she told me what happened when she came to visit you. I suppose it should astonish me that you would suppose she would *not* tell me, but it doesn't. Indeed, it's the only genuine fact surrounding the letter and its circumstances.

After Judy told me I was so angry I almost came to Chatham to kill you. Literally. But it is typical of me not to act hastily, and by now my anger is cooled to a point where I can at least write to you. Now I'm merely repelled and, in many ways, sorry for you.

You said you would drop the suit. Good. If you institute it again, I have your letter admitting it was unreasonable.

You asked if I would return as your agent. The answer is a categorical "no"—not if you were the last writer alive, and I was starving to death.

You asked, too, that I forgive you for your behavior toward Arthur. Once again the answer is "no," and, further, I do not forgive your behavior toward Judy, toward me, and most of all toward Anne and David. You act toward all of us out of selfishness and greed, without the slightest regard for the fact that we are

270

human beings—in Judy's and my case, thank God, independent ones.

I do not hate you. In you somewhere is the capacity for understanding and the ability to love. These elements are in your books —all but *Twilight*, and even in that there is understanding, if only of the dark.

The immense pity is that you put your humanity only into words. This is not, in my view, where humanity belongs.

This is the last time we will communicate. I hope, genuinely, that your books continue to be successful, that you mature still further as a writer, and that you win the Nobel Prize. I suspect you will.

But I will never again represent you, and I pray to God you will never again represent me.

Tony

23

Interestingly enough, the quantity of business, though by no means the quality, picked up for me. Everybody knew the reason I had been forced to close my offices, and I acquired two authors as clients who told me they would not have come if I had still represented Eric, figuring I would be devoting almost all my time to him. And almost, it seemed, out of sympathy, a few editor friends bought books from me they were undecided about.

Actually, I was feeling pretty proud of myself. There is satisfaction in knowing you've done the right thing, and the cleansing effect of my letter to Eric cheered me enormously.

Still, I felt a void, missing not only the prospect of money a new Meredith novel would bring, and not only Eric's proximity, which had so fascinated and stimulated me in the early days, but most of all the pleasure in the fact that I was associated with Eric's work, and through that association at least a peripheral part of the most important American writing of the decade.

True, it was Eric's talent and Eric's fame; all I had was the luck to have read and liked a manuscript and the privilege of taking charge of an author's business affairs. Nevertheless, I hated it when I could not tell strangers, asking me what I did, that I represented Eric Meredith. I missed the awe in their eyes. And I wondered if he had found a new agent, and if it was anyone I knew.

The pain became particularly intense when I read in *Publishers Weekly* that *Twilight* had been bought by Knopf for a million dollars, a price "negotiated by Anne Meredith, the author's wife, acting as his agent." (So he had done what he had told Judy he would. I could hardly believe it!) Knopf, the piece assured us, felt that this was Meredith's finest work to date, marking "new depths of profundity and eroticism for a man indisputably this country's most important writer."

It hurt me badly that none of my friends had told me about the sale (such information is available long before it is printed in *Publishers Weekly*). They were obviously shielding me out of kindness, but I resented their solicitude. I was a grown man and could take the bad news. Eric was a person from my past. I felt like somebody at the end of a love affair, when nobody brings up the name of the recently departed. It took Judy to reassure me that I was not a pariah. Her own pride in what I had done was sufficient balm.

About Eric himself I heard nothing more, until one day I got a call from Arthur, who had finally managed to get a job as senior editor (taking a substantial cut in salary, but *working*) with Locksley Books, a small press specializing in beautifully designed but esoteric works of fiction. I had tried to sell him a number of things; he had rejected them as "too mainstream." But we remained friends and his spirits had appreciably improved.

He had called to ask me for a copy of a book whose subject interested him, which one of my authors had written for a different publisher. It wasn't until some time into the conversation that he finally said, "I'm reluctant to bring up Eric."

"Why?" I asked, the catch in my voice belying my attempted casualness.

"Because I know you and I know me, and when he left me I was hurt to the core, as you must be."

We had discussed this before. "The pain's worn off," I told him.

"As it did for me. But the name still hurts when I hear it."

"Tell me what's happened," I said.

"Nothing to him directly. But David—"

"Go on."

"David's been institutionalized." The words were flat, a news broadcast. But they sent a shiver through me.

"Why?"

"Seems he tried to kill a classmate."

Again. Obviously, Arthur did not know about the first attempt. "How awful," I said, amazed that the shiver was all I felt. "Poor Anne."

"She's evidently broken up over it. Really destroyed."

"I'm not surprised. It would be horrible enough even in a more stable family. But with Eric for support—"

Arthur chuckled. "Yeah."

"How did you find out about it?" I asked.

"Connie Ferris told me about it. She's copy-editing *Twilight* for Knopf. He canceled a meeting with her yesterday."

"You mean David's more important than this book?"

Another chuckle. "The meeting's been rescheduled for Friday. And you shouldn't be bitter."

"Bitter? *Moi?*"

"So the pain *has* worn off, has it?" Arthur asked, irony dripping. "I'm glad to hear it."

"Fuck you," I said, laughing.

Judy's concern, when I told her that night, was, not unexpectedly, Anne. "A hospital's best for David," she told me. "They can do remarkable things with disturbed kids, especially ones where the families can afford one-on-one care. As long as they keep him away from his parents, he stands a chance." She sighed. "But think of Anne living alone with Eric. Think of her guilt. Who's to help her?"

"Not you," I said. "The only thing you could possibly do for her—that anybody can do for her—is get her out of that house, away from Eric. Well, she tried it herself once and went back. And they need each other now. He's all she has, with David away. She wouldn't leave Eric if we sent in the marines. Besides, even if she wanted to go, how could you face her, after what happened?"

She gravely bit at a thumbnail. "She'll die if she stays with him. Leaving's her only chance."

"You're not her savior," I reminded her.

Three days later, at a little before six in the morning, the phone rang. Since it sits on Judy's night table, she answered it, her voice dull with sleep, then sat up abruptly. The movement more than the sound shocked me awake.

"Yes of course he's here," Judy said. "I'm sure he'll speak to you." She covered the mouthpiece with her hand, mouthed the name, "Eric," and handed me the phone.

"Eric!" I said, utterly at a loss.

His voice was sepulchral; I could barely hear it. "Are you my friend?"

"*What?*"

"Are you? I need a friend."

Fury and shame—all of the past—vanished in the present. "Yes," I said, "What's happened?"

"Anne's dead. She killed herself."

"Oh Eric, no!" I cried. "Killed herself?" I looked at Judy. She had gotten out of bed and was quickly dressing. "How?"

"Can't talk," he said. "In shock. Can you help?"

I kept my voice brisk, businesslike. "What do you want us to do?"

There was a pause, then a little strangled cry, then a wail. "*Be with me!*"

From my bureau, Judy threw me underwear, socks, a shirt. "We're on our way," I assured him.

☯

It was too early for prowling traffic cops, so we drove the trip in less than two hours. Neither of us said much in the car; I found in discussing it later we were both trying to reconcile his responsibility for her death with the pity for them both the call engendered.

I had expected to see ambulances and police cars at the house, but only the Merediths' cars, forlorn in the morning mist, stood in the driveway. He must have been waiting for us by a window, for the door opened before we reached it, and he stepped out into the chill morning air to greet us.

He looked wasted. He wore a pair of faded blue jeans and a T-shirt; he was unshaven and uncombed, and his eyes, hidden behind sunglasses, but visible in profile, were red, as though he had been crying or drinking or both. His flesh tone was gray, and the jowl lines in his neck shone with moisture—I had the feeling it would be viscous, like glue.

He shuffled rather than walked toward us, his body grown fat and heavy, and his hand was wet when I shook it. If he was surprised at seeing Judy, he gave no indication of it, but rather shook her hand, too, as formally as if they had never met, and he gave a pathetic little bow.

"I've put on some coffee," he said, his voice weak, like a dying man's, "only I don't think I can control myself enough to pour it."

"I'll get it," Judy said. "But first I want to see Anne."

"There's no need," he said quickly.

"Where—?" I started.

He knew what I meant. "In the bedroom. I haven't touched her since I woke up this morning to find her—" He broke off and answered my unasked question. "She's dead all right. If you saw her, you'd know. She's dead. I'm sure of it."

He stood still, not looking at me, barely even blinking.

"You've called a doctor? The police?"

He shook his head. "I couldn't."

I stared at him. "But you called me."

"You're my friend," he said dully.

"But it's been *hours!*" Judy exclaimed. "You mean to tell me you've been alone with her all this time and done nothing?"

"I could only call a friend," he said, his head bowed. Suddenly he began to sob. " 'Cause the next call, I knew—you see, the next call would have to be to David."

My throat constricted; I could say nothing. Instead, I took his arm and turned him toward the door, then helped him into the hall. I thought of the time, many years ago, when my father had suffered a stroke and I had visited him in the hospital. He walked with that shuffling step, unable to move unless I led him. What right had Eric? I thought, and almost let go of his arm. But then I was able to act more rationally; with Eric leaning on me, we walked ahead, Judy leaving us to get the coffee.

And so for the third time I entered the sun porch. Rather than lifting, the mist had deepened in the few minutes we stood by the door, and now was so dense I could not see the maple.

With a slight gesture, Eric shook free of my hand and walked unsteadily to the bar. "I know it's morning," he said, "but I need a drink. Join me?"

I shook my head. "Just coffee." He poured himself a straight Scotch, without ice, his back to me. I waited until he turned before I said, "The first order of business is to call a doctor. The second is to call the police. Do you want to make the calls, or should I?"

He slumped into a chair, his hand trembling so violently that the drink spilled though it did not fill half the glass. "You, please, but not quite yet. I couldn't face a stranger yet."

"It's the law," I said, keeping my voice unemotional. "You'll get yourself into a heap of trouble if you don't call."

For the first time, he was animated. "Do you think I give a shit?" he asked, taking off his sunglasses and glaring at me.

I shrugged; he was right. Judy came in with the coffee and poured us each a cup. Eric put his aside, busy with the Scotch. I took an immediate sip, desperate to do *something*, and managed only to scald my tongue and then my hand when I hastily pulled the cup from my mouth. Judy sat beside me on the couch, looking at Eric noncommittally. The silence was as palpable as the fog.

Something prompted Eric to start talking—the duration of the silence, perhaps, or the gradual easing of his shock. But all at once words tumbled from him, slowly at first and then faster, as though they had been encased in slightly torn plastic, the rent made wider by the force of the flow.

"We had no fight, no argument. Last night we watched television, the PBS Shakespeare series, *Julius Caesar*. She seemed to enjoy it, but I was restless—Shakespeare makes me restless—and so I watched only a little bit and then went to the study to do some work. Eventually she shut off the set—she was watching in the bedroom with the door open, and I could hear the white sound of voices—but I kept right on going. I have an idea for a new novel, Tony! An idea which— Usually, Anne says good night—said good night—but last night she didn't, or maybe she did. I was so engrossed in the new book I wouldn't have noticed one way or the other.

"Anyway, at around two o'clock I got to sleep, and I undressed in the study so as not to wake Anne. I sleep in my underwear, so I simply washed and brushed my teeth, then crept into bed without disturbing her. It was all perfectly natural. I must have gone to sleep like that a thousand times. But the point was, I didn't turn on the light. *I didn't turn on the light!*" He sobbed once, but because he made an effort to stifle it, it came out an embarrassing hiccup, a weirdly touching sound. "If I had, I might have saved her."

He stopped, waiting for confirmation, but neither of us spoke. I thought, he killed her; he couldn't have saved her; sooner or later she would have died.

When he was convinced we weren't going to speak, he went on.

"When I'm working on a book, particularly at the beginning, three hours is just about all the sleep I need. So I wasn't surprised when I woke up at five—I was grateful, really, wanting to get back to work.

"But you know, there are times when, though everything seems normal, you *sense* there's something wrong? Well, I sensed it this morning, there in the pitch dark, even with my mind filled with sentences. There was something wrong. Yes. It took me a moment, but it came to me: Anne was lying far too peacefully; Anne was far too still. My God, Tony, I couldn't hear her breathing!"

He managed to down his Scotch in a swallow and quickly rose to pour himself another. I could see he was sweating, though I myself was shivering cold. "I turned on the light and looked at her. She was gray, her skin was pale gray, and her closed eyelids were almost black. I said her name, screamed it, already knowing she was dead, and then I looked down and saw the empty pill bottle by the side of the bed, and I knew what had happened. I touched her, shook her. God pity me, she was already cold. I lay on top of her trying to warm her, trying to breathe air into her mouth, but I couldn't even pry her teeth apart."

The Scotch must have helped, for his step was steadier as he returned to his chair, and when he went on, his voice was stronger. "I blanked out then. Really. I can't tell you what I did in the next half hour, whether I moved about the house or stayed in the room with her body. I don't remember, for instance, putting on these clothes. The next thing I knew was that I was opening the door to my study—I keep it locked, you know, so I had taken out my key —exactly as if it were a normal workday. The sight of the desk and the typewriter and the pile of paper seemed appalling, as though they constituted some physical threat. And only then did I think about Anne—I had literally erased her from my brain— and so I went to call you."

He sat back in his chair, breathing noisily, watching us with wary eyes.

"She hadn't seemed depressed?" Judy asked.

He waved a hand. "No, I didn't say that. She's been depressed since David went away. It's just that she didn't seem worse last night than any other."

"Did she leave a note? Any indication of why she did it?"

He shook his head. "No, unless I haven't come across it yet." He paused. "Funny, I hadn't thought of a note."

"Maybe her death was an accident," I said.

Again he shook his head. "That bottle was full the night before last. I saw it and asked her about it. She laughed and said she'd been having trouble sleeping again and so the doctor had phoned a refill prescription to the drugstore." He grimaced. "She said she had used up the last prescription. I believed it."

"Did she have trouble sleeping?" Judy asked.

"Oh, absolutely." He leaned forward confidentially. "You know, she really did beat her addiction. She didn't touch cocaine from the moment she came back from the Manchester. But the effort was tremendous; my God, what it cost her! She was jumpy, fidgety, couldn't stop moving. Then, at other times, her depressions got so bad she couldn't get out of bed. She was as obsessed by fighting her need as she was when getting coke was the most important thing in her life."

"I often wondered," Judy said, "how you persuaded her to come back to you. I thought you had bribed her with cocaine."

"I made her realize how much I needed her," he said simply. "How much she needed me. For all our quarrels, for all my inexcusable sins, we were as one." He shook his head. "I don't know how I can live without her."

His agony moved me deeply. He was not pretending now; despair governed him.

But Judy seemed untouched. "You'll manage." Her voice was low but firm. "Since you lived with her, surely her suicide can't be a complete surprise."

"I told you. She was depressed. But no more so yesterday than—"

"You brought her back to kill her," Judy said.

I could see him tense. "What do you mean by that?"

She didn't answer. "Tell me about David. He must have known there was something radically wrong with his mother."

"I can't speak to that."

For the first time, Judy's voice rose. "Well, if you can't, who can? You're his *father*!"

He put his hands over his ears and bowed his head. "An awful one."

Judy was having none of it. "Isn't it a little late for contrition? He's in the hospital because of you. Anne's dead because of you."

His head snapped up as though jolted with electricity. "That's wild," he said, his voice low, "wild and unfair. You're getting revenge because I made a pass at you."

She was ice. "Hardly a pass. A deal." She looked at me and smiled. "As you know, my business manager and I conferred and decided to turn you down." But the memory made her anger rise again. She turned back to him. "I'm not accusing you of murder. I'm accusing you of blindness, callousness, insensitivity, and a lack of empathy so colossal it drove your son mad and your wife to suicide."

My stomach twisted. He got out of his chair, his face darker and his hands, fists. "Bitch!" he screamed. "Cunt." But when I stood, my fists raised, to defend her, he sank back into his chair and once more cradled his face in his hands.

"I didn't want to lose her," he said. "She was my life."

Judy was implacable. "Your books were."

"Both," he said, "but she more than anything." He gave Judy a look of longing and what I swear was love, stood again, and stalked to the door. Then he turned and faced us both. "Wait. I'll prove it to you."

He disappeared and we heard him run up the stairs.

I took Judy's hand; it was trembling. We waited silently.

He was back in a few moments, carrying a short manuscript which he thrust into my hands. "Read the first page," he commanded. "What does it say?"

It was a title page. "'*Colossus*,'" I read, "'a novel by Eric Meredith.'"

He paced in his excitement. "Go on. Turn the page."

I complied. "'Chapter one.'"

I was about to read the text itself, but he interrupted. "Then you know what it is?"

"Of course. The start of a new novel."

"By whom?"

I couldn't fathom him. "You."

"You believe it's mine?"

"It has your name on it. And I recognize the typewriter."

He gave me a conspirator's grin. "It could be a forgery."

"It could," I said, "but it isn't."

"Right!" he exclaimed, slamming fist into palm and walking to a brass wastebasket, the contents of which—magazine wrappers, a newspaper, an empty liquor bottle—he dumped on the floor.

I glanced at Judy. She was watching Eric in horror, mouth slightly open with amazement.

"For my next act," he said, "I shall make a masterpiece disappear." Kneeling, he put the manuscript—fifty or sixty pages—into the basket, took a lighter from his jeans pocket, and set the paper ablaze.

"Good God!" I said, and Judy screamed, "Stop!" and he seemed oblivious to us both. Face flushed from the heat and his exertions, he stood and watched the book burn. He simply stood and watched, letting tears roll unchecked down his face. No one said a word until the flames had gone out and only smoke emerged from the basket, then Eric turned to us.

"If David can do it, so can I. As God is my witness," he said, "I'll never write a word again."

I believed him then.

"All this morning, sitting by her side, numb as I was and unconscious, the idea must have been growing. Yes, it's too late to save Anne, but David—there's David!" His eyes shone with an evangelist's zeal. "Thanks to you, Tony, I'm secure for the rest of my life. All I could write about now are horrors, but more than that, I can see now—I see it as clearly as a man can see—that my writing doesn't matter. David does." Eyes filling again, he faced Judy. "God pity me, you're right! I did kill her, as surely as if I'd slit her throat. And drove David mad." He paused for a moment, his gaze now on me. "And betrayed my friends, if only by not knowing who they are."

He was pleading now, for sympathy surely, but for something more; for acceptance, I thought, as a human being.

"I need writing," he said, "need it the way Anne needed cocaine. I'm addicted. But addictions can be cured—Anne could have been cured, was close to being cured, if I had watched and listened—supposedly when the user hits rock bottom. Well, that's where I am, and it's wet and it's cold, and it hurts now and it will hurt ten times worse tomorrow when the shock's worn off. But tomorrow I'll know more surely than I know now that my life must be David's. I've taken his mother's, I've almost taken his, but at least I can try to give it back to him."

There was no questioning his sincerity or his sorrow. He was not acting now, there was nothing here for effect. Judy, too, must have felt it, for she reached out to take my hand in lieu of his.

"What I'll need," Eric went on, "is friends. You, Tony. Most of all, you. I can't get through this alone." He gave me a look of such yearning and vulnerability that I felt it in my heart.

"You wouldn't be my agent anymore," he said, breathing quickly, his eyes never leaving my face. "There would be no need for a business relationship. I've stopped writing. But I need somebody to talk to, to see me through the bad patches. And I need somebody to have fun with when the bad times are gone." He paused, choosing his words meticulously. "Most of all, I need somebody besides David who can teach me how to give."

He tried to smile, but failed. "What do you say?" he asked me.

The question had been building throughout the meeting, and

WORKS OF GENIUS   283

for far longer than that. I remembered my own need for his friendship, and how he treated me and Judy and Anne. I remembered
the power of his written words and what they revealed of his soul.
I had thought about "what I would say," and my answer was
prepared.

Eric stood up and took a step toward me. I could feel Judy tense
on the couch beside me.

"No."

Eric staggered back; he had run full-tilt into a wall. Judy's sigh
was one of gratitude.

"Judy's right. You'll never give up writing," I said. "I don't
think you *should*. I don't think you'd save David even if you devoted full time to him. It's up to doctors now, not you. And you've
destroyed Anne, so there's no one left for you to harm. You'll
survive by writing, only by writing, and in that way you'll get
millions of people to go on loving you, even as I once loved you.
But Eric, I have ordinary friends. I wouldn't know what to do with
a friend like you. And if we did become close, if you were capable
of it, then when we were at our closest, I'd tell you to write, even
if it destroyed me."

Judy smiled at me, and that smile made my rejection of him
worthwhile.

Eric went berserk. I don't know how much he heard, how much
had penetrated. But he surely understood that I was denying him
at the most crucial moment in his life, and he became frenzied. An
ashtray flew by my head. Judy screamed. A lamp followed the ashtray, its short circuit sending sparks into the room. He had lost
control not only of his senses, but of his limbs, and soon he was
simply destroying the objects in the room, ripping up pillows, sending tables to the floor.

Terrified for Judy and our unborn child, I rushed to shield her.
He noticed the movement, for he stopped long enough to glare at
me with intense hatred. Then he howled—a wolf, a banshee—and
as if he were striking me, drove his fist into the wall. I could hear

his bones break, but his howl did not alter with the pain. He drew back his hand to strike again, but I did not watch. Judy had stood, and now I was pulling her across the room toward the doorway.

Through the hall we fled, past ominous doors and stairs, his howl reverberating in our ears, as though the entire house were its tuning fork. Then at last we were in open air, our car in the mist a haven in a surreal world. For a brief moment, it wouldn't start, and I had a fantasy of Eric rushing at us, changed into a wolf, still howling, howling, teeth bared, clawing at the windows, demanding that we look at him until the sight and sound of him were fixed forever in our dreams.

But then the motor turned over, and we drove off, knowing we would never see that house again. Judy laid her face against my shoulder, and I stroked it, not surprised to find it wet with tears. "Hadn't you better call the police?" she asked. "He won't, not for hours."

We pulled into the gas station, and I made the call. There had been a terrible tragedy, I reported, a suicide. I told them Eric's name and address. The husband was too distraught, so I was calling for him. I did not say where I was or why I had been to the house in the first place, and they did not ask. They merely took my phone number and said they would call if they needed me.

"The man's a famous writer," I said, concluding. "It would be best if this didn't get to the press."

There was a short silence at the other end. Then the sergeant said, "Eric Meredith? I've never heard of him."

For some reason that consoled me, and I walked back to the car feeling cleansed, enjoying the touch of the mist and the air. Judy, too, had revived, for she smiled when I opened the door and kissed me gently when I sat down. "Did we do right?" she asked.

"We had to save ourselves. You knew that long ago. I realized it only today."

We started to drive. She put her arm under mine and pressed against me. I drew her closer still, and we were quiet for a while.

"I wonder," Judy said at last, "how much of what we've just seen was real."

I thought about it. "All of it," I answered slowly. "He wasn't faking."

"I'm sure you're right," she said. Yet late that night, after we had made love and were lying in "our" position, her head nestled in my shoulder, my arm around her naked body, our faces close together so we could kiss if we wanted but did not have to—later, when we were happy and at peace, she said, "But I'll bet he kept a carbon."

twenty-one

COLOSSUS WON THE AMERICAN BOOK AWARD FOR hardcover fiction this year—but you know that. You know too that its reviews and sales were even more extravagant than those for any of the other novels and that Costa Gavras will make the movie. You'll have read the book, too, and recently, so there's no need for me to describe it to you. Like most of the reviewers, I think it's his best, more peaceful than the others, more composed (in both senses), more compassionate. It is as graphically erotic, but here the sex does not seem so driven, so combative. Its sex reminds me of Judy's and mine—all out, unafraid, trusting. *Colossus* represents the growth of that part of Eric which exists in his novels, and as such to his contemporaries it seemed clairvoyant.

I saw Eric at the American Book Awards ceremony at a distance, he on stage and I in the audience. It is unlikely that he saw me. Possibly we'll meet again, for we both move in "publishing circles," and their circumferences are not wide, but he will speak to me from now on only through his books. At the awards, I felt a pang of loneliness when he first came on stage, lit, as were the other winners, with harsh yellow theatricality, while the rest of us were in semidarkness. The moderators for the program were John Kenneth Galbraith and William F. Buckley, and their strained badinage made me reflect that I should not have heeded Judy's exhortation to attend. "You can't hide from him," she told me when I announced my decision not to go. "It's the most important public gathering of your profession, and you'll be missed if you're not there. Besides, it isn't as though you have to *talk* to him."

So there I sat, between Arthur (who had agreed to come only if I did) and a subsidiary rights saleswoman whose face was familiar but whose name was not, bored and slightly embarrassed, paranoiacally sensing that everybody in the auditorium, reminded by the view of Eric on stage, was thinking about the break between us, even if none of them knew the facts. I shifted uncomfortably in the hard Carnegie Hall seat, ashamed of my feelings, despising my weakness, wishing I were somewhere else.

At last the jokes stopped and the awards began. Each recipient was introduced by one or the other of the moderators, who read a scroll of praise prepared by the selection committee. Then the winners in the various categories (poetry, nonfiction, etc.) each gave a speech of thanks. They were supposed to talk for a maximum of ten minutes, but the children's book illustrator needed to deliver a vital political message, the biographer wished to let us know in detail of the painstaking research he had undertaken on behalf of his subject, and the essayist determined to inform us of how he had built his house in the country, and of the fieldstone that was the central metaphor of his book. All of them took twenty minutes or more, so the audience was stultified by the time the award for fiction, Eric's award, was announced.

I had been watching him throughout the ceremony. For the most part he sat absolutely still, his face grave even through the jokes; and when he did move, to applaud a winner or simply to shift position, it was as though he had rehearsed the movements beforehand. I didn't know if he was paying attention. Although his eyes were open, it was impossible to tell at what or whom he was looking.

Now he rose slowly from his chair and made his way toward the rostrum, his steps painful. But as he walked, the audience seemed to walk with him. Soon one man stood, and then another. A woman behind me shouted, "Bravo," and she too stood, and a man by her side joined her. The rest of the audience, publishers, writers, editors, and agents, all bound together in the alliance of words, rose, honoring their master, until to my astonishment Arthur and I were the only ones still seated. "Shouldn't we join them?" he whispered. "Better to be inconspicuous than truthful."

I thought about it for a second. I could claim, after all, that it was an act of respect for the art, not the man. "I'll sit, thank you," I said, and actually reached out to hold Arthur down as well.

There was no sign that Eric was moved by the demonstration. He stood passively, leaning slightly toward the microphone, and waited for the applause to stop. Although I could only see his face between the two men standing in front of me, I got the impression that I was looking at an old man or a defeated one, and I felt one last spasm of sympathy.

"Thank you," Eric said, when everybody was again seated, "for this great honor. To be recognized by the critics and the public brings enormous rewards, but to be recognized by my peers and colleagues brings the greatest rewards of all, for only you know how amazingly hard the work is, and how much one must give of one's soul." He hesitated a moment, but referred to no notes; the talk was ad lib. "I do not wish to make a long speech"—scattered, sarcastic hand-clapping—"but I do wish to say thank you."

He stopped and smiled. Thank you, I thought. If he's going to thank anybody, mustn't he thank me?

"Thanks go first to my mother and father" (mild laughter) "not for giving birth to me, for I'm not sure I welcome that. But for allowing me to become a writer, for not standing in my way." He cleared his throat, already emotional. There was a restlessness in the audience, but I sat still, anger rising behind my eyes. "Too, I thank my editors, first Arthur Collins and now lovely Frances Gaines, who put up with my rages and soothed me when the pain got too great."

"Fuck you," Arthur muttered at my side. I barely heard him.

"If I lashed out at you in that pain, I apologize. And I thank my son David, who is with me tonight—" he gestured toward the front row; I could see nothing "—and who was with me all through the writing of *Colossus*. He is my inspiration and my solace."

Heads around me strained to get a look at the wonder child. I sat back.

"And finally, I thank Anne. My Anne." Here his voice broke, but he shook himself and continued strong. "She died tragically as I was writing *Colossus*. I say to her now—I say to you all—that if I could trade this book for that life—if I could trade all the books, mine and Shakespeare's and Tolstoy's, all—I would do it without hesitation. It is indeed my deepest sorrow, my deepest pain, that it cannot be done."

I could see that many in the audience were moved, and this should have made me more resentful still. Yet remarkably all anger vanished, and I felt calm, even euphoric. He would not mention me. My negotiations on his behalf, my recognition of the extent of his talent before anyone else, my nursemaiding, my friendship, the compromising of myself and Judy, and even my love would go unacknowledged, and I did not care!

"Now I'll stand," I said to Arthur. "Coming with me?"

He looked up, surprised. "Where are you going?"

"Home to Judy. I find it oppressive in here."

Already I was sliding past the subsidiary rights director. Arthur half-stood, then seemed to change his mind, for he sat back down, leaving me alone in my departure. Eric was plunging ahead with his speech, and I doubt many noticed the distraction I was causing, but as I reached the aisle and headed for the exit, I saw some heads turn toward me, and a few of my friends pantomimed applause.

I reached the exit door, pushed it open, and stepped into the lobby, letting the door close behind me. I could still hear Eric's voice, but was unable to distinguish the words.

I stood for a moment with my back against the door, thinking of Eric as I first knew him and Eric gone mad. He was a great writer; he was a genius; and I rejoiced that I no longer needed his genius or him for my own fulfillment.

Had he seen me leave? I wondered. And if so, did he realize or care about my last act of defiance? It was a petty, adolescent gesture, I knew. But nevertheless, it brought me satisfaction.